A Kind of Warfare

To Brenda
with very best wishes

[signature]

A Kind of Warfare

Deborah Bosley

Duck Editions

First published in 2000 by
Duckworth Literary Entertainments, Ltd.
61 Frith Street, London W1D 3JL
Tel: 020 7434 4242
Fax: 020 7434 4420
email:DuckEd@duckworth-publishers.co.uk
www.ducknet.co.uk

A CIP catalogue record for this book is available
from the British Library

ISBN 0 7156 3001 6

Typeset by Ray Davies
Printed in Great Britain by
Redwood Books Ltd, Trowbridge

To Richard Ingrams

Contents

CHAPTER ONE

OUR LIVES HAD BECOME UNMANAGEABLE

Hello, my name is Mark and I am a sex addict. Or so Maria, my ex-fiancée, thinks. After a failed attempt to get me into therapy she now reckons I need to go the twelve-step route, stand up and put it on the line. Admit my powerlessness to a room full of sex offenders and saddos in some badly-lit, stale-smelling community centre or church hall. Share with the fellowship of Sex Addicts Anonymous the misery of a full and contented romantic career. I will come to see abundant and diverse sex with a lot of women not as great good fortune, but a cry for help. Once I surrender to God *as I understand him* I will discover peace of mind. No more the abject loneliness of concurrent sexual partners. I will enjoy the serenity of love and commitment to one woman.

I know, totally outrageous. This time she's really lost her sense of humour. I thought it was a simple case of straw-clutching when Maria suggested at that awful dinner last week that my behaviour, far from being the healthy expression of my natural desires, was a disease from which I could find relief. Admittedly, I encouraged this line of thinking as telling her the truth would have been too brutal. Like I was really going to come straight out with it and say, 'Maria, I'm sorry, but I can't marry you because I really don't want to, and I think I might have fallen in love with somebody else.' I mean please, I'm too chicken shit for the truth at the best of times, but on this occasion it was a vital case of damage limitation.

Once you get past the big I-am, Maria's nature bruises easily. She overcompensates by coming up with elaborate defences, the worst of which is treating love as if it were some system that can be analysed and fine tuned. She loves self-help and how-to books and even though I've told her a million times that studying the form at the dog-track is a more accurate science, she refuses to surrender to the unknowableness of love. To do so would be to admit that for all the manipulation and push-me pull-you, I am not for her. She sees my willingness to indulge in even the most fleeting sexual contact as proof of an illness and not the simple case of opportunism and greed which I would put my money on. The fact that she has managed to stay in love with me, or at least convince herself of it for so many years, is the heart's refusal to see the obvious. I am partly to blame, not least because I have gone along with some of her madder schemes for the sake of a quiet life. The biggest mistake was relenting to see a counsellor about a year ago. Unable to accept that the reason I hadn't stopped seeing other women or asked her to marry me was because I didn't really want to, Maria came up with the theory that I have psychological blocks to commitment which manifest themselves in bizarre sexual behaviour. She also suggested I reflect upon some of the destruction and heartache I have wrought upon womankind in my quest for satisfaction. She added rather cruelly that my last dose was a symptom of a much worse disease. I'm sorry, but find me one person in metropolitan London that hasn't had a brush with NSU, herpes or thrush. Only monks escape the itch, it stands to reason. Normally I'd have told her to go blow it out her arse, but she must have caught me on a bad day or the worse for drink, because I found myself agreeing to attend an appointment she'd made for me with one Henry Temple-Golden, a psycho-dynamic counsellor in Primrose Hill. It was such a measly ploy that I went along with it, reasoning that it couldn't hurt and rather than prejudicing my case, this guy might actually turn round and say that there was absolutely nothing wrong with me. Far from apprehensive, I trotted along punctually for my appointment thinking it might even be a laugh. I'd never seen a shrink in my life, not even really come across that many socially, not being a Hampstead Garden Suburb kind of man, and I had to admit to a soupçon of curiosity. Besides, I liked the sound of this guy. Henry Temple-Golden sounded a very solid, well-qualified kind of dude. I imagined him to be slim, greying at the temples and draped in expensive threads. His consulting room would be dark and masculine with a lot of expensive leather furniture. When the receptionist tells me Dr Temple-Golden is ready to see me if I'd like to go through, I enter a small, white room with large creamy scatter cushions on the floor. A candle which I presume to be the source of the room's cloying female aroma is flickering on the windowsill behind the good doctor's head. Everything is white and cream except for one very large orange cushion upon which Dr Temple-Golden is kneeling serenely. Dr Temple-Golden turns out to be a woman of about forty-five with waist-length black hair and a large beak. I swear to God, she's a human crow, all dressed in black with the long pointy hooter and ratty hair.

'Please sit down, Mark, and make yourself comfortable.' Her hands are crossed just so on her lap in a yogi pose and she smiles to reveal about five grand's worth of cosmetic dentistry. I can spot it a mile off. I'm just sort of standing there looking at her trying not to laugh and unsure of what to make of this little scene. She gives me a quizzical look with a cocked head and I scratch my own and say, 'Sorry, you're just not what I was expecting.'

'You were expecting a man?'

'Well, you know, Henry is a bit misleading.'

'I spell it with an "i". Do you have a problem with talking to women?'

'Not even slightly.' Cheeky cow. I lower myself onto a cushion. She studies my body language thoughtfully as if I've just done something very significant, cocking her head this way and that, looking more and more like a crow or a rook with every jerking motion. I catch her checking out my crotch which seems to mildly alarm her and I'm thinking, well excuse me, where exactly would you like me to put my bollocks, doctor? She raises an eyebrow at me as if to say, And just what is it you find so amusing? Involuntarily, I laugh. 'Sorry,' I say, 'this just seems a bit comic to me.'

'It's natural to feel uncomfortable talking about yourself for the first time. Why don't you just relax and tell me why you're here and what you hope psycho-dynamic therapy can do for you.' I bite back another broad grin that is trying to wrap itself across my face and hesitate, because it's a valid question. What the fuck am I doing here?

'It's not my idea. My friend Maria seems to think I need to talk to somebody.' She nods at me to continue, very sagely with a slight furrowing of the brow. It strikes me this might be a look she has rehearsed in the mirror. 'Basically, Maria's problem is I don't want to commit myself to her and I see other women.'

She holds up a hand to stop me and clears her throat. 'It's interesting that you refer to it as Maria's problem. Would you care to elaborate as to why you think it is her problem and if so, why she isn't the one sitting here.'

I think, you fucking aggressive feminist baggage and say, 'I don't know, doctor, maybe she doesn't like sitting on floors and while we're at it, how come your cushion is orange and all the others are white?'

'Orange is the colour of healing. I am a healer.' A pretty extravagant claim to make but I didn't pull her on it. All is quiet for a moment and she is deliberately not talking, waiting for me to crack first which of course I do.

'I'm not sure it is a problem to be non-committal, especially if you're entirely honest with everybody.'

'Mmmm,' she says, in that kind of Mmmm, interesting, pisstake way. 'Are you certain that you are always honest, Mark?'

'As much as possible.'

'But not entirely.'

'No, not entirely because it isn't always necessary.'

'You mean if you can get away with it, you will.'

'Bingo.' Far from grinning, I've got a bit of a snarl going now. Who does this bird think she is, my wife?

'Why are you frightened of your emotions, Mark?'

'I'm not.'

'So why stall at the chance of real intimacy with a woman? Why bombard your senses with multiple partners?'

'Put like that, it sounds rather good.'

'Mark, you are terribly defensive. You are exhibiting classic symptoms of denial. My job as your therapist, if we decide that is what we both want, is to challenge as well as support you. Do you understand?'

'No.'

'I sense that you are not yet ready to share but I think you would benefit from extensive medium-term therapy.' She's making notes while she says this, and I reckon she's working out what she could squeeze out of me.

'What's that gonna cost me then?'

'You don't see therapy as an investment in the rest of your life?'

'You didn't answer my question.'

'Three sessions a week for eighteen months. £90 a session.'

I've worked in a pub so I'm good at maths and I quickly calculate that I'm looking at a price point of around twenty grand for dubious mental health and now it's my turn to shake my head. 'I think we've got different values.'

'How much do you think you might spend on women in order to seduce them in the next eighteen months?'

'I make a point of never keeping track.'

'You're very sharp, Mark.'

'Thank you, doctor.'

'Your sarcasm doesn't shake me, Mark, I want to help you move beyond your fears into safe harbour where we can hold these issues up and examine them.'

She seems pretty sincere despite the fact that she talks total crapola, so I give her a few crumbs to be going on with, like admitting I sometimes wake up next to a woman in the morning with a terrible cold feeling of dread. I kind of lay it on a bit, thinking, go on then, I'll indulge you for fifty minutes, give you a chance to flex your little psycho-dynamic muscles. Course, she's on it in a blink, theorising every which way, and while she dissects my comments I take the time to really check her out. She has a pitted complexion and she isn't wearing a bra which in her case isn't wise. A bit too heavy to fly solo, if you know what I mean. I can see the end of her legs poking out from under her long black dress and the ankles are very thick and very white. I'm thinking, you could do with a few sessions down the gym and a couple of sunbeds, love. Her fingers are encrusted with silver jewellery, not a look I'm fond of, and I decide even if she was begging for it, I definitely wouldn't shag her. I must have drifted off for a while when she was talking because she leans over and touches my leg, and I mean the inside of my thigh, and looking into my eyes says very earnestly, 'I think we could work together, Mark.' I couldn't say for sure, being new to the talking cure, but she seemed to be making a pass at me. I look at her hand on my leg and she quickly draws it away and is suddenly businesslike and suggests I book an appointment on the way out. I stand up and shake her hand and say, 'I'll think about it, but thanks for your time.' She shifts just slightly, but there is a definite rattling of her composure before she whispers breathily and meaningfully, 'One day you'll have to stop running, Mark.' Not if you're behind me I won't, love. On the way out I drop four twenties and a ten on the receptionist's desk and take the lift down the stairs thinking, what a total and utter waste of readies.

I get home and there's a message on my machine from Henri Temple-Golden sounding a bit tense and asking me to please call, she wants to clear up a misunderstanding. Fucking bunny boiler that one, I'm giving her a wide berth. But when Maria calls to ask me how it went, I don't complain. I'm very low-key and say I didn't really think we had much rapport. I have to play it quite carefully with Maria because lurking in the back of my mind always is the guilty thought that I have shat on her for seventeen years and she still hasn't dumped me. It has to count for something.

I am restless during the evening and can't settle for long enough even to watch a bit of telly. I'm not good at being on my own, so I shower then jump in a cab up to the West End. I'm telling myself I've just come out for a beer and a change of scene, but as I plonk myself down at the bar in Signor Zilli's I know I won't be leaving here alone. Sure enough a group of girls, mid-twenties I'd say, are having a high old time of it on a table behind me. I spy on them undetected using the mirror behind the bar. The most attractive member of the group is also the most drunk and singing very loudly. She has a lovely dewy smile and a high-pitched laugh. She works her way over to the bar clutching a couple of twenties and squeezes in beside my stool. She hasn't clocked me, but there's such a crush at the bar that her shoulders are squeezed up against mine. She is wearing a sleeveless top and has lovely slim, silky arms. The kind of skin you just want to bite into. Her hair is long and glossy and despite the fact she smells like a brewery, she's well groomed with painted nails and a short summery dress. I've got mixed feelings about making a move on women who've been drinking, but I reckon she's a consenting adult and can make her own decisions, so when the barman looks at the sea of notes being waved at him by thirsty punters I speak up and say, 'Over here, mate, this lady was first.' She says thanks and we strike up a pretty jolly conversation while she's waiting for her bottle of champagne. Apparently she's on a leaving do for one of the girls at work and they've been on a mission since four o'clock that afternoon. She says she's shattered and that this is definitely her last drink, she needs to get home to her bed. She's very easygoing and pleasant so

I ask her where home is and she says Kensal Rise. Oh yeah, I say, you don't want to share a cab and drop me off on the way do you, I live in Maida Vale? She looks at me suspiciously and says she'll think about it, but I catch her checking me out in the mirror once she gets back to her table and she's catching my eye and smiling at my reflection in the mirror pretty frequently. After about twenty minutes I figure the time is ripe, so I stand up and give her a little wave and say, see ya. She looks a bit surprised and then goes into a huddle with her friends. I wait outside on the pavement and let a couple of cabs go past. Sure enough, she comes out of the bar and asks if I still want to share a cab. Sure, sweetheart. There's no point bothering with the small talk once you've settled into the back seat of a cab with a girl in a short dress, so I just lean over and kiss her very gently. Sorry, I say, I just had to do that. Don't be sorry, she says and responds with some enthusiasm. 'I don't usually do this kind of thing,' she says as we walk up the stairs to my flat, 'I don't want you to think that I go home with just any old bloke.' The sex is pretty average and to be honest I think she has trouble staying awake because she is so pissed. I dispatch her in a minicab to Kensal Rise about 2 a.m. As I close the door behind me, I realise that I don't even know her name. Before I turn out the light, I screw up the piece of paper with her number which she left by the bed and lob it into the bin in the corner.

A pretty typical encounter and one which I'd normally end up confessing to Maria some weeks after, laughing at my disgustingness. She'd just roll her eyes and make some pithy comment and then it would be business as usual. She's known me too long to think I'd ever take a vow of celibacy or even exclusivity but events of the last few months may finally have ground down the remaining stump of her affection for me. I am not just a shit because I sleep around but because this time I really made her believe that I was ready to settle. It wasn't deliberate cynicism. I wanted to believe it myself. There was no way of knowing that exactly one week after announcing our engagement I would fall bang in love with a complete stranger. Maria and I had the final showdown last week when I put her into a cab on Piccadilly at about midnight on Thursday and I didn't hear a peep until this morning. I was having a wank in the shower when the doorbell rang. I would have ignored it, but they were insistent, so I plod downstairs dripping in a towel to find Karl my postman looking dazed with a large package. I got on first name terms with my postman a few years ago because of wrongly delivered mail. Karl is a white Rasta with big dirty blond locks and is stoned from sun-up to closing time, hence the mix-ups with the post. I like him though, there's something very gentle about him and some days when I'm sick of being a journalist I look at Karl and think I wouldn't mind swapping lives. Up with the lark, nice joint and a cup of tea then off on my rounds, home by lunchtime. The simple life.

It took Karl a few seconds to compute my dripping state. 'Sorry, mate, but I knew you were in, your windows are open. I've got a big parcel for you.'

'I can see that.'

A slight pause. 'Yeah, right. Can you sign for it here?' I see from the writing on the box that it's from Maria and my spirits take a bit of a dive. It's bound to be some kind of let's-make-up present and I'm going to have to go through all this break-up shit again.

'Cheers, Karl.'

'Yeah, Peace.' I watch Karl trail off with his heavy sack, doing that kind of slow pimp-roll that he has perfected watching the local hoods. Today I want Karl's life. I don't want to deal with this box. But I take it upstairs and I open it and instead of a gift I find a jumper and a couple of books that Maria packed by mistake in her haste to move out a couple of weeks ago. With it is a note, *Get help Mark, your life is a mess* and a pamphlet.

IS SEX ADDICTS ANONYMOUS FOR YOU?
Twelve Questions Only You Can Answer.

For a moment I wonder if this is something she's knocked up on the computer at work, but I see from the address on the back it's a bona fide organisation with a crest and registered address. Most of the questions were fairly straightforward, along the lines of *Is sex affecting your ability to do your work effectively?* and *Have you ever decided to abstain from sex for a week or so, but only lasted for a couple of days?* and the obvious *Do you ever try to get extra sex from other partners because one partner does not give you enough?* But the corkers for me were Questions 5. *Do you envy people who can have sex without getting into trouble?* and 12. *Have you ever thought your life would be better if you did not have sex compulsively?* I ticked the yes box next to all the questions except for number 12 which I scribbled 'not sure' next to. I underlined Question 2, *Do you wish people would mind their own business about your sex-life – stop telling you what to do?* in red felt tip and put it in an envelope for posting.

I think highly of Maria – shit, I was supposed to marry her this month, June wedding at Chelsea Town Hall, the works – but of all her little quirks, none is more maddening than her belief that she really understands me. I've told her a million times to leave it, to stop pulling me apart, stop discussing everything, having to know the ins and outs, wanting to be the only one who really knows what makes me tick. She's pulled some desperate stunts in her time to get me to bend to her will, most of them I've gone along with for want of anything better to do but this time it's OVER and I can't go back to her out of laziness as I've always done before.

According to the literature, Step One of recovery is to admit that I am powerless over my sexual urges and that my life has become unmanageable. There is some truth in this. My problem has never been finding women – *au contraire* – but narrowing down my options. This leads, I must admit, to some complications. Rarely have I met a woman who is happy to be one of many in my life. The exception to this rule is a bird who is already committed herself, in which case it can be the sweetest of arrangements. But the law of averages dictates that the number of young, happily attached women – unhappily attached is no good because they see you as their ticket out of a bad set-up – who are attractive, willing to deal in untruths and shamelessly unconcerned about the fall-out from having an affair is thin on the ground. More often I have to content myself with lies and subterfuge. I don't like to think of myself as innately deceitful but it is necessary to keep the girls at least partially in the dark, if only to keep them interested.

The trick is to give away only as much as you need to. I always admit to the existence of the other women, but just slightly alter their context. For example if I have to tell X that I am having dinner with Y, I will explain that Y was a girl I used to have a relationship with but now we just meet for dinner a couple of times a year to stay in touch. I might follow this up with a line like, 'Yeah, it's a shame it didn't work out, because she's a nice girl, but I just don't fancy her.' Over dinner I will tell Y that X is somebody I see only occasionally as she already has a boyfriend – it's fun but it's not going anywhere, kind of thing. The fact that X is single and has been sleeping at my house every night for the last week is information surplus to requirements. Such conversations have the sheen of honesty and usually lead to improved communications inside and out of the bedroom. For the most part, this strategy works like a charm.

I believe we all, but especially women, when it comes to love, sex, infatuation, call it what you like, see only what we want to see and if I encourage them in these little falsehoods, all to the good. But it takes work, and over the last year I found myself feeling increasingly worn out from the effort of keeping so many balls in the air. For most of my life I've laboured under the big illusion that I was in some way special. I despised my colleagues for their semi-detached homes and their anodyne wives; I told myself I would rather be alone than suffer the long-littleness of married life in a London suburb. It was odd then that I should grow to envy their leaking cisterns, asshole children and bald patches. What started as a small niggle of dissatisfaction slowly accelerated into panic. I think Maria sensed the change in me and chose the moment to steam in. It was certainly true that I was growing tired of living alone. It had been six years since my one cohabiting relationship had ended in disaster and although in subsequent years various girlfriends had tentatively left toiletries in the bathroom and clothes in my wardrobe, I would always politely fold and return the items. The girl I lived with, Pilar, was Spanish and after three years of trying to acclimatise her to a life in London with me I gave up. Traces of her remain in the flat, the rug she chose for the living room, the glasses she bought from Portobello Road and, inexplicably, her straw hat which I have never quite been able to chuck out. I still see her from time to time, usually riding a wave of disenchantment with the other women in my life. It is always a last-minute decision to go, when the prospect of a weekend in London with a girlfriend I may be arguing with at the time, usually about my unwillingness to commit, fills me with dread. I go to Jerez de la Frontera to visit her and brave her father who nearly had my bollocks for breakfast when we broke up. I usually leave after two days grateful in the knowledge that we cannot ever be a couple, though there was a time when I couldn't imagine life with anyone else. She will never again leave Spain and I cannot imagine who I would turn into if I left London.

Besides her, there are/were a handful of other women in my life, three with whom I definitely did not envisage any kind of future but was reluctant to give up, serving as they did the very useful purpose of keeping my self-esteem buoyant and my body hard. I am nothing if not an ego-warrior. That left only one real contender for the title of Mrs Mark Tucker. I've been side-stepping the issue of Maria for almost as long as I've known her. We've been friends and on/off lovers since we were eighteen and in my way, I've been more faithful to Maria than any of the others. It didn't matter who else I was seeing, Maria never let me down. This made her both undesirable and indispensable. Women would come and go, some for a weekend, others like Pilar for three years, but through it all there was always Maria. I do not mean to imply that she hung around dog-like just waiting for me. Far from it. Maria's romantic career was as eventful as my own. She is not the type to sit around just cooling her heels and waiting for a call. Oh no. She is probably the most good-natured woman I have ever known, but I continued to stall on the final step of marriage.

As is often the way, it was something small and apparently insignificant which triggered me into action. I was watching, get this, *The Sound of Music* with my mum in her smoky, overheated front room one Sunday after lunch. Rain streamed down the double glazing and through it the streets of Croydon had never looked so miserable. My sister Bee and her three boys had just left, taking their outrageous decibel level with them and leaving just a load of sweet wrappers on the carpet and me and mum sitting mutely on that horrible Dralon sofa that always makes my arse sweat. Mum was getting all weepy over Julie Andrews and chain-smoking while I pretended to read the sports section of the Sunday paper so that I wouldn't have to talk to her. Suddenly, the nuns burst into 'How Do You Solve a Problem Like Maria?' It made me sit up. I definitely did have a problem, and her name *was* Maria. Mum's thoughts chimed with my own and as the song finished she asked pointedly, 'So, how is Maria?'

Over the years I have managed to fob off anybody who asked what my intentions were, but I can definitively pinpoint that dismal March afternoon as the time when the net began to close fast. I mumbled something about not really knowing, which was true because we'd had a big fight at the end of February and hadn't spoken since. Typical mum, wouldn't drop it: 'I don't know why you two don't just get married, you break up and go all round the houses just to get back together.'

'It's not that simple, mum.' Part of me wanted to tell her, but asking your mum for advice? Forget it. She offered it anyway.

'I think you youngsters complicate things and waste too much time. Your father and I had two kids by the time we were your age. All you've got when you wake up in the morning is a hangover and a guilty conscience.' This was good, but the next bit was the killer. She sighed and shook her head. 'I don't know what you're looking for, Mark, but I'll tell you this, life's too short to stuff a mushroom.' My mother has a fondness for quoting her favourite authors, a relatively recent habit she's developed since joining that reading club. I wandered into the kitchen to make some tea and while I fished around for teabags and sugar tut-tutting at mum's taste in earthenware – teddy bears on teapots, come on – the wheels in my brain started to spin. An inauspicious setting, my mum's kitchen, but I tell you it was there, leaning my head against the humming fridge door with my eyes closed, that I resigned myself to working with what I had instead of lusting after some imaginary future that probably didn't exist. Imaginary futures were fine at nineteen and even twenty-nine but when you're still going to mum's for Sunday dinner at thirty-four and waiting for life to start, it's a bit pathetic.

That afternoon I became possesed by the desire to 'get real'. Pare down and empty the net of romantic, all right then, sexual possibility I had cast so wide. The prospect of forcing change so decisively rather than waiting for things to happen was exciting and I felt as if the adrenaline switch had been flicked in my gut. Back in the front room with two steaming mugs I surprised myself by telling my mother all about the last time I had seen Maria and what we had fought about. My mother, a bit of a latecomer to feminism and newly empowered by Shirley Conran, is convinced of the unreasonableness of all men. I was on a hiding to nothing if it was sympathy I was after, but I thought I'd air it out anyway.

CHAPTER TWO

GRAVY TRAIN DERAILED

Before I get to the ins and outs of the row, which wasn't really a row, more of a stand-off, I should give you a bit of background. I'd dropped a bollock at work and came up with the idea of Maria hostessing – all right cooking – a bit of a dinner party for me so I could do some remedial politicking over a nice plate of grub and some decent wine. I work on the features desk of a London evening newspaper, a plateau in an undistinguished career which I started as a cub reporter on the *Croydon Advertiser* and which, via a series of infrequently upward but mostly sideways moves, has landed me in a sterile office block just off Kensington High Street. I am in the slightly unusual and not unenviable position of being half staff, half freelance, a post I managed to wheedle myself into eighteen months ago when I put it to my arsewipe of an editor Matthew Cullen that I needed more flexibility so that I might write a novel. So far the novel is a product of not even my imagination, but it's a delicious scam which has kept my salary disproportion-ately high for a fraction of the work. In my early days on the paper Cullen considered me to be young and promising. He arrived at this, I can only presume, by a process of elimination, reasoning that at least half his hacks over thirty were either drunks or deadbeats. As I was so far neither, it might do well to support whatever ambitions I had, however incredible my notions. Cullen agreed to me working three days a week commissioning and editing quick turnaround pieces on the back of news events and the rest of the time, when the demands of novel writing permitted, knocking off the odd restaurant review or travel piece to use as fillers.

As even the most mediocre journalist could tell you, this is money for old rope. Editing news features means simply that you read the other papers to find an item you could never have dreamed up yourself, then get a writer to crib it inserting a few original sentences and hope that the subs can come up with a nice rhetorical headline. Of course the set-up worked for me, money for jam, but I sensed that Cullen regretted his decision almost as soon as it was made. He has always had half a mind that I'm a piss-taker and some of my more industrious colleagues were loudly resentful that I'd been singled out for special treatment. I've got pretty thick skin and can take the digs at work in my stride, but it made Cullen look a bit of a prick, like I've really suckered him and he knows it. He spent a lot of time waiting for me to slip up, any excuse to revise the two-year agreement which he foolishly committed to paper after a good lunch. He didn't have long to wait. Of course the contract isn't really worth the paper it's written on and if he wanted to play hardball he could, but again, it's what it looks like that concerns Cullen. He has this idea of himself as an old Fleet Street legend, you know the coup, tough but fair, a gentleman and a bastard.

In common with every editor I have worked under, Cullen's judgement, however wobbly, is not to be questioned. My laconic presence lolling around the features desk is a constant reminder to him not to talk about staff contracts after 1 p.m. Those on the staff who do not think I'm a wanker find my brass neck amusing. It's not as if the paper can't afford it. With a wealthy stable of other daily titles behind it, Amalgamated Print are oozing cash. I'm not noticeably ambitious and do not have what it takes to be a hard-hitting, rough and ready newspaperman. I learned early to stick to what I can do easily, maintain a low profile and quietly take all the perks on offer. I tried to keep it simple and not get greedy, but we all love something for nothing and last October it looked like I'd finally gone too far. The gravy train was about to derail.

I was relaxing at the weekly features meeting, not really listening, when Cullen piped up with a suggestion that we do a politics with a twist item on the Italian general election. Fuck all to do with London, but we're not fussy, we've got pages to fill. Here was an opportunity to bring together all the worthless elements of good features – fashion, restaurants and European shagging etiquette. Stick a couple of tasty photos in and Bob's your uncle. Never one to miss an opportunity to get out of the office, I quickly sat up and tried to look as if I was on the ball. I volunteered to fly to Rome and find out what the smart, and I mean Armani-smart, not book-smart people were voting.

It's surprising how easy it can be to scam these trips. A lot of the guys, especially the married ones, can't really be bothered to drag their arses out to Heathrow and get on a plane for the sake of a few days. They'd rather be at home with some nice fat wife eating fish and chips and making plans to build a new shed in the garden. Can't say I blame them. Cullen did a thorough scan round the table for an alternative but there weren't any other takers. As I have neither the education nor the curiosity to write a decent political piece everybody agreed I was the perfect candidate to grab a few stylish Italians off the streets, ask them which way they would be voting and where they will be celebrating – or not – on the night of the elections. For greater depth I suggested the element of the Versace murder. Did anybody think he was bumped off because he was a Communist? Were allegations of his Mafia connections just a red-herring to throw us off the real scent of political skulduggery and assassination? I didn't believe this myself for one moment, but thought I'd run it up the flagpole. Cullen told me to stick to fashion, food and sexual mores, but agreed to my going. Satisfied with a good morning's work, I set about performing my time-honoured trick of cashing in one heavily discounted club-class plane ticket in exchange for two economy seats so that I could take

Stella Kennedy for a long weekend at Amalgamated's expense. Stella is a messed-up snob but she's fit and game and I was trying not to let the class issue get in the way. More of her later.

It was bad juju that I wasn't at my desk when the fax from the travel agent confirming the ticket changes came through. It was Cullen himself, perched on *my* desk talking to a couple of the blokes about the upcoming test match in South Africa, who spotted the offending document. It wasn't so much the bollocking from him that bothered me – a fair cop after all – but the slight taint of cheapness which still clings despite the good-natured jokes in the office. I ended up going to Rome with Stella and we had, as expected, a very live time of it, but it bothered me more than it usually does to be the butt of office jokes.

So I decided to host a dinner party for a couple of my colleagues from the newsdesk. News by its nature is more dynamic than features and this is reflected in the staff. On features we tend to be quite phlegmatic, facts are not after all vital to our success. The news boys are a lot more on the case and although neither Marcus Reid nor Andy Hicks are heavyweights on the paper they are popular. Andy in particular has the ear of Cullen and it was time to take steps, hence the dinner.

A good idea, except that I cannot, even by the most generous interpretation of my skills, cook to save my life. I manage to eat well enough doing restaurant reviews here and there and living on bacon sandwiches and takeaways the rest of the time. So I call in Maria who is, despite a long list of faults, something of a trophy-wife in the kitchen. I was a bit wound up about what was after all just a bit of dinner and in a fit of anxious generosity I gave Maria £100 to go shopping in Soho's finest delis to buy food. Maria is thrifty and could feed a football team on a pound of mince but that night I wanted to push the boat out and told her not to cut corners.

We agreed to meet at my flat in Maida Vale at 5 p.m. so that we could have a few liveners and take our time preparing the meal. At quarter to seven I was pacing the flat pulling out what is left of my hair when the doorbell rang. I buzzed her in and watched from the landing as she weaved her way up the stairs, weighed down with bags of shopping admittedly, but definitely not sober. I said nothing and waited for an apology which never came. I resolved to make the best of it and opened a bottle of champagne.

'You look nice, Maria,' I said, handing her a glass, but she missed the dig and regarded her jeans and some tatty long-sleeved top I've seen a hundred times before with pleasure.

'Thanks,' she said and raised her glass.

'Where the fuck have you been? You're almost two hours late.'

'I'm here now, aren't I?' Turning her back on me, she lit the gas, sparked up a fag and turned the radio on very loud and tuned it into Radio Four. I hate Radio Four and she knows it. Crafty cow was baiting me, knowing full well I couldn't retaliate because I needed her to sort the food out. Just like a bloody woman to see the advantage and milk it. I reckon if women want to live in a man's world, they ought to go about it in a more gentlemanly fashion, but that's an old beef I won't go into here.

'You did say five o'clock, Maria. If you'd said later, I could have gone down the gym and had a sauna instead of hanging about here waiting for you.'

'If you'd given me a key, you wouldn't have had to.'

So that's what it was about. I've been resisting Maria's requests for a set of keys to the flat for the very reason that I do not want her coming and going as and when she feels like it. It's delicate, because on nights like tonight and a good many more I want her here. But there are also nights and sometimes whole weekends when I don't. She knows that I sleep with other women, just as I know that she sleeps with other men, but we don't get specific or answer honestly when one of us asks, 'What did you get up to last night?'

I watched her unpack the shopping for a minute and it was obvious that I was surplus to requirements. She just went about her business studiously ignoring me. 'I'll just let you get on with it then, shall I?'

'If you wouldn't mind, Mark, you'll only get under my feet.'

It's a blessing and a curse to know somebody as intimately as I know Maria. On the one hand, you don't have to bother with all that pointless chit-chat, but then again it can get a bit flat, the way I imagine it does if you've been married for a long time. She seemed neither pleased nor put out to be cooking a meal for six people in my kitchen. But why should she? She has been cooking meals in my kitchen for years. Her indifference was entirely appropriate to the occasion.

I wandered into the living room, taking the bottle with me just to annoy her. I mooched around, checking myself in the big mirror above my gas coal-effect fire, and picking bits of fluff off the furniture. I was combing my mediocre CD collection with its embarrassing Best Of … compilations looking for something suitable to play when the doorbell rang. I pressed the buzzer on the intercom and waited on the landing, recognising the man's voice as Marcus's, but was unable to pick out the soft tones of his female companion. It wasn't until they reached my flight of stairs that I saw it was Iona from the fashion desk, whom I've always half-fancied fucking. I wondered if he was giving it to her or whether she'd just agreed to be his date. If I was edgy they didn't seem to notice and it was a relief that Marcus found something he wanted to listen to among my CDs. Marcus is black, posh and, though I try not to be impressed, pretty cool. He comes from a powerful family in Antigua where his dad is High Commissioner or something. Whatever it is he does, he's in charge, runs the joint and gets plenty of readies for his trouble. The old man sent Marcus to England to be educated at Ampleforth with the result that Marcus is an enviable mixture of learning and laid-back island boy. He is a classic example of Amalgamated's unwritten rule that black people are only hired if they've been to public school.

I'd planned champagne for early drinks, but Maria knocked up some very above average Martinis and the evening took off with a bit more acceleration than I'd hoped for. Maria and Marcus have met on several occasions, Christmas parties and what have you, and I've noticed that they flirt quite a lot. She went right over and gave him a big smacker and they laughed and joked a little. If she was trying to wind me up she was going the right way about it. Marcus would go for Maria like a shot, but I take care to maintain just enough ownership over her to ward off any suitors from the paper. I don't want things getting messy and if she wants to screw other men, let her find her own punters, is my philosophy.

The Martinis really were excellent though, and I prayed that Maria would stop at two, because by now she has engaged the pencil-slim Iona in conversation about the cigarette-pants from Joseph she is wearing and saying things like, 'I love your trousers but I can never get my arse into any of his stuff.' Marcus looks at Maria's ample derrière and I can tell whose arse he prefers out of the two. 'I've never really managed to get my look together, I've never given it the time.' She cleverly puts Iona in her place by apparently lamenting her own lack of fashion sense when in fact she is really highlighting what a pointless label-slut Iona is. Maria is gloriously, self-righteously unfashionable and truly doesn't care. I like her attitude, but I wish she'd take a bit more care with her appearance. I said to her one morning in bed, looking at her dark hair highlighted with henna and a set of roots well overdue for attention, 'How often do you get your hair done?'

'When I can be bothered,' she replied.

'You should get into a routine with it, Maria, book an appointment every six weeks so that it always looks good.'

'For someone with so little hair, you've got pretty strong opinions.' Bitch. She knows I'm touchy about my hairline. That's the thing with Maria, she can't take constructive criticism about her appearance and it definitely holds her back in the style stakes.

We'd already seen off our second round of Martinis by the time Andy and his wife Rebecca tip up, so naturally we have a third.

They really are a nice couple. They have two young children and Rebecca packed in work to stay at home with them, which to my mind is the right thing to do. She used to work at Radio Four as a producer, so she's no divvy but she doesn't go around boasting about her intelligence either. Maria could do with taking a few lessons in humility from Rebecca rather than going around picking arguments and flexing her intellectual muscles. I find opinionated women very unattractive. There's no need for it. Maria and Rebecca greet one another warmly despite having only met once before and I feel touched that Maria is making such an effort on my behalf. I began to relax as the drinks work their magic, though by this time I am developing acid heartburn, a chronic reminder of a duodenal ulcer I have been nurturing with spirits and fried food for fifteen years. That bloody shrink, Henri Temple-Golden, reckoned my ulcer was a symptom of a permanent acidic hunger for sex. I pointed out that Rennies did the trick most of the time and left it at that.

Like all couples with kids Andy and Rebecca arrive late and quickly explain that they have to leave early because the babysitter is only fifteen and not allowed out after eleven. This gave Maria the nudge she needed to get some grub coming and within minutes she was gliding in and out of the kitchen with little plates of blinis and merguez sausage slices, a controversial choice for canapés but they went down well. After bringing in the food she would pause for a cigarette and crack everybody up with some *bon mot* or snippet she'd heard at work – TV production is not just hot but ripe for credible gossip – before sliding back into her secret cage of steam for more food. I tell you, it's impressive and I'm not the only one to notice. Andy in particular keeps giving me that 'She's brilliant, why don't you marry her?' look. That's my problem really. Everybody likes her, even other women I'm sleeping with. If she lost a stone and stopped trying to boss me around I probably would marry her.

Andy's wife began to look a bit anxious after another hour of drinks and more canapés, and reading the situation Maria abruptly announced that dinner was ready if we'd like to sit down. I love the way she can work a room and make everybody in it feel good. Even Iona felt looked after. Socially Maria is a fish that can swim in any sea and while she is capable of fantastic bitchiness towards me, with other people she has a sure touch. It was, by the most modest estimate, a very successful evening. Not only was the food good – pork tenderloin with spicy red cabbage – but there was a heart-warming interlude round about the third bottle of wine when Marcus, Andy and myself slaughtered Cullen and declared ourselves brothers in arms against the evil tyranny of his perk-trimming regime.

'What you need to remember about Matthew,' says Andy, 'is that he doesn't really give a shit what you get up to as long as you keep it low key.'

'I am low key,' I reply, innocence itself.

'Not when you tried to pull little Lucy at the Christmas party you weren't,' Marcus pipes up.

'I had no idea that was his daughter.' We all laugh except for Maria who looks surprised and hurt. Fuck. She didn't know about that little episode and it's only bad luck she found out tonight. It occurs to me this might have been deliberate on Marcus's part, trying to discredit the opposition as it were.

Maria quickly recovers her composure and captivates the table with her story about the Conservative MP who was simultaneously a major shareholder with a massive brewery and a member of AA. She is shamingly up on current events and usually manages to put a comic spin on it. There was only one moment when I felt myself blanch. There is a joke she is very fond of telling which involves, to my mind, too much swearing and a very accurate description of a man's moves in the bedroom. It's like she really *knows* this and it makes me wonder who else she is sleeping with because none of what she describes comes from my admittedly meat and potatoes repertoire. The dreadful thought strikes that even though I have more sex than she does, she might actually be better at it. She is remarkably open about sex and not in the least bothered by its absence. Unlike me who can't go a fortnight without suffering headaches and losing my temper, I have known Maria go for two years, during one of our just-friends phases, without being actively beastly. She admits to masturbation though I wish she wouldn't in company.

So everybody was having a high old time of it and nobody objected when I sloshed large measures of pukka Armagnac into their glasses to follow a spectacular bread and butter pudding. The food was great but doing a quick tally, there was no way it cost £100. I'd already bought the booze so I knew bloody well she'd shopped wisely and kept the change. Marcus had given up paying even the most scant attention to Iona and spent the last hour rolling joints and watching Maria. He was giving her the strong silent come-on which I reckon all spades are probably a dab hand at.

Inevitably the conversation moved, as it does at a media gathering, to film. I figured out years ago that women will rave about films and songs that they think somehow capture their essence. It's a tool you can usefully deploy to get a pretty accurate picture of the kind of woman she thinks she is by taking an interest in her cinematic and musical tastes. What is harmlessly interpreted by the woman as a lively interest can in fact be vital information. When I asked Iona what her favourite film was and she replied, *Last Tango in Paris*, it was all I could do not to get the butter out of the fridge. I filed the info away for future reference. Any woman who not only relates to Maria Schneider but could fuck a lardy like Brando likes sex, let me tell you.

Maria claims the following as her favourites: *The Mirror* by Andrei Tarkovsky, *Days of Heaven* by Terence Malick and *The Long Good Friday* starring Bob Hoskins. It's a convincingly eclectic list to all but the most seasoned of Maria's spectators, but I put her selection down to pure posturing. She can be very pretentious about film, especially since she has been with that groovy production company. My favourite films are *The Day of the Jackal* and *Shane* and I'm not embarrassed to admit it. Intellectually, Maria and I are about level-pegging, that is to say bright, but never bothered to work hard enough to get to a good university. If she has the edge on me at all it's because she works at it. I've told her a hundred times that I'm a journalist and simply don't have the time to read. I am not being glib when I say this. I freely confess to being a magpie who steals his ideas from whatever readily available source I can. On a good day this might amount to ten minutes news on the telly and a furtive scan through *Arena* on the toilet. This and a lot of lunchtime gossip is all I need to commission and edit passable features for a London evening paper. As for the novel, every jerk that ever held a pen thinks he has a novel inside him. It's total madness.

People do not, on the whole, enter into journalism because they have original thoughts in their head and I am no exception. One more mediocre novel about London in the Nineties? I don't think so. But when it comes to the birds, what you write is immaterial. It's not as if you ever have to show it to anybody unless you want it published. The simple fact of supposedly being in the process of writing is like catnip to women. I've yet to meet the female whose eyes don't sparkle when you mention that you're a writer. I think they really go for that idea of being the muse who inspires her man to write The Great Novel. Even Maria to whom I have confessed regularly to having no literary ambitions has said that she would, in theory, be prepared to support a husband she believed to be talented.

Although she doesn't give much indication that she thinks me talented, the key word here is husband. More than anybody I've ever met Maria wants to get married. In many ways an independent girl, she is probably the least capable of surviving without a life partner. She has confidence, but it depends on her being chosen within the next few years. She's over-concerned with her shelf life and that kind of neurosis is very off-putting. She pursues the ideal of marriage with a tenacity that is hard to fathom. What's more it's impossible to reconcile her ideals with her lifestyle. She wants to come and go as she pleases, treat me like her private bank and fuck other men, but she also likes to coochy-coo over passing pushchairs and drop not very subtle hints about her biological clock. After seventeen years I still have no idea of what our love for one another – and I do not deny that I love her – is really about. For a start, is it really me she wants or will anybody eligible do? She might talk a good story and act the part of a liberated woman, whatever that is, but beneath it she has more than a touch of a clinging suburban-princess. She dates mainly creative men. They could be anyone from a runner in a film company to a publishing director. Fucking media women ... they won't look at a guy who earns £30,000 a year doing quantity surveying, but any old tosspot with a pony tail and a couple of Martin Amis novels and they're like a rat up a drainpipe. It makes me puke.

But I digress. I was flirting with Iona, for something to do as much as anything else, but it was Marcus who had thrown down the romantic gauntlet that night. Soon after Andy and Rebecca left he started making cosy with Maria on my big cushion on the floor by the CD player and put on some schmaltzy track along the lines of 'Baby, all the things your man won't do ... I'll do it for you.' An obvious rebuke to my treatment of Maria which is sadly often indifferent, but his interest pissed me off enough to order a minicab for him and Iona so that I could get Maria to myself. When everybody had finished proclaiming her genius with food and thanking *her* for such a lovely evening, I relished the prospect of getting her alone. I had a full belly and was nicely chilled on the drink. A good rump would have rounded the evening off perfectly, though I knew I'd probably have to do some explaining about the Lucy Cullen incident before I got the green light. She cleared the plates while I made more coffee and poured large Armagnacs for us both. We had this oddly intimate moment in the kitchen. She was stacking plates in the sink, her face red with drink, and I was waiting for the kettle to boil. I felt suddenly very tender toward her. 'That was brilliant, Maria, thanks.' Instead of making some clever remark like she usually does, she smiled so sweetly, if I hadn't known better, I'd have sworn she was shy. I kissed her head and inhaled the fading aroma of her perfume. Her hair was slightly damp with steam coming up from the sink and the veins on the back of her hands stood out with the heat of the water. I nearly proposed then and there, but held back knowing that I was drunk and my sentimental feelings would pass. Best to play safe and settle for a sleepover. You can never tell which way the wind is going to blow with that one when it comes to sleeping arrangements. You can't push Maria, she has to be in the mood. As I felt myself wanting her, an image of Stella and me shagging on a cliff in Cornwall the previous summer came to mind. I swear Maria is a witch and can read my mind because out of the blue she suddenly asked, 'Do you always use a condom when you have sex?' I thought of lying but you can't get much past Maria. She has spooky antennae that always catch me out. I tried to skirt it by saying, 'Most of the time ...' but I knew the game was up. She turned very slowly from her place at the sink to regard me with cool distaste. She carefully wiped her hands on a tea-towel and said, 'Do what you like with your life, Mark, but don't put mine in danger.' There's no answer to that so I just stood there, feeling like a complete arsehole as she gathered up her belongings, a tatty shoulder bag and worn jacket I bought her once in Browns in a bloody expensive attempt to smarten her up. She checked for her keys and fags and without saying a word or even looking back at me quietly closed the door behind her.

I hadn't seen her since. A month is a long time for us to have no contact whatsoever, but each of us is, I suppose, nursing wounded feelings and waiting for the other to make the first move. Truth be told, I feel a bit of a slimy cunt and I'd rather she'd just punched me in the face that night than walking quietly away looking deflated. There was no point pretending everything was cushty and giving her a bell to see if she fancied a drink. I sensed that Maria was really putting it on the line this time. If I got in touch at all it had to be to offer her commitment or finish it for good. We had gone on too long, growing stale in our open arrangement. It was just too confusing.

She was my friend but she wanted to marry me. She was the person I couldn't imagine life without, but didn't always want to sleep with. During the course of an average dinner alone together our conversation will generally run as follows: Maria will tell me what is wrong with me over starters and the main course and I will return the favour over lengthy coffee and brandy sessions where we both slowly slump closer to the table. We often wonder why we bother. It makes no difference whether or not we are being sexual, we always behave as though we are. Even when we are seeing other people we are proprietary, jealous and unfailingly rude about each other's choice of partner. She is exceptional and I know I should grab it while it's going but I just don't want her enough. This is going to give me away for the shallow bastard that I am but I blow hot and cold on her physical desirability. She is quite tall, almost as tall as me and in heels she makes me feel like I've got a two-inch dick. She has no breasts to speak of which would be OK if she had an equally lithe lower half, but she is classic English pear. Funny, but I don't mind a big bottom on short women, attracted as I am to busty petites, but the combination of height and hips I have never warmed to. Her dark hair is usually worn in several variations on the same basic, short, messy style and her hands are big and gnarly and she never gives them any attention. I do like a bit of nail polish. I know it's slutty because my mum told me so, but I like it all the same. On the plus side she has very long legs, but it is her face which is her passport. Her nearly-black eyes and aquiline nose are pleasing but the mouth is particularly good. Her lips are short but full, suggesting both cruelty and passion. It was the need to get at that mouth that precipitated the inauspicious beginning of our sexual relationship at the age of eighteen. The first time I fucked her was in her bedroom at her mum and dad's who were downstairs in the garden trying to get the barbecue going. I was rushing because I didn't want to get caught out and when it was over she said, 'Don't ever do that again.' I think she was disappointed by the casual brevity of it.

Oh, yes, there was a lot of history between us and it was time to resolve it once and for all. Mum said she wasn't surprised Maria was unhappy. 'Come on, Mark, she doesn't know if she's batting or bowling with you. You've either got to make up your mind just to get on with it or let her go so she can meet somebody nice.'

'You saying I'm not nice?'

'No, Mark. You're my son, I think you're lovely. But if I was Maria, I'd have given you up as a bad lot. If you think you could be happy together, make your move. She won't hang around waiting for you for ever, Mark, she'll get to the point where she's had enough and take up with somebody else.' Put like that, I had to agree on the need to act decisively.

CHAPTER THREE

SHIT OR GET OFF THE POT

I left mum's in a fairly determined frame of mind, though I still wasn't clear which way the dice were going to fall until I reached the traffic lights on Streatham Hill. I was motoring along at a fair clip and would have shot the lights which were just changing had it not been for an old man who stepped off the pavement causing me to brake sharply. He was your classic old geezer, mid-seventies I reckon, in a smart herringbone coat that he'd obviously had for donkey's years, a brown felt trilby and one of those leatherette shopping bags in a shade of shit brown. His scarf was knotted tight around his neck and the lower half of his face to fend off the March winds. I found him strangely fascinating and began to wonder what I'd look like in forty years' time. I wish I hadn't been watching him so closely because then I wouldn't have witnessed a blue Sierra with about seven kids inside it come tearing across the junction, swerve sharply to overtake another car and knock him up in the air. You knew before he hit the deck there was no way he was coming out of it alive. I saw the driver's face freeze in horror for a couple of seconds before he drove off. I had time to memorise the plates, for all the good it would do as the car had obviously been nicked. I jumped out of the car and went and knelt by the old boy with a woman passer-by who was feeling for a pulse. I don't know what made me do it, but I picked up his left hand; it was papery and fragile and cold, the nails hard, yellowing and in need of a trim. I couldn't let go. He wasn't wearing a wedding ring but you just knew that there was somebody waiting at home for him. Somebody he'd probably been married to for over fifty years. I kept rubbing his hand as if by doing so I could put some life into it. I couldn't get over how cold and bony it was, like he'd already been dead a long time. His brow was furrowed as if he were cross, maybe about to shake a fist at the kids in the car driving too fast and about to shout out the time-honoured 'They could kill somebody driving like that.' The police were on the scene in what seemed like seconds though it must have been longer. I could hear it all going on around me, the cars and crackly radios, but I was fixated on this old guy and wanted to know his life story, wanted him to wake up. I really wanted to know if he was married, this fact seemed extremely important to me. Come back, mate, just for a minute and tell me how it was. I noticed that his shoes were wrinkled with age but polished to a high shine, like he'd just run the brush over them before leaving the house. 'Let go, son,' a voice behind me said. A middle-aged copper with a kind expression peeled my fingers off the old man's hand and pulled me up to standing. I must have looked wobbly because he put his arm gently across my shoulders and led me away from the body so that the ambulancemen could get to him. 'Did you see what happened, son?'

'Yeah.' I rattled off the licence plate number and told him just what I'd seen. He wanted details, details. How many kids, what direction were they coming from, going to, description of the driver, my name and address in case it came up in court.

'Yeah right, what are the chances of that?'

'I've got to do my job, sir.' Not his son any more then. I'm sir now. Sir in a snide, don't piss me off sir, voice. I was growing agitated and could feel my head going hot the way it does just before I lose my temper. The copper must have clocked it and after taking my number at work, let me go.

I got in the car, drove two hundred yards up the road, pulled over and cried like a baby. It must have been the shock, because on the whole I don't do tears, but when I go, I really go. Eyes like slits, snot, the works. I'm filled with outrage and righteous fucking fury. Was that it then for that poor old boy? Is that all a life adds up to? You work hard, maybe even serve in the War, then struggle to bring up a family. He was a hard worker, you could tell from the way he was dressed, like he'd been a productive, thorough kind of bloke. 'If a job's worth doing, it's worth doing properly' sort of man. Old school, the sort that polishes his shoes before going down the shops. Then one Sunday afternoon he pops out for a pint of milk and some crumpets, dodging the dog-shit on the pavement, when some fucking juvenile, probably high as a kite and never done a day's work in his life, comes tearing along and ends it all for him. Done him out of his stroke, or heart attack or cancer or whatever else it would have been that brought his life to a natural close. No chance of that poor sod's kids sitting round the sickbed and saying, 'I love you, dad,' before he shuffled off. The next time they saw him he would be laid out in the chapel of rest, a *fait accompli*. It all seemed so fucking wrong, so totally, mind-numbingly pointless. Like there had been some cosmic cock-up and he'd been given the wrong ending by mistake. He looked the sort of man who would be missed, who'd fill a church at his funeral. Who was there to miss me if I met with sudden death? My mum and my sister, it goes without saying, but dad's gone and apart from that there is nobody. Zilch. Nada. Except for Maria. I don't have particularly close male friends given the amount of time I've devoted to the women in my life and half of them hate me. Maria's the only person outside my family who would cry if I died. I got the mobile out to call her, but thought better of it. She'd probably tell me to fuck off. I'm better off just turning up and taking my chances. Least that way there's a chance of getting a foot in the door and now would be a good time to catch her. She's always home on a Sunday afternoon – likes to get ready for work on Monday, makes notes, does her washing, that kind of thing. She's very conscientious like that, very organised. I dry my eyes and drive to North London.

Maria lives in a large shared house in Belsize Park. Nice house, nice neighbourhood, shame about the flatmates. I'm no homophobe, but those two queers she rents a room from really grate on my nerves. Terry and Joseph they're called. Chronic case of creeping campness. They were probably all right when they were younger but even in the five years I've been acquainted with them they've grown more shrill, more brittle, too faggy by half. Not hard up though. They've been together for about fifteen years and bought the house when it was a run-down shell. You should see it now. The place is like something out of *Architectural Digest* – immaculate. They say they let Maria's room for extra cash, but there's no way those two are struggling, they're totally minted. I think they keep Maria around because they're bored, haven't got any kids to distract them and like to check out the straight geezers she brings home. An ungenerous interpretation of the arrangement, but one I'd put my money on.

All the lights were on when I got there, so I knew somebody was home. There was loud music playing and the sound of voices, like there was a party going on. It took a while for someone to answer the door and when they did it was Joseph dressed up as a Wren, Vera Lynn hairdo, stockings with seams up the back, the lot. 'Hello, stranger,' he drawled in a what-the-fuck-are-you-doing-here? tone.

'Looking fit, Joseph.'

His hands flew to his wig in mock horror and he beckoned me inside, babbling rapidly about some fancy dress do for the Terence Higgins Trust they were off to that night. He sounded wired. You wouldn't believe what I found in the kitchen. About eight blokes in various states of undress, fixing tiaras, doing make-up, going for the full drag. There was make-up and enough cans of hairspray, styling products and heated rollers to stock a salon. The counter tops were littered with empty bottles of champagne and half-eaten snacks. In the middle of the kitchen table was a mirror smeared with left-over cocaine and some cut-up straws, so I guessed right about Joseph. No sign of Maria.

'Oh, look, it's the Prince of Darkness.' Terry comes in the kitchen, looking quite out of place in his trousers and crisply ironed shirt, kisses me on the cheek, which I actually don't mind, and points to the ceiling. 'In her room.'

'You not dressing up then, Terry?'

'What, and go out with this bunch of girls? No thank you. I'll be perfectly happy at home with a pot of tea and Pussy.' See what I mean about the campness? If a little girl had a cat called Pussy, I'd think it was sweet, but a forty-five-year-old man who sniggers every time he calls his cat. Give me a fucking break. 'All right if I go up, Terry?'

He waves his hands theatrically. 'Go, go, go and do something with that creature. She's been moping around for weeks. All your doing, I presume?'

'I'll let you know if I find out.'

The house is one of those big bastards embellished with stained glass that has four floors and an attic space above which they converted into a games room with pool table, marble chess set, backgammon boards, the full deck. There isn't an inch of this house that hasn't been gone over and renovated with a one-hair paintbrush. Maria's room is at the top of the house and as I get closer my heart starts banging in my chest. I can't pass it off as the altitude and it feels strangely good to be shitting myself. It's reassuring to think something more than habit got me here. Her door is slightly ajar and I can hear voices on the radio, the sound of papers being shuffled and a drawer closing. I knock. Thinking it must be Terry or Joseph she calls out, 'I hope you're bringing me a cup of tea.'

I step inside. She is standing at her chest of drawers with her back to me putting folders in a pile. I knew she'd be doing her homework. She's wearing pyjamas and her hair is wet. A fag with about two inches of ash is burning away in the ashtray at the side of her bed. 'Maria, it's me.' She freezes and doesn't turn for a few seconds. When she does her expression is blank and she says nothing. She stands stock still, waiting. This is the Maria I see all too rarely. No make-up, no bra, fresh-faced, vulnerable, fleshy. She looks about twelve years old and I get a rush for her. My Maria. All the years I've fucked her around and look at her, so perfect in her ordinariness. I think there's a great misconception among women of what they think men find attractive. I don't turn my nose up at good clothes and a nice haircut. Course I don't. Waxed legs and knickers that cost £60 a go are always pleasing, I grant you. But there's something about a woman without adornment that brings out my more tender side. I like to see girls the way they were made, not how they look after a day at the spa. I like a bit of sweat, a roll of flesh, a couple of hairs she missed with the tweezers, something I can relate to. Maria looks elemental, angelic even. I can think of plenty occasions when she's been demonic and poisonous but that's not why I'm here. I have a debt to pay, a loyalty to reward, and at the risk of laying it on with a trowel, a life to build. I'm breathless with the significance of what I'm about to say, but it feels right so I just come out with it. 'Will you marry me, Maria?' She looks puzzled and hurt and I think I've lost it, she's going to say no. But then her expression changes, she starts to look more like the old Maria, a kind of wry, knowing smile on her face. I can't help myself, I smile back.

'This is a bit of a turn-up isn't it, Mark?' She's circumspect, part of her thinks it's a wind-up, I can tell.

'I've been doing a lot of thinking and I reckon we should make a go of it. I've missed you. I always miss you when you're not around.' This much is true. I can tell by the look on her face that she's not sure what to think now. She motions for me to sit on the bed. I sit on one side, she lowers herself gently, as far away from me as she can, on the other.

'Did you see your mum today?' Right on the button. She's a live one, my Maria.

'Yeah, but that's not why I'm here.' She nods but I can see she's not convinced.

'I'm really flattered, Mark, but I don't know if it's a good idea.' Now she's going to make me work for it. Can't say I blame her, but that doesn't mean I have to oblige. I say nothing for a minute or two and you can tell she's just dying for me to ask a bit harder. She might be deserving of hearts and flowers but she'll be waiting a long time if she's after the down on one knee treatment, it's not my style.

'The ball's in your court, Maria. Think about it and let me know.' I stand up and you can tell she's surprised to see me back off so quick. I'm not deliberately trying to play it cool, but I've said what I came to say. If she wants to play silly buggers, let her. I might be a lot of things, but I'm no drama queen. I hate people who have to milk a moment. Keep it short, keep it sweet.

'OK then, I'll be in touch.'

'Yeah, call me.'

We don't hug, we don't kiss, there's no whooping and screaming and ripping each other's clothes off which I'd kind of imagined, but I sense it's in the bag. I trot down the steps all nimble on my toes and pass Terry coming up. He starts flapping his hands, 'Go back, go back, it's unlucky to cross on the stairs.' But I keep going and shout over my shoulder, 'Luck's got nothing to do with it, Terry. I'll see ya.'

I leave the house without bothering to say goodbye to the freakshow in the kitchen and jog along the road towards the car. I'm feeling good, pumped up. I think I'll go back to the flat, get my kit and fuck off to the gym for a sauna. I don't want to be hanging around indoors for a call. I'd always imagined that the desire to marry a woman would be about deep love, desire and the absolutely certainty that she was the one. In the absence of these, maturity and resignation sufficed. It felt surprisingly good. If we cannot let go, I reasoned, we may as well be together. I think of the old man whom I saw killed and I feel like ringing up Henri Temple-Golden and telling her the good news about overcoming my commitment phobia. Doubtless she'd say I was suffering from post-traumatic stress disorder; they have a way of raining on your parade, those people. I only get as far as Chalk Farm when the mobile rings. Maria's number flashes up on the display.

'Hello, darling,' I say.

'Mrs Tucker to you.'

CHAPTER FOUR

TERMS OF ENGAGEMENT

The next day Maria bunked off work to cart her multitudinous possessions from Belsize Park into my compact Maida Vale flat. It was a decision which I neither encouraged nor discouraged but handled with the vapid ambiguity which came to be the hallmark of our choppy union. I agreed to take the Monday and Friday of that week as my working from home days. Not that I ever did any work from home, but it pays to maintain even a little bit of pretence. Monday for moving, Friday for buying the ring and becoming officially engaged. I wasn't aware that you needed an official date to become engaged, but Maria assured me it was the case. I suppose it made sense to get Maria rocked-up before we told our families the news. Maria seemed to think that I should go down to Woking to ask her dad for her hand in marriage. I'm traditional in a lot of ways, but it seemed ridiculous when you consider that we'd been together on and off for as long as we had. Besides, I don't like her dad. A nicer bloke I could have been persuaded to do it for out of courtesy; old Manolo, Pilar's dad, for example, but not that arsehole. He'd get the news delivered as a done deal and if he didn't like it he knew where he could shove it.

The Monday she moved in was a beautiful spring day and I took the prevailing weather conditions as an auspicious sign. I was feet up in the front room nursing a can of Tennants and waiting for her to turn up. Every now and then I'd get up and go to the window to see if she was coming, like looking would make her get there any quicker. I felt slightly tingly and very chilled from the night before when I entertained a bit of madness, otherwise known as Stella, in my front room. The timing was perfect, I'd have been a mug to let it pass me by. Just after I get off the mobile to Maria, the phone rings instantly and it's Stella. I'm tempted to tell her the news, but think fuck it, that can wait, for tonight I'd like to see that skinny little body working away on top of me. It was all very civilised; she called from her flat on Ladbroke Grove and said she could meet me in Maida Vale in half an hour. I told her to make it an hour, so I could shower and change, but yes definitely, do come over. So she did, she came, she came and she left. She's attractively heartless, Stella, but when her cab came to whisk her back to Ladbroke Grove in that snakeskin raincoat with nothing underneath it was a relief to close the car door and wave her off. I slept like a baby afterwards and woke up this morning feeling very contented. Last night was no big deal and besides I wasn't officially engaged just yet. A technicality maybe, but a crucial one.

I grew very impatient waiting for Maria to arrive, looking at my watch and willing her to get here faster. I couldn't settle for long enough even to read the paper and took instead to pacing the room. The sky clouded over for a short April shower and I leaned my head against the window feeling briefly melancholic. The cherry blossom was being rained off the trees, covering the pavement below in a carpet of pink petals, and daffodils were bursting out of window boxes. I've never been much of a nature lover, preferring the feel of concrete beneath my feet, but it all seemed so poignant, standing there cherishing the dying moments of my civilised bachelor existence and thinking of my poor old dad. Shame he didn't live to see this. He only met Maria a couple of times before he died, but he liked her cheek. She had a touch of Bee about her in her forthrightness and that made him laugh. He always loved the mouthy girls, my dad.

Soon to be my wife or not, I'd told Maria no way was she borrowing my spotless Saab to move her gear. I refused on the grounds that the car wasn't big enough but the truth is she's a shit driver and chain smokes while she's at it. I love that car – my nerves wouldn't take it. So she'd been forced to beg around until she found a friend willing to lend her one. I was onto my third can of Tennants when I saw a large, battered Volvo estate turn the corner into Delaware Road, its indicators signalling the end of my life as I knew it. I walked heavily down the two flights of stairs to the lobby and jammed open the main front door with a stack of Yellow Pages which nobody had yet bothered to pick up. Taking a deep breath I thought, OK, Mark, this is the future, just move with it. I walked over to the car as Maria was opening the back door and a load of clothes tumbled out of a black plastic sack onto the road. Now if that had been me, all my clothes would have been folded or put on hangers and placed in the car in such a way that they reached their destination looking as good as when I'd packed them. Not Maria. Everything had just been stuffed into bin liners and old Tesco bags, complete chaos.

I kissed her hello and my immediate irritation melted when she held me tight and said, 'Oh, Mark, I'm so happy, just so happy.' I've always had enough love for Maria to be pleased for her when she's up so I gave myself a mental ticking off and started hauling gear up the stairs. After six trips to the second floor carrying lampshades, saucepans, a foot-spa, facial steamer and, inexplicably, a large mirror with Kermit the bloody Frog on it, I thought we'd cracked it, but Maria moves round to the driver's side and said she was off to get the next load. I just lost it.

'And where the fuck is all this gear supposed to go, Maria?' There wasn't enough room to swing a cat in my flat even after a good clear-up and already every room was stacked with bags and boxes.

Maria looked hurt. 'But what about all my books and records, Mark?'

I know for a fact that this woman has about three hundred albums and her bedroom in Belsize Park was piled high with books. I wasn't having it. 'Fucking hell, Maria, don't you think you might have discussed this with me first?'

Bad timing. Mrs Murray who lives underneath me on the first floor was just coming out of the door to walk her miniature poodle. There's a rule about animals in our block, but she's an old lady and the dog's no bigger than a rat, so we've all turned a blind eye. But she's the first to complain if somebody has got their telly on after midnight or I'm playing my music too loud. Mrs Murray gave me a frosty look and said, 'Come on, Snowy' to the poodle.

This is all I need. We have a kind of courtesy arrangement whereby we're supposed to inform the other residents in the block if we're moving somebody in with us, or changing our cleaning lady or whatever. Supposedly it's for security purposes but I reckon Mrs Murray just wants to keep abreast of all the comings and goings. I hadn't said a dicky bird to anybody about Maria moving in, I hadn't had a chance, we'd only decided the night before and after that I got kind of busy. Mrs Murray is the chairwoman of our little residents' group and although I never attend any of the meetings I just know that a curt little reprimand is on its way through my letterbox before the week is out. Never one to miss a trick, Maria quickly tries turning the heat off herself.

'Who's that nosy old bag?'

'Never mind her, there's no way you're bringing any more gear in this flat, Maria, you're taking the piss.' She stands there by the car door for a minute looking like a little girl who's just had the back of her legs slapped and I can see that I'm putting a big downer on what should be a happy occasion, so I soften a little and walk round the car and say gently, 'Come on, don't worry about your stuff, we'll figure it out later, yeah? Come upstairs to your new home.'

I give her a bit of a smile and she smiles back and says, 'Go on, then, as long as you go down the offy and get me a bottle of champagne.'

'There's one in the fridge.' I take her hand and lead her up the stairs but she hesitates by the front door. I pull her arm but she doesn't move. 'What's up?'

'Aren't you going to carry me over the threshold?'

I take a big swallow and say, 'It's bad luck to do it before you get married,' but really, I'm assessing Maria and thinking she has to be around the eleven stone mark at the moment and I'm not sure I could do it without straining which wouldn't make either of us feel too good. So instead I push her roughly inside, slam the door and then pin her up against it and get stuck in. We have some pretty fantastic sex right there in the hallway, about the only place with more than two square feet of floor space in the entire flat. She's wearing that bra that cost me £250 to have made to measure and although she's dressed in jeans for moving house, I can tell from the bra she's in the mood. Afterwards, we're lying in the hallway, our clothes half-on half-off, having a laugh and drinking champagne from the bottle. She apologises about the amount of gear she's brought with her and promises to take most of it down to her mum and dad's over the weekend and store it there until we get a bigger place. Pleased with this concession I start kissing her again and she's very responsive, pushing herself against me and wrapping her legs right up around my waist. Maria's really game about quickies. Not all women are by a long chalk, so I'm silently congratulating myself on making such a good choice of wife, feeling all warm and loved-up, thinking to myself, this is going to be all right, it really is.

Maria's enthusiasm for our lives together was infectious. After the shock of waking up to find her next to me every morning and the wireless permanently tuned to Radio Four from my preferred GLR, I was even beginning to enjoy cohabitation. Personally, I think Radio Four is a load of boring wank, but Maria is convinced that you can really learn something by listening to Jeremy Paxman on a Monday morning. She's always fancied Jeremy Paxman. I think he's a conceited knob, but then I would. Things were rocking along quite nicely, the only spanner in the works being Maria's suggestion – or should I say condition – that before we wed I should give Henri Temple-Golden another shot, just to clear up any lingering issues. 'I want you to be sure about this, Mark,' she said during one of our lovemaking sessions. It's very hard to refuse a woman who has your penis in her hand, so the next morning I made an appointment to see her the following week. No harm in keeping Maria happy, besides, I was looking forward to seeing the crow's face when I told her I had successfully 'surmounted all my blocks to real intimacy.' Ha, ha, fucking ha. I was a bit surprised when I got a call at home from Temple-Golden's secretary that evening saying that she'd had a cancellation and could see me at 5.30 p.m. the following day, but I thought it best just to do it and be done with it. It wasn't quite the triumphant session I was expecting. I turned up full of swagger, thinking, right then, love, stick this in your pipe and smoke it, but rather than congratulating me on my forthcoming nuptials she just looked a bit put out and said that I must be sure I wasn't rushing into anything.

'Quick fixes are rarely the solution to our problems, Mark.'

'I wouldn't say seventeen years was too hasty.'

'But you were still having major issues with commitment only months ago. What happened to change your mind?'

'I dunno, I grew up I guess.'

'Growth is a permanent part of living, we can never consider our work on ourselves complete.' Her mouth twisted into a mean little smile when she said this, but I put it down to her irritation at not being able to squeeze multiples of ninety quid out of me. She urged me to consider therapy as an ongoing process, something that could be incorporated into married as well as single life. I told her I wasn't getting married so I could pay another woman to tell me what to do, but she didn't see the joke. I thanked her politely for her concern and left her on her orange cushion. Leaving her office I gave a silent prayer of thanks and thought, thank fuck that's over with.

On the three days I went to the office that week I worked until

44

seven or eight o'clock at night, marking up features for the next day's issue, and it was nice to come home and find Maria on the sofa greeting me with the words, 'Your dinner's in the oven' just the way my mum used to greet my dad when he'd come back late after a game of crib down the pub. Things were good, really good. We were having a lot of sex which helped quell my paranoia that the minute you shack up, the fucking stops. That's what happened all those years ago with Pilar and I still get sad at the memory. Her beautiful face set in stone, nursing some silent grievance and refusing absolutely to let me make it up to her in bed. Foreign holidays though, that was a different matter. Pilar was my first real love, but a total drain on all my resources, financial, emotional and social. But that's in the past and now I have Maria, my oldest friend and now fiancée who's a major bonus socially, a real mate emotionally but in common with every woman I have ever known, a bit of a worry when it comes to money.

We hadn't got as far as the joint account stage yet, but I'd said that anything she bought for the house she should stick on her credit card and I would pay the bill. Big mistake. Maria earns only slightly less than me so there is a good argument for fifty-fifty, but I was stuck on the idea that you had to give your wife housekeeping of some sort. My mum got hers regular as clockwork on a Friday night when dad came home with the fish and chips, so it's kind of indelibly stamped in my mind that this is the right thing to do. Are women pathologically incapable of being sensible with money? Is it some prehistoric urge to fleece the cave-man of his carcass the minute he comes back from a day of hunting and gathering? From day one of her moving in Maria was pushing hard for a party which I did not really fancy at all. If we were to have any kind of celebration I wanted to keep it small. I did not feel much inclined to shout the happy news from the rooftops as to do so in any style would be at least a couple of grand down the Swanee. I finally persuaded Maria that finances did not allow for a large do, but this turned out to be a bad bit of strategy because she then countered with the suggestion that we let her parents host a party for us down at the Veg Palace in Woking, home of Maria's parents, Graham and Diane Weller.

Maria's faith in marriage comes directly from her parents' thirty-seven years together, bypassing every bit of common sense she has. If ever there was a couple who should have jacked it in years ago, it is Graham and Diane. Maria admits that apart from brief periods when she was young they have never been very happy. 'But the point is, Mark, they stuck it out.' I am not convinced that this in itself is a virtue. Graham, or the Veg King as I like to call him, started selling cabbages and bananas from the back of his van on Brixton Hill in the Sixties and now has a chain of over twenty greengrocers dotted around London. Graham and Diane are lower-middle-class alcoholics with pretensions to grandeur. They live in a large detached home on the outskirts of Woking, guarded by electronic gates and their beloved Dobermanns Flash and Radar. Graham, Woking's own Banana Rajah, is your classic ignorant pig who sits in his large armchair cradling a tumbler of scotch on top of his sizeable paunch and sounding off about immigrants, single mothers and people who land themselves in professions, like journalism, where the potential to make obscene amounts of money is limited. He likes an entrepreneur, a cash-merchant, a boy who's in on the swindle somewhere along the line. He greeted the news of our engagement over the phone by telling Maria, 'He'd better start making a decent living then.'

Maria's mum, Diane, is a nice enough woman, but nervous from years of living with the Cucumber Kaiser and his unpredictable temper. She talks non-stop for the simple reason that nobody ever listens to her. She then retreats to her kitchen and knocks back bottles of Chardonnay as she cooks up elaborate meals that her husband never thanks her for. He really is the most detestable pig, though Diane talking non-stop for nearly forty years could try the patience of a saint. I have my theories as to why they stay together. Most of the time they are too pissed to get themselves up the stairs to bed at night without the other one holding their arm, but more importantly Graham would be highly reluctant to carve up his, by now, considerable veg assets to give Diane the kiss-off, much as he clearly despises her. Poor Diane's nerves are shot to shit and the idea of starting over again with a reduced standard of living probably terrifies her. She is the best recommendation I can think of for women having an interest outside the home. Diane has never worked, choosing instead to stay at home with Maria all through her childhood and later turning the keeping of their large house into a full-time occupation. The place is spotless, worryingly so. When she isn't cooking or cleaning she witters on endlessly about who did what and she said to him, he said to her etc, etc. She is fascinated by the minutiae of other people's lives and spends hours on the phone amassing detail from Joyce, Carol, Barbara or any other poor sod who finds herself captive to her drunken phone calls. Maria thinks her mum and dad have a great relationship, a model we should emulate, you know, good times and bad, hell and high water. Frankly, if I thought I was going to end up like those two I'd throw the towel in now.

Maria is quite mean to her mum and treats her like a bird-brain which I suppose she is, but all the same it doesn't seem right and I think she could do with showing Diane a bit more respect. Maria is an only child and it shows. Everything she wants she thinks she should get. Me included. Her mum had some kind of gynaecological complication after Maria which meant no more kids and I reckon that's at the root of a lot of the Veg King's contempt for his wife. You know, never getting the longed-for son and heir to prove his virility. Maria says it never bothered her not having brothers and sisters, she had plenty of mates and no shortage of toys. It's a miracle she isn't more spoiled than she is. Her dad she idolises unreservedly – she's a textbook daddy's girl – and together they chat endlessly about work. Graham is constantly devising schemes for Maria to get more money out of the independent production company she works for. 'Fucking long-haired prats, you wanna fleece 'em, love.' He is such a major arsehole that I have to keep my mouth shut every time she starts up about what a great guy he is. For someone as sharp as Maria, and even allowing for parental infatuation, I cannot fathom that she doesn't cop even a little bit to his nastiness and narrow-minded bile.

So anyway, the party idea was being kicked around for a day or two and I start to think that maybe it's not such a bad idea to let her old man cop for the lot. So on the Sunday after we get the ring, a solitaire diamond costing £2,500 (could have been worse), Maria and I drive out to Woking for a roast dinner and a planning session with the Banana Rajah. It is a beautiful day, daffodils and crocuses bursting out of every front garden we pass, and I have to admit that the Veg Palace looks pretty magnificent if over-wrought mock-Tudor and a fresh yellow paint-job every other summer is your idea of good taste. Flash and Radar are there to greet the car, menacing-looking bastards, baring their teeth, looking all sinew and steel like they'd take your leg off if you made a wrong move, which of course is the whole point of them. Maria jumps out of the car and greets them like a couple of bunny rabbits, 'Hello, baby, darling, come and give me a kiss, oh yes, I've missed you two so much.' I just swerved and strolled over to the Veg King who's standing in the doorway of his home looking like a suburban Yul Brynner with the sun on his big shiny dome and a lairy silk shirt he probably picked up on a jolly to the Far East. I'd lay money that he fucks young girls on his 'business trips' – really young girls. He looks the type and besides I can't think of any other explanation for a greengrocer in Bangkok.

'Hello, Graham, how's tricks?' We pump a handshake but he doesn't say anything, just looks at me, giving me a bit of an evil eye above the tight smile. He's doing his, 'fuck my daughter around and I'll have your bollocks for breakfast' number but I don't care because he's already half cut and when he gets bored with me he'll go back to picking on his wife. When Maria finally finishes snogging those disgusting animals she flings her arms around daddy's neck and it's all cuddles and 'How are you, princess?' – he actually calls her princess – and 'I hope this herbert is looking after you?' He's smiling but he means it.

Relief comes in the form of Maria's mum who's actually looking very bright and well and welcomes us in extravagantly. 'Ask them in, Graham, keeping them standing there on the doorstep, honestly.' Me and Diane have a cuddle and she cups my face and looks into my eyes and says, really meaning it, 'I'm so pleased, Mark, I really am. I've always hoped you two would settle down. Come on, come in, let's get the champagne going.'

Diane leads us into the front room which is about half the size of an Olympic swimming pool, decorated quite nicely for middle-aged suburbanites, with lots of reproduction furniture and reeking of Mr Sheen. One end of the room is all glass with doors which lead out to a very formal garden with lots of topiary and rose-beds and behind that a large yew hedge which conceals the swimming pool and tennis court. You could do a lot worse than marry into a family with this kind of dough, and as Diane brings the champagne in my crafty little mind starts to mull the possibilities of a wedding present. A deposit on a house perhaps? No one will ever be good enough for his daughter, but whoever she plots up with, Graham would never see Maria go short.

I'm feeling quite cheerful with all this affluence around me. Not only that there's a beautiful smell of roast dinner coming from the kitchen and life feels more than all right. Diane brings in the tray with the champagne and glasses and as she bends down to set it on the table I can see the price-tag sticking out the back of her skirt. It must have been bought brand new for the occasion and this little detail moves me. Her cheeks are flushed and my guess is that this is not her first drink.

Graham still doesn't address me directly, referring to me through Maria. 'So is he going to start working full-time now that he's nearly a married man?'

'Ask him yourself, dad, he's sitting about six feet away from you.' Nice one, Maria.

With this, the Veg King turns his fat red face on me and does a passable impersonation of a man trying to be civil. 'So then, son, no more part-time for you, eh?'

I'm thinking, don't call me son, you cunt, my dad was worth ten of you, but I reply, 'I don't see why things need to change. It's not as if I'd be earning much more if I did go full-time. Anyway I want to finish the novel first.' This is blatant bullshit, but I'm in the mood for a wind-up.

'Oh, yeah, what's it about then, this "novel" of yours?'

A slight smirk plays on his face and the only thing that holds me back apart from the fear of being crushed by this fat horrible bastard is the anxious look on Maria's face. I've never come right out and told her that I think her dad is a total arse, but she senses my attitude and is determined for us to be friends. 'Crime,' I say and leave it at that, savouring the slight shock which registers on his ugly boat. The Veg King has legitimate enterprises all right, but all his cash gets spun a few times before it comes out the right side of legit.

The Veg King recovers his composure and asks in a snide voice, 'Know a lot about crime then, do you, Mark?'

'Well, you don't have to be Einstein to figure out that things are rarely what they seem.'

By this point we're having a bit of a stand-off, pure hatred vibrating back and forth across the room. Diane, love her, comes in and saves the day. 'Dinner's ready.' Maria gives me one of those please don't fall out with my dad looks and so over the course of lunch I make an effort to ask him about the business and if he still plays golf. Those fancy fruits, mangoes, starfruit, papaya etc, recently arrived on the British shopping list are proving to be a nice earner and trade is good. 'We just stick fucking organic stickers on everything, double the price and it's walking out of the shops.' Nothing like a businessman with ethics, eh?

Next to us, Maria and her mum and are discussing the party and I've got one ear cocked trying to figure out how much this is going to cost me, because it still isn't clear who's picking up the bill. The champagne and the good wine were obviously working because apropos of nothing, I come out with, 'Look, Graham, it's good of you to host a party for us but you must let me pay for all the food and drink.'

This is a piece of nonsense because I have just about fuck-all in the bank after our little trip to Hatton Garden on Friday, but my gesture goes down well and the Veg King cradles my shoulder in something approaching warmth and says, 'I appreciate the offer, son. As you know, I cannot tolerate a ponce, but this one's on us.' With this he gives me a big wink. 'But cheers anyway. I appreciate the offer. Did you hear that, Diane? Not frightened to put his hand in his pocket.' He winks at me again. Diane and Maria are beaming now, relieved that we've crossed the wire of tension.

For bonding purposes, Graham takes me down the golf club after lunch, not for a few holes, just a few more drinks, and treats me to his philosophy on life and marriage. He lights up a big cigar and is pointing it at me meaningfully, narrowing his eyes and giving me the world according to Graham Weller. 'What you got to remember about women, son, is that they might scream and shout and give you all kinds of shit, but they need to know that you're the boss, that you're going to look after them. I don't care what they say about men having to be more sensitive, that's a load of bollocks, they need someone they can trust and look up to. Lose the respect of your wife and what the fuck have you got, eh?'

'But Maria's pretty independent, Graham, it's one of the things I like about her, I don't think I'd get away with giving it the cave-man.'

'Never mind all that independent shit, that's just something they do until they find a geezer who can take care of them. And you are going to take care of her, aren't you, Mark?'

This is more of a threat than a question so I'm nodding away going, 'Sure, sure, absolutely.' Some of his mates come into the bar, all of them escapees from the post-Sunday lunch domestic scene, and he's introducing me right, left and centre, looking at moments almost proud. Without exception, they all want to know what I do for a living. When I tell them I'm a journalist there's a bit of teasing, but I can feel the respect. I shouldn't think half the men in this bar ever learned to read and write properly and even though none of them look hard up, life has probably been a struggle one way or another. I'd never been to a golf club before, but I'd imagined it was all bank managers and accountants. Instead I'm drinking with a clutch of suburban thieves and I have to smile to myself.

By six o'clock Graham is seriously pissed and I'm not feeling too clever myself. I suggest that we start making tracks but he's having none of it so I ask him what his number is so that I can ring Maria and let her know where we are. 'That's very considerate of you, son, very considerate,' says Graham laughing, then to his mates, 'She's got him right under the fucking thumb, ain't she?'

The phone rings for ages, but finally Maria picks up and I tell her to come and get me right away. I've had about all I can take of the Veg King and his lairy mates. My head hurts and I feel a bit sick. I'm on early tomorrow morning and it's the editorial meeting at 9 a.m. I do not want to be feeling shabby because Cullen is still watching me like a hawk and in a couple of weeks I'm going to ask for more money. Change in domestic circumstances and what have you. Maria's keen for me to stay and bond with daddy but I put my foot down just like Veg King told me to and it yields surprising results. 'All right, I'll be there in five minutes. Mum and I have finished up here, I just want to get a few things out of my old room.'

'Oh, for fuck's sake, Maria, not more stuff.'

'Just my old teddy.' Great, now I've got to sleep with her bloody teddy.

'Just be quick about it, Maria.'

'Mark ...'

'What?'

'I really love you, babe.' I'm pissed enough to smile at this.

'Yeah, me too.'

My back gets slapped so much when we say our goodbyes in the golf club bar that I'm going to check in the mirror for bruising when I get home, but at least we leave the Veg King in good heart and we've avoided a major row, so all in all we can claim the day as a success. Without consulting me, Maria has settled on a date for the party, a fortnight Saturday, but I'm too drunk to care and I'm resigned to just going along with it. It might even be quite good. This way I can invite all my mates from work and get the family involved. Everybody is happy. Life is good. Just got to tell my family now.

CHAPTER FIVE

A FAMILY AFFAIR

I find idolatry in any shape or form distasteful, but I can't help hero-worshipping my sister Bee. Temperamentally, she's more of a mother than my real one. Although she's only a year older than me Bee has always been very much the big sister, pushing me around, sticking up for me and very free with her opinions. Her real name, Veronica, was used only when filling in forms or by my mum when she lost her rag, 'Veronica! Pick your bloody shoes up' etc, and I'm quite proud that her nickname comes from me. My dad used to call her V and as a baby trying to copy him I hit upon the B sound and it stuck. I'm very close to my sister, which is handy because my relationship with my mum can get a bit fraught. I'd do anything for my mum but she pisses me off in ways I can't fathom. There's a resentment there that I don't like to contemplate too deeply and certainly nothing I would care to explore with the rook on the orange cushion. Any problems, I go to Bee. Any announcements, it's Bee I tell first. It was natural that she should find out I'd got engaged before I broke the news to mum.

My sister is tall and skinny with a bossy, protective nature. Bee was always quick to thump any child that came near me. This was a glorious sensation at five, six, seven and even ten, but by my twelfth year she was still doing it and it wasn't such a good look. There was one term during my first year at grammar school when I was being bullied by a group of boys who went to the comprehensive. We travelled on the same bus and they used to like a

55

wind-up. It was nothing serious, just a bit of shoving and name-calling. Certainly nothing bad enough to complain about, but Bee got wind of it from a mate and every day for a month she insisted on riding with me to school and then half-way back again to her own, which was a mere ten-minute walk from our house. My protests fell on deaf ears and even when dad took the unusual step of intervening and telling Bee to 'let him fight his own battles' she ignored him. Every morning she would march me upstairs on the bus and make us sit ostentatiously on the seats at the back, typically the hard boys' place. She'd narrow her eyes menacingly at anyone who looked our way and shout down the bus, 'Yeah, you want some?' I would spend the entire fifteen-minute journey staring out of the window and edging away from my sister. Some of those boys were quite big, say fourteen or fifteen, but Bee didn't give a shit. She certainly showed no fear. Can you imagine the agony? A pubescent boy with a stringy sister as security? But there was method in her madness and very soon my tormentors backed off. Didn't even look in my direction. The memory of it makes me cringe to this day.

We lived in a street of terraced houses sandwiched between an edgy council estate and a flush suburban ghetto. Socially we were neither fish nor fowl. My dad was a park-keeper for the council so economically we had more in common with people on the estate but Patsy, my mother, had aspirations which stretched southwards into the sun where the neatly shaved lawns of detached homes were tickled by the sweep of willow. She tried to gentrify our house by having mock leaded-light double glazing installed and festooning the front garden with hostas which she'd heard were the 'smart choice' among plant-lovers. I don't have any recollection of wanting to live in a bigger house and I could never understand my mother's dissatisfaction. One of her habitual complaints was not having a 'pantry' for storing dry goods. Her friend Barbara at work had one and didn't know how my mother managed without. My dad used to murmur in agreement when she went off on one but never got around to building the extension which would house the multiple-buy special offers at Sainsbury's – Tesco's though closer was too downmarket – she was so fond of. We weren't rich, but we weren't dirt poor either. What I knew seemed normal to me.

A natural politician, Bee played the game well enough to keep my mother happy and still get away with murder. Like me, she was a grammar school pupil, and most of her friends came from respectable families. But when her homework was done and she'd helped mum with the washing up after dinner, she would slip into her beloved ankle-length leather trench coat, the sleeve concealing a slim pack of ten cigarettes, and saunter off to The Centre. The Centre was the nucleus of the neighbouring estate, a small Co-losseum of graffiti-etched shops, a pub, community centre, library, four phoneboxes and some large concrete tubs robbed of their shrubs and replaced with dog-ends and Coke tins. There she would loll on the benches with girls she'd known from junior school and watch the boys go by. Everybody smoked, some drank cider, but only Bee could nonchalantly sit on the directories in the phone box and make reverse charge calls to unknown people in Canada and Belize simply by inventing the numbers. The rest of her gang were at the comprehensive together so Bee was a bit of an outsider but that suited her. She lacked the ringleader ambition, preferring to sit quietly on the sidelines amusing herself. By the time she was fourteen she was not only visiting The Centre every night, but slipping into the downstairs lounge of the pub, the now burnt-out Merry Go Round, where a quick turnover of defeated landlords turned a blind eye to the ceaseless tide of underage drinkers. Bee had developed quite a persona by her early teens and I remember her clearly at that age, dressed always in her long leather coat with the pack of ten John Player Blue in her sleeve, shovelling ten pence pieces into the jukebox. A soul-girl, she favoured Fred Perry tops, gold jewellery and a soft shag perm. Her favourite song was Jermaine Jackson's 'Let's Get Serious'. By this age she'd adopted vodka and lime as her drink of choice though I never saw her drunk. She had the most immaculately cared for nails, always painted a daring shade of red which drove my mother totally nuts. Every day at school, she'd get dragged off by one of the lab technicians who would remove it with acetone which turned her nails black. Every afternoon she'd come home and paint them again. She wasn't a come-and-get-it troublemaker, but quietly determined to go her own way.

Bee isn't classically fanciable and never really had boyfriends as such, but she was matey with all the blokes and they treated her with a lot of respect. Especially the older ones. I suppose they could see that she was sharp, not just another dolly bird. Bee's intelligence took the form of native wit, an exhaustive knowledge of jazz funk and a sharp tongue. Mum would send me off on my bike to look for her if she wasn't home by half-past nine. I always knew where to find her and would loiter outside the pub, inhaling that seductive aroma of beer and cigarettes, trying to catch her attention through the window. I didn't like going in to get the piss ripped out of me by her crowd. Bee would have harsh words for anyone who tried it on, but I preferred not to be defended by my sister, especially since I had already grown taller than her by the age of thirteen. It wasn't so much that I was a wimp but lazy, as in all things, when it came to confrontation. Bee was, still is, an intriguing mix of good-girl bad-girl, saucy but safe. She passed among her peer group by adopting the mannerisms and dress of the pack, but she was never really one of them. Bee had her own agenda though you were never quite sure what it was exactly. A lot of her friends are losers but she seems to like them best that way. She has the same mates today as she did back then with a few additions from her years in nursing. They are all variously skint, down on their luck or, to my mind, bloody chancers who take advantage of her generosity and good nature. You could build all kind of worthless theories as to why she is the way she is and I daresay Henri Temple-Golden would have a field day, but whatever the explanation she has a natural sympathy for the underdog. I don't know how else to account for a pitifully paid career in nursing and her bewildering marriage to Coxy. Dean Cox, first boyfriend and now husband. As far as I'm aware he's the only man she's ever slept with, but with Bee you can never tell. She's a dark horse, my sister. I think she was probably quietly in love with Coxy from about the age of twelve when she first started hanging around at The Centre. Dean would have been about sixteen then and had already left school to work with his dad as a roofer. Not a typical hard-man but very much of that gang, he didn't take much notice of Bee in the early days, engrossed as he was with bedding estate dollies. Most of them were older than Bee and some already had children. But when Bee left school at sixteen and lived-in up at St George's to do her nurses' training, Coxy started turning up at the house at weekends to see if she'd come home. He'd never taken much notice before but once she was gone he must have missed her. I think Bee's decision to move into nurses' accommodation might have been a deliberate move to force Coxy's hand. She'd hung around patiently for four years waiting for him to take notice of her and then left, knowing full well he would follow in her slipstream. Her life has never, as far as I can see, been complicated and I envy her. Coxy, like Bee, has a simple unchanging character that allows him to be happy living around the corner from the house he grew up in, still working with his dad in the roofing game and drinking with the same crowd he went to school with. It's no secret that I think Bee could have done a lot better for herself and on this one mum and me are united. Throughout Bee's training mum had hopes that she would make a match with a doctor or ambulanceman, 'somebody decent' were her exact words. But Bee just steadily went on with Coxy and is still doing the same today. I remember coming home from football on Saturdays to find him stretched out on the settee watching sport on the telly while Bee read her nursing books. His languid presence used to wind mum up no end. She never quite had the nerve to court Bee's wrath by barring him from the house but she refused to sit in the same room and would fidget around the kitchen, cleaning out cupboards and banging saucepans all the time he was there. If I went in to fetch a drink or biscuit she would hiss, 'Look at him, he's just bloody ignorant, lying on my settee like that!' To give Coxy his due he had pretty good manners even if he wasn't what you'd describe as a scintillating conversationalist. Typically taking the line of least resistance, dad was pretty sanguine about Coxy, figuring that he'd never been in trouble with the police and was too frightened of Bee to mess her around. It all seemed fairly ordinary family stuff at the time, alternately irritating and boring, but once it fell apart, I'd have cut my leg off to get it back.

The breakdown of my parents' marriage seemed to come out of nowhere and what galls me to this day is that there was no good reason for it. Mum seemed to get in a panic as she approached fifty. She felt she'd done nothing with her life save work, run a house and struggle to bring up children. All true. She began to run around like a headless chicken, taking up keep fit classes and anything that would get her out of the house. Her frustrations, which had always simmered just beneath the surface, began to explode into angry verbal scenes where she would rail against the three of us for taking her for granted and treating the house like a hotel. She changed her name from Pat to Patsy and began to favour daring colour schemes in her clothes. She encouraged dad to take up golf, presumably so that he'd be busy enough not to notice her absence, but it didn't work. Dad gamely trudged around the golf course at Mitcham a few wet afternoons, but he wasn't stupid and knew the score. If not yet physically, emotionally mum had flown the nest.

Months of barely disguised tension broke one afternoon in October 1983 when I came home from sixth form college to find my dad stretched out on the settee in tears. It was a shocking discovery on a number of levels. For a start, dad was never at home during the day. Only serious illness or our annual fortnight's holiday in Spain would keep him away from the small six-acre park he managed for Croydon Borough Council. So it was suspicious that he should be at home, let alone prostrate on the settee crying his eyes out. His face was swollen and contorted, I had never seen my dad cry before and I didn't like it. He wasn't a hard man, quite the opposite, but he was quiet and private, a thoughtful person with a rich interior life I would say. Seeing him like that freaked me out and I remember running around making weak mugs of tea because I couldn't keep still for long enough to let the teabags brew. 'It's over, Mark, she lied to me, it's over.' All this on the strength of one phone call to her office at 2.30 to find that she was not back from lunch, but his hunch proved right. My mum didn't have another man exactly, but she had gone out to lunch with one. She'd never lied to my dad before in their entire marriage, but knowing full well he wouldn't swing for her having a pub lunch in the country with another man, she'd told a porky. The worst thing was, I'd encouraged her to do it. She'd been going on for some time what a laugh she had with the reps at the car parts factory where she worked as a secretary and how one of them, Dennis I think his name was, wanted to take her for a pub lunch in the country one day, just to say thank you for all the back-up work she did for him. This might just have been an excuse, but she wasn't going anyway so it didn't make any difference. 'I can't go, you know what your dad's like, he wouldn't understand.' She had a point. Dad was possessive with mum simply because when he married her he felt he finally had something that was his own. My dad was the youngest of four orphaned brothers who drifted in and out of children's homes until the maternal grandmother, having seen off the last of her own seven children, took them in. He suffered no shortage of love in his life, but every item of clothing or toy had been used by at least three kids before him. He left school at fourteen and worked in a greengrocers saving enough for his treasured Norton motorbike. But it was my mum, to whom he became engaged at the age of eighteen, that was the real prize.

His Pat. He managed to hold on to her for twenty-four years, but just shy of their silver wedding anniversary she slipped from his grasp.

A brief shouting match ensued when she came home and within days dad was walking out of the front door with his suitcase. It all seemed to happen so quickly and I remember him leaving early on a Sunday morning and, in particular, the smell of his shaving cream as I kissed him goodbye. It was raining, and as I watched him throw his case in the van and drive off, I knew my childhood had ended. I would never live with my dad again. He kept his composure well enough but the sorrow was so thick it was choking. He went to live in a bedsit in Mitcham, rinsing out his socks and drying them on the radiator overnight so he could put them back on his tired feet and go off to work the next day and continue to support the woman who had asked him to leave their home. I was appalled at the way he just rolled over and did as he was told. No fucking way is this ever going to happen to me, I vowed. I don't know how he managed to stay so reasonable, for me and Bee I suppose, but there was never any question of my dad being sticky over the house. Whatever she'd done, she was our mother and she needed the house to finish bringing up my sister and me. We were almost off her hands. Bee was eighteen and only had a year to go before she finished her nurse's training. I was seventeen and half-way through my A levels.

I have never, like some sons, put my mother on a pedestal, preferring instead the quiet steadiness of my dad, but until then we'd rubbed along well enough. In a practical sense she was a very good mother. The house was always clean, our clothes washed and pressed and a hot meal on the table every night. Mum was always the strict one, the disciplinarian, the worrier. She was hard-working and highly responsible but for a while I hated her with a passion and wanted to get as far away from her as possible. Physically, this was impossible as the three of us all had to live together, but emotionally I withdrew the little affection I had been willing to give her up till then. Don't get me wrong, I love my mum, but she broke my dad's heart and splintered our lives in the process, so I don't think I was being unreasonable to hold it against her.

In the early weeks after he left my sister and I walked around in a daze, not quite believing what had happened. Mum was in a highly strung state, either vigorously defending her decision or breaking down in tears. Bee managed to comfort her without ever agreeing when she tried to convince us that she'd 'done the right thing'. I couldn't stand to be around it and would find more and more reasons not to be at home, either going to friends' houses for my dinner or just hanging around at college kicking a ball until it was dark. If all else failed, I took refuge in the chip shop up the road where I would play the fruit machine and drink tins of Coke until they closed at 10 p.m. Ironically, the whirlwind of activity outside the home that prompted the split came to a halt. As far as I knew, Dennis was not on the scene and the keep fit classes also stopped. Mum just used to sit, morose, in front of the telly looking thin and unhappy every night after work. Bee moved back from St George's and occasionally I would sit up in her room, lounging on the bed while she crouched over the tiny desk my dad had built her making notes. Like dad, Bee has a very solid, calm quality about her and all the time I was up in her room on the bed I felt safe. For the first year after the split, she single-handedly kept what was left of our family on an even keel. She never said much about the split beyond the simple diagnosis that mum was 'going through the change'.

Dad reliably came to pick me up every Sunday and took me off to play football during the season. The summer was trickier. I was too old to cart off to the zoo and more often than not we would find ourselves sitting in a Berni eating a £4.99 roast lunch special, dad trying to be cheerful and me feeling like my heart was going to break. I was never invited to visit his bedsit but I know that Bee used to pop in on her way home from St George's. You could always tell when she'd been to see him, because she'd come home very downcast. I'm certain that her decision to get married was done as much in desperation to get away from the situation at home as it was a mark of her commitment to Coxy. I'm not saying she wouldn't have married him anyway, but the idea seemed to come out of nowhere. The evening she made her announcement was a classic in family drama. She surprised mum by saying that she'd invited dad home for his tea because there was something she wanted to tell us together as a family. This was a first as dad usually refused to come into the house at all. Mum would stand in the doorway on Sundays and call out to his waiting van on the kerb, 'Do you want to come in and have a cup of tea while you're waiting for Mark?' Dad would shake his head and keep staring straight ahead as if something fascinating was happening further along the road. Mum desperately seemed to seek dad's forgiveness and I hoped for a while that her contrition was a sign that she wanted to get back with him On the evening in question dad turned up at 6.30 sharp and shifted uncomfortably on the threshold of what used to be his home. He looked so out of place, it didn't seem possible that only months before he used to walk through that door whistling every night. Dad knew what was coming because he'd obviously gone back to the bedsit after work, had a shave and changed into a clean shirt.

'Hello, Pat.'

'Come in, John. Sit down, do you fancy a cup of tea?' Mum fluttered around smiling and trying to keep busy. Dad took a seat on the settee, deliberately avoiding the worn armchair that had been his place for as long as I can remember. Dad's chair was sacrosanct and if either Bee or I sat on it we would be told by mum, 'Get out of there, that's your father's chair.' Neither mum nor I had any clue of what was about to happen, though mum had suggested earlier in the kitchen that maybe Bee was planning to go and work in America after her training. She'd always had a thing about Bee going out to the States or the Middle East where nurses can earn very good money. She probably imagined Bee making a good marriage to some nice rich doctor over there, getting out of the drudge of suburban living. Mum had very high hopes for both of us and you could argue that this was handy as I don't remember my dad even looking up from his paper when I opened my O Level results to find I'd passed all nine. I think he just mumbled something like, 'That's good, well done.' He really didn't give a shit what we did for a living as long as we were happy. Patsy, on the other hand, cared very much about her children having careers and I think she convinced herself that Bee had landed some wonderful opportunity. She was buzzing in anticipation of a big announcement. But it was dad I remember most vividly that evening. His wet hair combed back and a clean, stiff shirt collar rubbing against his freshly shaved throat. He was the picture of grace despite his obvious discomfort. When my mother put his dinner down in front of him he said, 'This looks nice, Pat,' the way he used to do every teatime before they split, and I felt sick with misery.

If Bee felt it too, she didn't let on and methodically set about carving up her dinner into little cubes, as she always does, the whole bloody plateful, before she starts to eat. Patsy, never a very patient person, couldn't stand the suspense and vigorously sprinkling salt onto her dinner asked, 'Well, what's this news you have for us then, Veronica?' The use of my sister's proper name was a dead giveaway that mum was jonesing.

Bee casually finished chewing her mouthful of chicken and mushroom pie while we all looked at her expectantly. A hypnotically slow eater, when finally she swallowed, she announced baldly, 'Dean and I are getting married next May.'

Dad, who was sitting next to her, put a big arm around her shoulders and, pulling her close to him, kissed her head and said, 'Brilliant news, love, I'm really pleased for you both.' Mum was a study in shock and disappointment.

'But you can't get married, you're only eighteen!'

'So, it's legal and anyway I'll be nineteen by next May.'

'But you're too young, what about your training, it's such a waste.'

'Being married doesn't stop you from working, mum.'

Mum looked anxiously across at dad for support but none came. Like Bee he was smiling and calmly continuing to eat his dinner. 'Lovely pie, Pat.'

'You knew about this, didn't you, John?' Mum's voice began to climb dangerously.

'Well, it is traditional for the groom to ask the father for his daughter's hand.' I don't think he was deliberately baiting my mother, just proud of the fact.

'And you said yes, just like that, without speaking to me first?'

'Those days are over, Pat,' my father said quietly. 'Besides, he's a decent young bloke, goes to work and he loves Bee. I don't see what you're so worried about.'

'Oh well, that's just charming, I'm the last to know about anything. I can't believe you didn't speak to me about it. We may not be together any more, but she's still our daughter, John.' My mother pushed her dinner away from her sulkily and lit a cigarette.

'I'm sorry, mum, but this isn't your decision to make, or dad's for that matter. Even if he'd said no, I'd still be marrying Dean.' In Bee's eyes I saw a glint of malevolence and it looked like it felt good. To this day, I don't know if she was motivated by her love for Coxy or the desire to stick the boot in, but I think it all came crashing down for my mum that night, the full realisation that we were no longer a family.

'I suppose you knew about it as well.' Mum looked at me accusingly.

I spoke for the first time. 'Don't look at me, I didn't know.' This was the truth and although I was almost as disappointed as my mother, I was enjoying seeing her suffer a bit.

'Well, you don't have to worry about money, I'll take care of the wedding costs,' my Dad said.

Bee knew full well that he was struggling and said quickly, 'Don't worry about it, dad, Dean and I have got some savings and his mum and dad have said they'd help, what with, you know, you and mum ...'

'Oh, so it's all my fault, is it, that your dad can't pay for your wedding?' Tears of outrage ran down my mother's cheeks.

'Bee didn't say that, Pat. Besides, Dean's mum and dad don't have to worry, I'm the father of the bride and I'm paying. I've only got one daughter and she'll get a proper wedding.' He looked lovingly at my sister. 'You and Dean save your money for a house.'

'You're loving this, aren't you, John?'

'If you mean am I happy that our daughter is getting married, then yes, Pat, I am.' Dad put his knife and fork together then, winking at me, said, 'Wouldn't mind a cup of tea, son.'

I stood up to put the kettle on and then without quite knowing why, pulled my sister's hair and said, 'I hope you're not thinking of getting married in white?'

'Cheeky little sod.' It was the only time I remember seeing my sister blush.

*

The day of Bee's wedding was emotional for all of us. I'm not usually sentimental, but I clung on to each moment of that day, savouring the family togetherness and genuine happiness we all felt. Mum niggled up to the last minute, knowing full well she was defeated but wanting the last word. Come the day she seemed resigned and even happy. It was held on the Saturday before the Whitsun Bank Holiday and the sun shone high and glorious over St Mary's Beddington. I remember dad turning up outside the family home looking like a film star. He'd obviously spent a few quid on a new suit for the occasion, his hair was very carefully combed back and his shirt as stiff as a board. The thought of him ironing his shirt with a can of spray starch and preparing for such a big occasion in that little bedsit on his own made me a bit thoughtful. It wasn't right. I sat in the kitchen with mum and dad drinking Baileys while we listened to the shrieks coming from Bee's room upstairs, where she was holed up with Linda, her maid of honour. The back door of the kitchen was open and outside, birds sang in the sunshine. Mum and dad were easy with one another, enjoying the house filled with laughter and shouting as it used to be. In the front room, Coxy's sister Sue was trying to dress her twin daughters, who were only about four at the time, in their finery. Records were blaring from upstairs and at one point mum went up to see how they were getting on and shouted at them to 'turn that bloody thing down!' It was great sitting there with mum in her rollers and dressing gown smoking cigarettes and reminiscing easily with dad, talking about their own wedding day over twenty-five years before without any apparent sign of strain. 'Do you remember your gran not letting you go to church until she'd smothered you in that bloody hair tonic?' My mum laughed. 'I could smell you as I came up the aisle.'

An hour before the ceremony mum slipped upstairs to dress and put her make-up on, leaving dad and me feeling stiff in our collars and ties in the kitchen polishing off the last of the Baileys. 'We might as well, Mark,' said dad, sloshing refills into our glasses, 'nobody's driving and it's not every day your sister gets married, is it?'

Mum came down looking really good in a pale green dress with matching handbag, shoes and hat. She looked at my dad and said, 'Will I do?'

'You look smashing, Pat.' Dad's voice was quiet and I can only imagine what was going through his mind. What a day. Your only daughter getting married and you're with your wife, but not with your wife. Mum and dad looked like a couple of awkward youngsters on their first date, but then we heard a beeping. The cars had arrived.

I know all brides are supposed to look beautiful on their

wedding day, but I've seen some dogs walk the plank in my time. Not my sister though, she really did look the business. The dress and veil were very simple, more classy than I would have given her credit for, and her hair was piled up on top of her head Dusty Springfield style. She didn't wear typical bride's make-up – all that peachy Princess Di shit – but went instead for a Sixties look with dark eyes and pale lips. Really fucking tasty, I almost fancied her myself. She completed the look with a fag dangling from her fingers. 'For crying out loud, Bee, put that fag out, you'll stink,' mum screeched. Dad just stared at her silently, looking a bit awed by his daughter.

'What do you think then, dad?'

'You look beautiful, love.'

'Is that our car I just heard?'

'In your own time. Feeling nervous?'

'Not really. Wouldn't mind a vodka though. Dog that out for me, Mark,' said Bee passing me her half-smoked fag.

'Oh for goodness sake, Veronica, you'll smell like an old pub by the time you get there.' Mum flapped about straightening her veil.

'Come on, mum, let's go.' I took my mother's hand and led her out to the car, feeling like a man, though of course, not in my dad's league. True to his word, and I have no idea where he got the cash, he paid for a slap-up do. Bee arrived at church with my dad in a vintage Rolls and walked the plank on his arm looking as women are supposed to on such occasions – totally radiant. Even Coxy looked half decent in a navy blue suit and silvery grey tie. I didn't notice the details until Bee passed me on the aisle when I saw the little silk daisies stitched onto her veil and about fifty pearl buttons down the back of the dress. Her lanky frame seemed to have filled out in the weeks preceding the wedding. She was considerably fuller in the bust and even her face had a plump sheen. Although we didn't know it then, she was already four months pregnant with her first son, though this didn't stop her necking champagne like a trucker. At one point during the reception, I caught her outside the hall smoking a joint with the maid of honour. Quite a picture they made in their silk and satin with a large spliff glowing in the dark.

Watching my parents sitting a few seats away from one another on the top table was like going back in time. Those who didn't know they'd split would never have guessed they weren't together. They even had a slow dance when the band struck up and looked as if they were enjoying themselves. After Bee and Coxy had left for their honeymoon in Devon, mum and dad went around thanking all the guests for coming. 'I'll call us a cab then, shall I, Pat?' He tenderly led my mum into the car and they sat in the back together, with me in the front. Dad opened the cab door for mum when it pulled up outside the house.

'Do you want to come in, John?'

'Go on then, just a quick coffee.'

Mum seemed pleased. Like me she didn't want the day to end. The three of us sat up drinking coffee and some disgusting liqueur mum dragged out of the back of a cupboard. I remember dad asking her for an aspirin, but we thought it was just because he'd been drinking all day. He did look a bit washed out when he left, but neither mum nor I really gave it much thought. 'You can stay if you like, John?'

'No, I'll get back and change out of this suit. But I'll come round in the morning to pick up the van and we'll collect their presents from the hall.' He hesitated. 'Maybe the three of us could go for a pub lunch, eh?'

'I'm certainly not up to cooking a roast after today.' We took that as a yes and dad gave me a big wink when mum wasn't looking. After he left we sat up for about an hour watching some shit film on the telly and doing a post-mortem on the day. I was pretty well oiled and just came right out and asked her, 'Do you think you and dad will get back together, mum?'

'I don't know, Mark.'

'But you enjoyed yourselves today, didn't you?'

'Yes, we did, love.'

I felt very warm towards her and for a while all was forgiven. It must have been about two in the morning when we fell into bed and I must have just dropped off when the doorbell rang and I heard mum clomping down the stairs to answer it. There was a few seconds' conversation that I couldn't really hear and then an awful kind of animal groan coming from my mum. It wasn't a scream exactly, but I knew it had to be bad news. I got downstairs to find mum sobbing and the cab driver who'd picked up dad with his arm around her.

'What's going on?'

The cabbie, a middle-aged guy, looked very upset and stammered, 'It's that bloke I picked up.'

'What's happened?'

'He just collapsed in the back of the cab. I took him to St Helier's but he was dead by the time we got there.'

Mum recovered her composure and went into coping-mode quite suddenly. 'Get your clothes on, Mark.' We both dressed quickly and sat silently in the back of the cab on the same seat where my dad had just died. The cabbie kept saying how sorry he was, though God knows it wasn't his fault. When we got there dad was stretched out under a sheet in casualty still dressed in his suit, only his collar undone and his tie stuffed into his jacket pocket. The look on his face was one of mild puzzlement, as if he couldn't quite believe what was happening to him. The post-mortem revealed that he had died instantly of a massive stroke.

So the last wedding in our family was blighted by tragedy. Bee's honeymoon was over within twenty four-hours and what with the shock of it all she started bleeding. For a while it looked like she would lose the baby. Coxy turned up trumps and got his mum and dad to take care of all the funeral arrangements. Mum and Bee were in bits, and at this point I'd already met Maria and had taken to going round to her parents' old house in Coulsdon and having a lot of sex. Maria was brilliant and seemed to sense exactly what

I needed which was to cry and to come. Her parents kept a respectful distance because of my bereavement and this bought us a lot of privacy for a few months. Bee's pregnancy was touch and go throughout and she kept getting admitted to hospital with every complication imaginable. Mum went a bit religious for a while and when the baby was born she kept saying, 'The Lord giveth and the Lord taketh away,' with this sort of nutty gleam in her eye. The baby was a boy and even though I've always thought it was bollocks when people claimed that babies looked like people, this one really was a ringer for my dad, so naturally he was called John. John Cox. It suits him. He's fifteen now and even has dad's mannerisms. It's weird because Bee's other two boys look just like Coxy, with those Neanderthal heads and matching temperaments, but John's got bearing and a touch of class. He's a bit of a gentleman, our John. He's tall and would look good in a suit too, so I asked him to be my Best Man.

CHAPTER SIX

THEM AND US

I must have seen her a dozen times before we spoke properly. She works on the flower stall opposite my office on the corner of Kensington Church Street and the High Street. I've often nipped over for a floral tribute if I'm off to meet a woman after work or in Maria's case need to apologise for something. I know a lot of men think buying flowers is suspect, but ten or fifteen quid spent wisely buys a lot of goodwill, if you know what I mean.

Like I say, I must have seen this flower girl quite a bit on and off over the couple of years I've worked on the paper but I'd never really looked at her before, not properly. She's not the fittest girl in the world, slightly chubby arms, but nicely upholstered as far as I could tell underneath the padded gilet and apron she always wore. She has a very pretty face, fresh and young-looking with dimples either side of her mouth which are very pronounced when she smiles. I've seen more beautiful women in my life but perhaps not many as wholesomely pretty. Maybe it was something to do with the aroma of flowers surrounding her, but she looked so clean it was almost dazzling. It was the Monday after the Friday that I became engaged to Maria and I'm off for a lunch with Stella Kennedy to tell her that she's history on account of my recent betrothal. I could have mentioned it the last time I saw her, but it seemed impolite at one in the morning after vigorous sex. Stella is one of a type that I classify as West London Shrews. They're everywhere, an easily identifiable breed who are nearly always thin, dressed either upper-class scruffy or dripping Ghost and working in the arts if at all. They only bother making friends with other fashionable people and most of them have tenuous family links in the media or publishing which they use ruthlessly to exploit the little talent they have. They seem to spend an awful lot of time slagging off people that they greet warmly and saying things like 'but please don't let on that I mentioned her abortion.' For such supposedly well-bred girls every one of them I've come across has been viciously disloyal and a bit too fond of a nose-up for my tastes. Perhaps the two go hand in hand. I'm not against drugs per se, but they're a bit of a waste of time and make you talk bollocks. I'd sooner get pissed.

But anyway, the Stella thing had been dragging on intermittently for about eighteen months and I'm glad of the excuse to kick our slightly sour affair into touch. We don't really like one another. I met her at the Features Christmas party when I first came to work on the paper. She was invited along as a contributor on the strength of a piece she wrote about the hipness of small handbags. I think I'm lazy, but Stella puts a whole new spin on the term leisured. She has a private income, a flat on Ladbroke Grove and a twelve-year-old daughter from her marriage to some fucked-up minor-aristo. She and her husband will never divorce because neither wants to have to sell off bits of their sizeable estate which includes a house and some three thousand acres in Shropshire. They live separate lives, he staying in the country so he can hunt, shoot and fish while she minces around town being urban. She's very coy about her age, but I'd say she's closer to forty than thirty.

It was a sex thing pure and simple for me and Stella. I'm of no use whatsoever to her as a long-term partner due to lack of breeding and readies, and if I took her home Patsy would have a fit – 'Who's that flighty bit with her nose in the air?' – but we definitely had a bit of chemistry in the early days. She's one of those women who really doesn't care who else I fuck as long as she gets her portion, when she wants it, how she wants it. She's very assertive like that and for a while it really made me hard. But what with my little personal crisis and all it was bordering on the sleazy. I was glad to be getting married if only to start putting some of these bad choices behind me. And even though I've never been one to stint on the expenses that come with women, I was getting very resentful over Stella's refusal to put her hand in her pocket. She thinks it's some kind of insult to her femininity to get her purse out and it was pissing me off.

So anyway, there's a bit of a queue at the flower stall and while I'm waiting I'm looking at this girl thinking what a sweet face she has. Style-wise she's no big shakes and reminds me of the Croydon girls of my youth, Bee in particular. She's got long brown permed hair pulled tight back off her face in a pony tail and a pair of those big hoop earrings. I look at the hands expecting to see each finger encrusted with gold, but they are bare except for a plain gold band on the little finger of her right hand. She's not wearing any make-up except for a bit of mascara and she looks scrubbed and spotless. You know just by looking at her that she smells good. The flowers on the stall behind her form a backdrop of fresh-mintedness. There's an old guy working the stall with her and I'm wondering whether he's her dad. He has large smiling brown eyes like hers and is having a joke with a younger bloke who is unloading boxes of flowers from a white van parked up on the double yellows with its hazards flashing. I finally nudge my way to the head of the queue and she looks at me very brightly and smiles. Her hands are dug deep in her apron which holds all the money, it looks like it weighs a ton, and for a minute I've forgotten why I'm there.

'Who are they for and how much do you want to spend?' she asks. Her voice has a definite London twang, but she's no indigenous cockney.

'They're for an old girlfriend. At least she will be in about half an hour.' I laugh to cover up the fact that I feel a complete prick for telling her that I'm about to bin a bird. I want her to know that

I'm single, my engagement four days ago conveniently consigned to the recesses of my dirty little mind.

'Oh, right, so you want "row-her-out" flowers. You'd be surprised how many of those I do in a week.' She's brisk but there's humour in the voice and she's smiling to herself, like she's got some private joke she's chewing on. I can see straight away that this girl is good for a laugh and I feel strangely relaxed and unhurried even though I'm running late. The tops of her fingers roam the buckets of flowers looking for the right thing. Long clean hands with short nails. Not my usual taste, but I like it. It suits her. 'Well you don't want to give her anything too flash, otherwise it's going to look like a consolation prize and she'll chuck them back at you. Go for something meaningful.' She gets the picture. I'm impressed.

'Like what?'

'Well, lilies are always for death and I suppose it is a death of sorts. You could put them with some irises, irises mean promise. Iris was the Greek messenger of the gods. You're bringing a promise of death, see? But they're pretty and they smell good, so hopefully she won't figure it out till she gets home, then she can have a good cry.'

Somehow I don't think my West London Shrew has cried since she was a baby but it's a touching thought. 'Bloody hell, you're good.'

'Yeah, well, like I say, I do a lot of them. £12.50 sound all right?' I nod in agreement though I'd only planned on spending a tenner. She's a good saleswoman, this one, and I come over all intrigued. She goes about her business quickly, cutting the stalks, tying the base of the bouquet together with plastic and ribbon, her fingers moving nimbly, her eyes darting up to check on the queue behind me and then calling out to the man I think might be her dad. He's leaning against the white van, smoking a roll-up and slapping his leg in merriment at something the driver has said to him. 'Come on, Pete, shake a leg, we've got people waiting.' She's firm but she doesn't bellow like some women can. It makes me wince when they do that. I hate fishwives. I fiddle around in my wallet separating the fifties and counting only three of them, when I know I had ten on Friday. It had been a bloody expensive weekend and if Maria's spending form on Saturday is anything to go by, marriage is going to consist of one long overdraft. The flower girl hands me the bouquet and taking the fifty says, 'So, do you work over the road on the paper then?'

'Yeah, how can you tell?'

'You get to be a bit of an expert doing this job, you blokes have all got a similar look.'

'What's that then?'

'I dunno, kind of stressed but lazy at the same time.' I have to laugh because she's spot on and the big grin on her face tells me that she goes in for this line of cheek. 'Do you know anything about books?' She hands me back my change and is already looking at the punter behind me in the queue when I reply,

'Yeah some, why?'

'Would you look at something for me?'

'Well, it depends what it is.' I immediately regret saying this, because it's obvious this girl has written something and I sound snotty. She looks at me very level, very cool, no expression on her face but you can see she's reading my mind. 'I mean, I might not be able to help you,' I add quickly, but she's not having it.

'What's your name?' I'm a bit taken aback by this change of tack but I tell her. 'Can you read, Mark?' She's lukewarm sarcastic, but her eyes are shining and she's got me on the back foot. The girl is a total fox.

'Yeah, not bad if you don't rush me.' I think I'm being witty but it sounds like a loaded statement and then my cheeks go hot. I can't believe this is happening. I'm blushing. I feel like a right plum standing there in front of her with my big bunch of flowers.

'You'll do then. No rush but next time you're passing I might give you something to have a look at.' I see a yellow light approaching so I give her the nod and trot off to hail the cab.

On the way to Notting Hill I'm turning this scene over and over in my head. I rationalise. You've just bought a bunch of flowers from some cheeky minx, that's all. But I'm getting hot though I'm only wearing a suit and it's chilly enough for a coat. I can still smell her stall and its heady perfume. What could she have written? Then I get it. She's asking on behalf of someone else. It's got to be the boyfriend, some plumber or jailbird that fancies himself as a bit of a Jean Genet. I've met the type before, ten a penny. Excitement over. The cab is pulling up outside 192 where I'm meeting Stella for lunch so I focus on the business at hand. I pay the cabbie and tip him way over the odds just because I can't be fucked to stand around on the pavement waiting for change. As I walk into the restaurant I see immediately that it's a bad choice because the tables are too close together and the place is packed. I can't elbow the shrew with everyone listening. For once in her idle life Stella is on time, waiting impatiently and looking pinched with a cigarette. A bottle of champagne in a bucket is next to the table and I'm thinking there goes the last two fifties in my wallet, I'll probably have to take the tube home tonight. This is typical Stella. She never wants to eat anywhere normal like a pub or café, it has to be some West London money-drain. She always orders champagne which is never the house stuff and expensive meals which she doesn't eat. She just sits there chain-smoking, moaning and looking bored while I tuck in. Stella takes the flowers without thanking me or even looking at them and offers me a lean cheek to kiss, her smoke wafting up into my face. Any nagging guilt about ditching her is gone and I'm thinking, I'm going to be pleased to see the back of you, you anorexic head-case. Cheer up, you fucking miserable cow, and get some normal clothes and stop doing coke and take up with some herbert from your own wretched circle and stop giving me brain damage, because you were only ever any good in the sack and even that got weird when you wanted me to start

78

slapping you around. I just can't do that to a woman, even ones like Stella that I half hate. But of course, I just say, 'How you doing?'

We engage in some desultory chat, she moaning about the forthcoming Easter holidays and how she's going to have to look after her own daughter because the boarding school are chucking out for a month. You'd think she had a job or something the way she goes on about it. When the waiter comes to take our order I ask him to give us five more minutes because I'm not going to go through with this charade. I'm going to do it now, quick and clean, and she can pay for her own fucking champagne because I'm off for a pint and a sandwich. She looks at me very disapprovingly when I dismiss the waiter and suddenly I've hit my limit and can't take any more. I'm very slippery and bad at this sort of thing but not today. I close my menu and say, 'Look, Stella, there's no point sitting here pretending because I've come to tell you that I won't be seeing you any more. I got engaged to Maria last Friday. I'm getting married, Stella.' It's really brutal, but it's out and I feel better already.

Her face starts to crumple with shock and the sudden realisation that she will no longer be able to summon me from my bed at 3 a.m. so that I can go over and fuck her very hard. 'Congratulations,' she says, 'I see she got her own way in the end.'

I regret telling Stella about how pushy Maria is and though I'm tempted to launch into a defence of my fiancée I don't see that I owe Stella any explanations. It was always what we called the most adult of arrangements, to try and dredge up a bit of emotion now would be pointless. We sit silently for a minute or so and I toy with the idea of giving her a fifty for the champagne, but then I think, fuck her, and stand up and say, 'Look after yourself, Stella.' She doesn't look up, so I walk towards the door and then I'm gone, out onto Kensington Park Road. I'm nearly running up it with adrenaline and juvenile pleasure thinking, I'm free of that bloody witch and all her rotten, boring, fucked-up mates. A number 23 bus comes round the corner and I jump on it not caring where it's going. I'm thinking about her on the bus as it chugs down West-bourne Grove and I'm looking out of the window at all the people and I know that what really bothered me the most about Stella was not the fact that she was messed up in the head, or took too many drugs, or that she was skinny, or lazy, and a bloody awful mother who was into kinky sex, but class pure and simple. She was the wrong class.

Unacknowledged but definitely there was the feeling between Stella and me that our two worlds should not collide and we arranged it so that they never had to. She is the daughter of a high-court judge, I am the son of a park-keeper. She is separated with a daughter away at boarding school. She dabbles in writing and can afford to as her income is private and secure. To my knowledge she has only had one piece published and that was by us – the handbag item. She is the kind of under-fed, pretentious, badly dressed woman that leaves me cold, but at that Christmas party she made her interest too obvious for me to ignore. I am nothing if not an opportunist. Stella is not the first bit of posh to wander into my orbit and it tickles me that I am attractive to a certain type of allegedly well-bred woman. It make me wonder if the entire patrician class of this country are crap in bed, though it's doubtful that even the Trojans among them could keep up with Stella's demands. I have never met a woman who loves sex so much. Not even sex as I think of it, but being fucked as hard and as heartlessly as I could manage. We came up with a mutually pleasing arrangement where either she would come to my flat in Maida Vale or I would go to hers in Ladbroke Grove which I was less keen on because it was such a filthy tip. She had a cleaning lady who came in once a week to try and make a dent in the mess but Stella was the sort of slut who didn't wash up her cups for days and wouldn't dream of cleaning the bath. She would leave her soiled underwear lying around without seeming the least embar-rassed or motivated to pick it up. I wouldn't say she was the type to set aside an afternoon a week for laundry. But the worst of it was her body odour, nothing overpowering but stale and yeasty and it made me wonder what she ate, if anything. She was a grubby bitch really, but as we never spent that much time together it didn't seem worth commenting on. I used to tip up at her place to find her dressed in expensive underwear and not much else. Foreplay was frowned upon and sometimes I thought it was asking a bit much to expect me to steam in through the front door with a raging hard on. I stopped enjoying our meetings after the first half a dozen times, yet Stella became a source of bizarre fascination for me. There was no tenderness in our couplings and she was so disdainful of even kissing that I began to wonder if I was the one with the hygiene problem. One evening I surprised her by having prepared a meal for when she arrived. She seemed offended and when I pointed out that maybe some food and conversation might be a nice preamble to our increasingly cold and brutal sessions, she pointed out, 'I come here to fuck, Mark, not eat.'

Another great thing about getting married meant that I could swear off the posh birds for life. I've always had a thing about them, like I had to prove something. I suspect the the real reason I did it was because I hated them. Sometimes fucking somebody is a very good way to express contempt. Maria's parents are caked but that's not the same thing as being posh. I used to have a slightly indulgent notion of the upper classes being basically nice people who lack dress sense, but my time with Stella and her mates crystallised the nearly visceral hatred I came to feel. I look up and the bus is at Paddington Station which is not where I want to be, so I jump out and go into the Pride of Paddington and order a pint. The place is only half full, but it has a nice rumble about it. A few people with cases either on their way to the station or just off the train, a few labourers dotted here and there with their *Sporting Lifes* and their roll-ups. I sit down at a table beside a group of three old ladies. They must be in their sixties or seventies and they've all got those sort of chiffon headscarves over their shampoo and sets.

81

One of them is drinking a stout, another a port and lemonade and the third is having a Babycham. Only one smokes, but they all cough. I look at their wrinkled hands, dried out and leathery from years of cleaning, no doubt, and I feel very affectionate toward these three old birds and it hits me that it's because they are *my* people. I always thought that tribal working-class London thing was sentimental wank, but there's no denying that we share a language and an attitude. It's been slowly dawning on me that there's nothing like going out with the wrong person to make you feel dislocated from your life.

The rot set in last summer when Stella persuaded me to join her in Cornwall for a long weekend to stay with old friends. 'Jazz and Muffin are having a houseparty.' Jazz and Muffin, I ask you. 'It's always open house for the first three weeks of summer, then August they simply holiday *en famille*.' It was phrases like that – '*en famille*', or even use of the word 'simply' – that used to make me want to slap her. She was deliberately vague about the characters making up this houseparty and the only thing I knew with any certainty was that none of them would have proper names. Like I said, for the eighteen months of our affair we sensibly avoided each other's friends, but I figured it couldn't do any harm to escape from London and get some ozone down my lungs. We were to be joined by at least six other adults and an assortment of kids, so I knew in advance that this is no poky little bungalow five miles from the sea. Stella had been going on about Rock in North Cornwall for a while, what a great place it was and the fabulous surfing. I nearly choked on my beer when she mentioned the surfing as I really couldn't imagine Stella doing anything more strenuous than mounting the escalator at Harvey Nichols, but maybe she had a sporty side I didn't know about. Last summer was very humid in London, lots of those days when you feel grimy and sweaty ten minutes after stepping out of the shower. I was getting very tired of the city and needed a break. A few days of fresh air, sunshine and good food. How bad could it be?

Real bad. We arrived late on the Thursday evening in the pitch dark after a long crawl out of London and a big delay at Exeter, to find a sprawling gaff, which Stella felt obliged to point out was *tiny* compared to their Chelsea townhouse. It was positioned very high on a cliff, alone except for some lights twinkling from a farmhouse in the distance. It was divided into a main house and an annexe with four bedrooms which they had built on to accommodate guests. Nothing like a spare room, eh? The main house had six bedrooms where Jazz, Muffin and their four children, a couple called Sabrina and Belly – don't ask, I haven't got a clue – and their three daughters with the Slovakian nanny in tow, plus a single father, Rupert, his five-year-old son and their Australian nanny were staying. The adults were to sleep in the main house, the nannies and children in the annexe. Stella's daughter was in Shropshire with her dad, which I was relieved about, as I didn't fancy playing stepfather in my free time. Even so, it was quite a crowd.

They're all pretty pissed when we get there and I'm really knackered so even though they strike me as totally obnoxious I tell myself to defer judgement on these characters until I've had a decent kip. The next morning only I and the nannies get up with the kids, all the other grown-ups are still sleeping it off and Stella, of course, never rises before noon. The kids seem nice enough, they're just kids after all, and once I and the nannies have finished sloshing out the Rice Krispies and giving them a free hand in the biscuit tin (strictly verboten by the parents) they're off running about the garden with some water pistols and having a high old time of it. The nannies are really sweet and even though the Slovakian one doesn't speak much English, the Australian one is a giggle. Emma, she was called, big fat girl with a freckly face. I liked her a lot. I asked her why she and the Slovak didn't eat with everybody else the night before and she answered, 'You're kidding, no ways we're allowed to share a table with them. We have to eat with the kids and make ourselves disappear after we've put them to bed.'

'What, they don't even put their own kids to bed?'

'Not that I've noticed, but I've only been working for them for two years. Wouldn't like to draw any premature conclusions.' I'd only been there five minutes and I was slagging off my hosts already. A tremendous feeling.

The grown-ups get up around noon and suddenly there's lots of shouting at the children to get their surfing kit together, we're all off to the beach after Bloody Marys. We travel down there in a convoy, two dusty Land-Rovers, an Audi estate and my Saab winding along the narrow lanes to the sea at quite a clip and I'm hoping all these flying bits of rock and stones don't knacker the paint-job on the car. I enjoyed myself at the beach, not paying too much attention to anybody, just dozing in the sun and looking at Stella in her bikini and wondering what she'd look like if she ate. The blokes all surfed and even though I declined the opportunity to make a complete prat of myself in a wetsuit, we chatted easily enough. I wasn't too sure about my host Jazz, there was something sly about him, but the other blokes were pretty relaxed and very generous with their cooler of beers. The women I kind of avoided, even though they weren't bad-looking. They all sat huddled in a little group anyway, like they were having this private conversation all day which I thought was a bit rude. The bits I heard were not generous, 'Rehab is a complete waste of time for her' and 'She's terribly common, not at all the sort of woman he should be with, far too aggressive.' A right bunch of charmers, these girls, but I was too chilled out in the warmth of the sun to worry. No, the day was fine, it was the dinner in the evening I couldn't stomach.

It's about nine o'clock and we're all getting stuck into some pretty far-out seafood, proper *fruits de mer* with good white wine, and as all present except for me are parents, naturally the subject turns to kids. It goes without saying that every single one of their children is privately educated, but that doesn't bother me, it's the way they talk about them as if they're some bloody nuisance that inteferes with their lifestyle. To give her credit, Muffin, the wife, wasn't too bad. She seemed like quite a sweet mum and I spied her hugging her sons once or twice during the day on the beach. The others merely gave their children cold looks whenever they got near.

'I work like stink to give those girls a shot at something beyond the norm, but all they can do is crave this bourgeois middle-class existence. They'll just have to accept that I'm not the kind of mother who considers fresh milk in the fridge and Cornflakes for breakfast a priority.' Thus spoke Sabrina Longfellow, oldest and best friend of Stella, or Estella as this group call her. I'm tempted to speak up, but reckon I'm better off keeping my head down. One of the other women is complaining that she *simply cannot cope* since the nanny walked out and she's indignant at the thought of paying 'another chippy bloody nanny' £250 a week.

'Get an au pair. £40 a week and they do everything. They're not as eaten up with loathing and resentment as the qualified nannies. I'm afraid you need to go Eastern Bloc if you want to avoid the chippy ones who think they're too good to wash the kitchen floor,' says Sabrina. I bloody hate that word chippy. It's really offensive and I think it says more about the person using it than the one it's directed at.

'But what about the children?' asks the other woman. 'Won't it be difficult for them if the au pair doesn't speak English? And I've heard that a lot of these Eastern European girls who are coming over at the moment don't speak a word.'

'Nonsense,' says Sabrina firmly. 'You don't need to communicate with them. Children are whores, they don't care who they get love from.'

'Yes, you're probably right,' the other woman agrees.

I'm still keeping schtum at this point. I don't have any kids, so I'm no authority on what they do and don't need, but I'd lay money that this lot's kids aren't getting it, whatever it is. The conversation moves from kids to sport and I'm thinking things are looking up, they might even be into a bit of football. Jazz treats us to a homily on his relationship with his surfboard – 'I really connect when I'm in the water on that board, it's when I'm most alive.' He laughs at some hilarious thought that has popped into his head. 'Actually I'm most alive when I'm either fucking my wife or making money.' I nearly choke on this one. All the others laugh, amused at his daring streak with the dinner party badinage. I'm thinking I'd have the right fucking 'ump if I was the wife. He then goes on to give us the benefit of his theories on how easy it is to make money. I find the moment to speak up.

'So, do you have to be a good accountant to really know your way around buying and selling businesses?'

'Good God, no. I'm a venture capitalist, not a mathematician. You don't need to be good with figures as long as you have a Mr Singh or Mr Patel who is. That's what I say.' I am normally a pretty chatty guest, but where's the half-way point that I could actually meet a total wanker like this in conversation? I soldier on for a bit, thinking, you're here now, Mark, and you're eating his grub and drinking his booze, you gotta be polite.

'So where did you go to school then, Jazz?'

'Slough Grammar.' I kind of shake my head as if to say, no, I haven't heard of that one, and then all the others start sniggering. Muffin puts me out of my misery by explaining that Slough Grammar is a euphemism for Eton. I look at Jazz and think, you cunt. He goes on in his irritating upper-class cockney accent about clubs and drugs and I think, fuck off, you impostor. I don't mind toffs, but they should know their place which is not adopting the speech and dress of those he claims to despise – we all hate a tourist. I was fuming, but alone like that, I felt beached, stranded, totally out of my depth. I desperately wished for Maria. If she'd been there, together we would have slaughtered them. For starters, she'd never stand for an ex-Etonian with a South London accent. It could have been a lovely parlour drama. I would have opened up with a few well-placed barbs and Maria fuelled by white wine would march in behind with the big guns. It's poetry in motion watching Maria have an argument. She's got this terrier-streak that just doesn't let up if she sniffs victory. Brutal but strangely beautiful. She's got good ethics, has Maria, and a sharp brain to back them up. I badly wanted her there to help fight off an unaccustomed drain on my good humour. It was as if the life was slowly seeping out of me. These people were spirit-stealers. I'm no Che Guevara but that night I felt it growing like a tumour in my chest, this incoherent visceral hatred. I'd come across toffs before, ten a penny in media, but they'd never bothered me. I'd seen them as some kind of benign anachronism living harmlessly, if frivolously, on the fringes of a society that just laughed at them. But here I was surrounded. There was something poisonous and nasty about these people that really brought me down. It's difficult to explain, but I felt saturated and dirty.

I shivered at the recollection as I sat there finishing my pint in the Pride of Paddington. Forget it, I told myself. It's all over now, you don't have to go there again. She's tail lights, history, finito benito. Thank fuck. The old ladies next to me were really stretching out their drinks the way these old girls do, and now they were having a game of cards, playing ten card brag for coppers, so I offered to get them another drink and they all chimed in unison, 'Ahh, you are a love, yes please.' Something about the vibe in that pub made me feel good. I was all cosied up against the radiator on the wall next to my chair and the sun was streaming in through the windows, so I thought I'd stay for another pint and just daydream for a while. Stella wasn't the only one getting her marching orders. There were a couple of other women that I used to see every now and then, nothing serious, but I should probably have the decency to tell them that I was getting married. Both worked in town, so I could be weasely and do it at lunchtime – long enough to deliver the blow, but not so long that I'd have to stick around and mop up the mess. I wouldn't have to account for my whereabouts to Maria either. Even better I had a couple more excuses to visit the flower stall and see the girl with the manuscript and the dimples. The crafty little canister was working overtime now, but suddenly I remembered that I had one other person to inform of my impending marriage. Shit, Pilar.

CHAPTER SEVEN

UNFINISHED SYMPATHY

Where do I start with Pilar? Pilar Medio. Pilar Maria José Malela Dolores Medio Cachafeiro, to be precise. Quite a mouthful, eh? Bee says my relationship with Pilar was a simple case of destiny, some love lesson she reckoned I needed to learn. She's a bit cosmic and out there sometimes, my sister. I'm undecided on the destiny theory and reckon it's a bit of a women's issue anyway. Astrology, the occult, mysticism, call it what you want but it's all a branch of gynaecology in my book. But there are times when even a cynical bastard like me has to bear witness to the hand of God. I met Pilar when I was travelling through Spain. It was one of those chance encounters that make you concede to the possibility of fate. Travel always adds a lustre to any romance but I suspect even without the sunshine and the Spanish landscape, even if I'd met her at King's Cross, I'd have flipped for this one.

Being abroad doesn't stop you from having a really shit time, and I was having a really shit time, a right bad day of it. It was about four o'clock in the afternoon and I was sitting on a cliff top above the Gulf of Cadiz. Below me the Med stretched south to Morocco where I was supposed to be heading. To be honest I was sick of travelling. I'd fancied myself as a bit of a backpacker but I'm just not cut out for roughing it. A victim of my own bad planning, I studied my map for the tenth time that day in awe at my ability to get myself to all the wrong places. I was supposed to be in Algeciras, some two hours or so to the east, so that I could

89

catch the boat to Morocco. I'd originally planned to hitchhike from Madrid where I'd been staying in a flea-ridden youth hostel with squat toilets, but at the last minute I chickened out and managed to blow my budget by boarding the wrong bus. I tried to tell myself that it didn't matter, that travelling was about getting there, not being there, but I'm not like that. I like to get to where I'm going quickly and in comfort. For people like me travelling for its own sake is a nonsense. I'm too lazy to be anything but a resort man. As I sat sweating buckets on that cliff, I don't mind admitting that I felt a bit of a tool.

On the beach below I could see small pin figures of people moving around and I thought I was probably going to have to go down and beg a ride from one of them. I counted my money again, hoping to find more than a ton of coins and a few sweaty notes which would get me dinner and a night in a pension if I was lucky. What kind of wanker goes off travelling around Europe without a guide book and a proper budget? I'd reckoned on making £500 last for about three months – I'm hearing stories of people doing it on less by hitchhiking and sleeping on the beach – but I managed to dribble away all but £30 of it on good food and decent hotels in seventeen days. I'd been determined to hitchhike and camp, working here and there to pick up enough money to get me to the next place, but the moment I stepped off the boat in Calais I opted for a fast comfortable train to the south. I looked at my fellow travellers leaving the boat and thought no bloody way. A crowd of skinny students weighed down with their massive rucksacks wandering aimlessly around the lorry park hoping for a lift – not my style, thank you. I was not, I told myself, some gap-year student going on holiday without mum and dad for the first time. I was a mature professional, if being twenty-four and working as a cub reporter on the *Croydon Advertiser* counted. I'd left there in a cloud of disenchantment, my Hemingway-esque ambitions trampled by mediocrity. I was cut out for more than visiting a retirement home in Addiscombe to get a quote on the secrets of longevity from Mrs Gladys Woodhouse as she celebrated her hundredth birthday. Every Ford Granada parked outside a semi-detached house in the London Borough of Croydon was an affront to my outsider status. I'd been reading a bit of Camus and it had gone to my head. I needed an adventure.

So anyway, I'm stuck up this fucking cliff because after six hours of being on the wrong bus, I get it into my head that I should jump off and thumb a lift. Instead of doing the sensible thing and staying on the bus as far as Jerez, then changing to another that could take me to the boat at Algeciras, I decide to get off as we're driving along a mountain pass above the sea. Really fucking smart, Mark. I was too hot and pissed off to scramble down to the beach and spent a very long time watching the sun slowly sink and the people on the beach gradually pack up and drift. I became aware of rapid little steps behind me and turned to see a small child hurtling at full speed towards the cliff edge, his little brown face ecstatic with freedom. I turned just in time to grab his arm and as I did so heard a woman's voice cry out in panic, '*Luis! Luis! Luis No! Ven aqui Luis!*' The little boy struggled to get free, but I had the little sod and wasn't letting go. He could have fucking killed himself. I'm half shitting it and blinking into the distance from which a girl is running fast, screaming at the child. Without looking at me, she wrenches the boy from my grasp and delivers an almighty wallop to the back of his legs. It was impressive in a weird child-slapping way. After she smacked him, she drew the kid close to her and started sobbing into his hair and rocking his little body back and forth as she thanked me fulsomely in rapid Spanish. It was all a bit of a drama in which I had become the unwitting hero. I'd always been pretty good at languages in school and although I was a little rusty I had a pop at some conversational Spanish by asking her how old her son was. '*Quantos anos tiene su hijo?*'

'*No, no es mi hijo, es mi hermano.*' Right, so he's your brother, not your son. It figured. She looked young, maybe my age or a bit older, and was the owner of a striking, if not classically beautiful face. She had a rather mean little mouth which forced itself into a strange rictus in place of a smile. I later found out that she was a bit self-conscious about her teeth which were small, uneven and slightly brown. If this makes her sound hideous, I should point out that she had these really bloody mesmerising green eyes and a lovely olive complexion. She was petite and slim and was wearing a pair of cut-off denim shorts and one of those string bikini tops that just about held her small but shapely tits. Really nice – the kind of girl you want to pick up and throw down on a bed.

After we'd checked each other out a bit, done some eyeballing, we made awkward and, in her case, slightly breathless introductions and she told me that her name was Pilar. I'm having a bit of a giggle inside at this because she sounds like something you'd order at the curry house. But she *was* attractive and what really got me horny was the way she pronounced my name. Mark in most languages is pretty bald, not too many options with the old pronunciation, but when she said it I felt like somebody else, a totally new man. The way she rolled the r and hit the k really hard at the end got me going. Coming from her mouth Mark sounded masculine and important. Everybody raves about the French language, but it's like a plate of blancmange compared to Spanish. They really fucking wallop their consonants when they speak, those Spaniards. They're punchy, expressive and passionate and I love that firecracker rhythm. It's more up my street than all that gurgling in the back of the throat that you get with the French. I have a physical reaction when I hear French sometimes. To me they always sound like they've got a load of gob backed up in their mouths. It makes me nauseous.

I managed to stutter out a few sentences explaining how I came to be stuck up a cliff and that I was from England. '*Viajando, de Inglaterra.*'

'*Ingles!*' she cried and told me in almost letter perfect English that she had studied 'your beautiful language' at the University of Seville for two years. The little boy was getting impatient and

92

started yanking her hair. She insisted that I join her and her family for supper that evening, bossing me back along the cliff path with her. That's what I like about these foreign birds, they just come out with it. If that had been an English girl we'd have stood there giving each other the eye but wouldn't even exchange numbers when it was time for goodbye. As I followed behind I had a chance to really check out her figure and I tell you, I did not find it wanting in any way. She had long hair tied back in a plait and a kind of swinging gait. Nothing shabby about this one.

When we get to the car, we have to go through the introductions with her family which takes about half an hour, but they're really friendly, really warm. The car seated six and had me, the little boy, the mother and father and two young girls. The other four children including Pilar were made to walk the mile and a half to their remote farmhouse inland from the sea. Pilar's family, I discovered that evening, are the kind that have largely disappeared into legend. At twenty-three, Pilar was the eldest of seven children. The youngest, Luis, the would-be sky-diver was only eighteen months. It was quite a set-up and at the head of it was Pilar's dad, Manolo. He was a bit of a character, old Manolo. Maybe because I missed my own dad so much, or maybe just because Manolo was so charismatic, I quickly fell under his spell and followed him around like some love-struck puppy as he gave me the tour of the house. A large, rather ramshackle flint and plaster construction, it was nonetheless spotlessly clean and smelt strongly of bleach. Dotted around the house were a few giveaway signs of the modern age. A television and video recorder were pointed out, 'Es maravilla no?'

Manolo, I came to learn, was a great lover of gadgets and modern inventions. When a large piece of meat was brought out for dinner, Manolo stood at the head of the table revving his electric carving knife like some nutter in a chainsaw flick, looking to me for approval. It was a man thing, I suppose. Though a mere five feet five inches in his Cuban heels, Manolo is a spry, dapper figure with a small pencil-thin moustache and buckets of attitude.

He couldn't have been more than forty-five when I first met him, but his face was leathery from the sun and his greased-back hair was liberally peppered with white. The family clearly didn't have a lot of money, but his trousers and shirt were crisply ironed, the sleeves rolled up not hastily, but exactly to finish just shy of his elbows. It was a calculated look and I liked it. Manolo is your textbook patriarch, largely ignoring his wife and ruling his kids with a rod of iron. While the rest of the family bobbed about getting the dinner ready, Manolo relaxed in a large chair on his veranda making expansive gestures as he explained that their little patch of land had been farmed by his family for nearly two hundred years and what a tragedy it was that the younger genera-tion were fleeing country life and almond-growing to find work in towns. He pointed to a small ridge to the west of their land and explained that it used to be chock-a-block with donkeys – a thriving mule track till about ten years ago – but now the children (he waves dismissively at his brood) all want cars. Terrible, a way of life gone for ever. I couldn't quite square his attitude with his love of modern inventions, but as a set piece of theatre he was bloody good. He'd break the monologue occasionally to bark some order at his kids and I was witness that evening to the way he frequently touched his children. There was a lot of hugging going on, but discipline was not in short supply. I thought he was a bit of a god, a bit of a guru, old Manolo. It would break my heart a few years down the line to fall out with him so horribly. It rankles to this day.

The mother looked quite old, probably not surprising after seven children. She'd turned to fat and didn't trouble colouring her grey hair which made her look much older than her forty years. She bore little resemblance to the teenage bride I spied in a black and white photo in their home. A more remote and dis-tracted figure than Manolo, she was continually occupied and if she wasn't working her way through a pile of laundry at a stone sink, she was cutting up basketfuls of veg and slicing chunks from a leg of ham to sling into a big pot she had on the go. Diffident and polite, she quietly went about her business, never failing to keep Manolo's drinks topped up and fetching him a fresh pack of Fortunas as he finished off the old one. Pilar seemed to be second in command, organising her brothers and sisters and helping her mother in the kitchen.

Manolo monopolised my time, getting off on his captive audience, but on the sly I kept an eye on Pilar, really studied her. I couldn't imagine any of the English girls I knew doing so much housework wordlessly and without complaint. I should probably come clean at this point and show my chauvinistic hand because it was definitely her more traditional feminine role – along with that lithe little bod – that attracted me to her. She was quieter and more composed than the girls I had been used to and by the end of that first evening I was bang into her. She knew straight away how I felt about her and would look at me across the table, then lower her lids demurely when she caught my gaze. She seemed to know how to handle herself and I got the distinct impression that this was no virgin I was dealing with. She looked like a woman who knew her shit. I like that a lot.

After a late dinner, Manolo outlined his philosophy of life to me, which from what I could make out depended on good weather, good burros, good women and lots of home-made wine. I was trying to be polite and listen, but I was really knackered and thinking, come on, mate, turn it in, I need some kip. Finally at 2 a.m. he extended the offer of dossing down on the veranda. I got to love that veranda and each night slept under the stars with just a light blanket. It was really hot and what with the crickets, and the smell of night-blooming jasmine on the breeze, very atmospheric. I really loved lying out there on my jack thinking of all the things I'd like to do to Pilar.

I once made the mistake of offering to help her mother with the dishes after dinner. Manolo gave me this look that asked, what are you, some kind of fucking homo? I think he saw it as his personal duty to school me in how to be a real man.

This meant getting up at four o'clock in the morning with him. If Manolo suffered from hangovers it didn't show. He used to wake me up with a small cup of black coffee, a glass of the sticky sweet wine he always had on the go and a chunk of fattty ham for breakfast. I thought I was going to lose my ring the first time he stuck it under my nose, but once I'd forced it down, I felt quite vigorously awake. I stepped out with a purposeful stride down the valley to tend to the first chores of the day. Fucking mountain man, or what? We marked out the olive groves that were ready for harvest and moved the twenty or so sheep he had down to the bottom of the valley where they could get a drink from the river. At 7 a.m. we would stop for more wine and about ten fags for Manolo and he would declare our work complete. 'And now, we rest.' We got into a little rhythm, me and Manolo, and as the days passed I grew more confident with my Spanish. After a week we were having some pretty deep discussions. He would tell me often what a wonderful wife Pilar would make, though if he was trying to marry her off he wasn't allowing much time for any kind of courtship to develop. It's so obvious now that he engineered the entire thing. For all his talk of a woman's place being in the home, Manolo was clearly in awe of his eldest child and must have known that she wasn't cut out for peasant culture. He was proud of her education, she'd done two years of a degree in English and he must have known that sooner or later she would tire of helping her mother run a remote farmhouse. Pilar had dropped out of college when Manolo had a heart attack. He was as fit as a bloody fiddle if you ask me, but she obviously felt that until the exit visa of marriage came along, it was to her family that she was beholden. Finding me that day in the car-park must have been heaven-sent for Manolo. Not only did he have a bit of entertainment and a prospect for his daughter, but it was harvest time and he could use the extra pair of hands.

Before university Pilar had served a one-year apprenticeship as a seamstress with a tailor in Jerez de la Frontera which is probably where she got her dress sense. She had few clothes, but they were all hand-stitched classic styles and, like her dad, she was spotlessly clean and pressed. She had a lot of style and *savoir-faire* and I thought she was smart enough to cut it in London. We got it together the night before I left to come back to England. Manolo stood up after dinner and said he has business to attend to in Jerez, but I reckon he just fucked off for a game of cards so that we could spend a bit of time together. The mother and younger children were turning in for the night and we listened to his car bump along the track and waited until we could hear him accelerate onto the road at the top of the track before we got to it on the veranda. That night as we talked and kissed and finally made love under the stars, we made plans for Pilar to come to England. I had to get home, get a job and somewhere to live. A tall order but after two weeks in Spain I was feeling a bit macho and kind of no problem about everything.

The solution to my raft of problems was bittersweet. Two weeks after I got back to England my mother asked Bee to come round for her tea on her own without Coxy and the kids. She needed to talk to us. We sat down around the kitchen table while mum pulled a lot of papers from folders and spread them out before her. Apparently dad had been paying into three separate life insurance policies before he died. My dad had been dead for over six years but this was the first we'd heard of it. Mum explained that, as dad's executor, the distribution of the monies had been her responsibility and rather than give the money to us straight away she had invested it and we had both earned interest.

'I expect you want to know how much you've got?' mum said. 'Originally you were both left almost £9,000.' This was big money and me and Bee had a little gasp, but there was more to come. Mum continued, 'I went and spoke to the building society and they put it into a high-yield something. Here are your cheques.' She

97

pushed the pieces of paper across the table and to this day I can remember the figures in the box on the right-hand side of that cheque. £13,632.17p. I don't think it had occurred to either me or Bee that there could be any profit from death. It had literally never crossed our minds, but it came at a really good time for both of us. A right little windfall. Bee and Coxy used the money to move to a bigger house, perfectly equidistant from mum and Coxy's parents. For me the change was more radical and I was to move from my mum's in Croydon to a bachelor pad in Maida Vale. Fired up by my unexpected good fortune I applied for literally hundreds of jobs – broadsheets, tabloids, nationals, locals, everything. It was time to take my career in journalism seriously, out of respect for my dad if nothing else. When I received a call from *The Times* asking me to interview for the post of editorial assistant on the Obituaries page my life turned the corner fully. Two months after arriving back in England I had a decent job with a salary respect-able enough to approach a bank manager for a mortgage and a hefty deposit to help persuade him. I didn't really know London at the time, but I chose instinctively well when I picked Maida Vale. It was expensive and though I could have got a bigger place somewhere like Clapham, who the fuck wants to live there? My ego kept pace with my swift progression and I was feeling pretty good about the change from suburban nobody to Slick Willie. All I needed now was the beautiful foreign bird to complete the picture. I'm not saying that my feelings for Pilar weren't genuine, but I have always been concerned with how things look and there is no doubt that Pilar fitted into the perfect picture of my enviable life. Nice job, nice flat, nice bird. Before Pilar came to live with me all I knew about her was that she was beautiful, understated, good at washing up and had always wanted to come to England. It seemed enough at the time.

I was loving work. You reckon on a place like *The Times* being stuffed with a load of hoorays but it was much more diverse than I imagined and I absolutely fucking loved it. My editor on the Obs or the Stiffs as they're known in the trade, Bill Evans, was an old-style newspaperman and knew everything and everybody. He was a bit of an old timer, by today's standards nearly ancient at fifty-five, and we used to love getting Bill on the wind-up. When Freddie Mercury died it was too good to resist. Bill's never heard of the bloke. Bill's a classical man and really couldn't give a shit about pop music. Contemporary music for Bill meant the Beatles. So we tell him that Freddie Mercury was one of the most important musicians of the twentieth century – seminal, Bill, seminal – and that 'Bohemian Rhapsody' was an opera composed in the early 1970s, an avant garde hit. Bill's getting really agitated at this gap in his knowledge and we later find out that he sneaks off to HMV at lunchtime and asks them where he can find the Freddie Mercury section. He glances through the racks to find not some dour Eastern European composer but a prancing homosexual rock and roller in a clingy cat suit slit to the navel. While he's out we fuck about with his voice-mail and record a few seconds of Queen singing 'We Are The Champions'. *The Times* was really good like that for practical jokes and I learned something as well. I really know my way around a library and I can source the most obscure figure and give you their life in detail. I'm not sure how useful that is, but I loved learning it. It was a good education working on *The Times*, no doubt about it. Only later would I discover that they didn't really consider me a serious career prospect. No offence, you're just not broadsheet material, Tucker. Those early days were good though. Really good. Life at home with Pilar was sweet. We were at it night and day. I never wanted it to end. It ended.

If I had to distil our three-year affair into one sentence I would say it was a process of slowly discovering that you are living with a stranger. Maida Vale is not, even on a good day, remotely like Jerez de la Frontera and for the first year most of our problems I put down to the weather. I earned a respectable salary which enabled me to pay a mortgage of £400 a month and still have funds left over for the odd restaurant dinner, the cinema and a couple of really good holidays. Not just Spain to visit the folks either, I'm talking Mombasa, I'm talking Bali. She should have been happy. I didn't push her to look for a job to start with because I assumed that she would slowly find her feet, make some friends and look for work. But she didn't make friends easily because she never went anywhere to meet any. She assumed the domestic mantle from day one and I'd silently gone along with it thinking, good, now I don't have to iron my own shirts. But I thought she should get a job all the same. One day I casually suggested that she look for work – get you out the house, babe, give you something to do, a bit of pocket money – and she flew into a Latin temper. Who the hell did I think she was? Was that any way to talk to your woman? Don't you think my place is taking care of you, taking care of our home? It was really fucking heavy the first time she blew her lid because I had no idea that that's what she really felt and could do so with such depth. When she went, she really lost it. Tears, wailing, uncontrollable outbursts where she'd fly at me with her fists. She's only tiny so it's not as if she could have done any damage, but it was fucking scary I don't mind telling you.

She was wildly unsocial and after a couple of years that took its toll on me big time. I had thought in Jerez that she didn't like going out because she had to play the game with her old man about. It's a different gig in Spain and I respected that. But she didn't like going out in London either. She just didn't like going out, period. Like a twat I played along with it, keeping her sweet, not rocking the boat, thinking, I love her, she'll be OK, she'll settle. I really did love her and felt fantastically protective of her and our love for each other, especially when Maria was being critical. I spent two of our three years trying to convince myself it would be the making of me to not go out so much. I had somebody to come home to. I would be productive and really accomplish things with my life. Our life. That was what I thought being in love was about. You meet the right person and they effect the magic change you couldn't make happen for yourself. I know now that if you can't face yourself down and take responsibility for your own happiness, it is plainly unreasonable to expect some other poor sod to come along and do it for you. Male or female, it makes no difference, we all seem to fuck up on this issue.

Pilar kept telling me, 'It is very easy for you, Mark, you think it is easy for me too, but I tell you, it is not.' So I learned not to push and tried to understand the culture shock of moving to London when all you'd known apart from a couple of years in Seville was rural Spain. She objected to my friends, insisting they were not even polite to her, but how are you supposed to have a conversation with a bird who spends the whole night giving you the evil eye? That girl could give you a look that would freeze a martini across a crowded room. She was very socially unbalanced and used to go about cutting people, flouncing off over some imagined slight, one hundred per cent bang-on insecure, and it drove me fucking nuts in the end. She was paranoid that I fancied other women (little did she know) and was at her most frosty with my female friends. I don't like that bitchy shit between women, it's embarrassing. There are a lot of birds in journalism and everybody flirts all the time because it's something to do and for fuck's sake we're alive. But I found that I kept checking myself, making sure I didn't do or say anything that might upset her. I was becoming two different people and I suppose that was when I first began honing my now famous slippery side. If I ever told her the truth, something like, 'I got pissed at lunchtime with Judy, we had a right giggle,' my life became a minefield and I'd have to fend off accusations of sleeping around, which at that point I definitely was not, though the search had begun albeit furtively. She became very needy, looking to me not only for financial, but total emotional security. I really started to suffocate with it all. What I thought was the woman of my dreams turned out to be a very fuckable child. But of course by then the sex had gone to pieces. Physically she withdrew from me, while simultaneously asking for more and more emotional support. I wasn't getting laid and she wondered why I didn't feel like being her best friend and daddy. I'm not up for being anybody's dad. I still loved the girl, but I needed to lose some protein.

Cue Maria. I don't have to go into details, but needless to say the whole fucking house of cards tumbled. Pilar was always paranoid about Maria for the very good reason that in the beginning I made the mistake of telling her the truth about our strange relationship. I really did swear off Maria for the first two years with Pilar, or rather she swore off me saying she didn't want to play second fiddle. Fair enough. But one afternoon I'm sitting at work and I really can't face the thought of going home to Pilar's miserable boat, so I call Maria and arrange a meet. In those days, before she broke into film production, Maria was working as a receptionist at Scribes West, Terry Venables' old club on Ken High Street. The club was about a thirty-second walk from my office, but she never invited me down for a drink on the grounds that it was members only. On the two occasions I just turned up to find her, there was no one else in the place, so I didn't see how Venables could afford to be so picky. She was mentally social at this stage and you could never catch her in. I tell her to sit tight at the club and not fucking move until I get there. I haven't seen Maria for a few months at this point not just because she never lets me in her club, but because I'm busy playing Romeo and Juliet in Maida Vale. So I have no idea that she's invested in a very cute leather mini-skirt to show off those gazelle-like gams. I'm sitting in the reception watching a few lagging boats go by when she appears in that skirt and cocks her head towards a door and says, 'Let's go into the staff room.' She has a bottle of red wine in her hand and very dark red lips. I know before I take the first step that tonight's the night.

We catch up quick in the staff room, moving onto a second bottle of wine within the half-hour and enjoying some very sparkling conversation. She's on tremendous form and I'm absolutely pissing myself which I haven't done in a long time. By the end of the second bottle I've brought her up to date and she knows that all is not sweet in loveland. So like the friend she is, she takes me to her bed. It only happened a couple of times with Maria, but I got the taste for it and had a couple of discreet but ultimately destructive affairs. Pilar found me out because I wanted to be found out. I'd had enough. It ended and I wept fucking buckets. I mean, really, really cried like I hadn't since I was little. But there was worse to come. I took her home on a plane to help carry the few belongings she'd gathered and make sure she got there in one piece. I knew I wasn't in for an easy ride when I tried to explain myself to Manolo, but it was more than a bollocking. He accused me of using his daughter, bringing his family name into disrepute and 'spoiling' her for other men. I foolishly tried to point out that I was not her first but wished I'd kept my mouth shut because then he really went for me. I was to leave his home and never set foot in his country again – seriously, his country. I was English scum and I should go home and marry an English slut. I began to understand where Pilar got her temper from. Without giving Pilar and me a chance to say goodbye properly, he ordered me into his car and drove at breakneck speed to Malaga airport for a solid two hours. He said nothing as he drove, but his face was set like stone and I wanted to beg his forgiveness. I've pissed people off before but he really hated me, there was no room for doubt. The whole thing really shook me up and made me wonder for a while if I really was a bastard. I've seen Manolo on two occasions since and he's been polite but nothing more. No more throwing his arms around me and telling me interminably long stories. I miss that enormously. There was nothing for it but to throw myself into my new-found freedom with gusto, getting laid right, left and centre, but I was totally dead for a while. I'm over it now, we both are, but when I see her there's still a kind of tug on the guts that tells you you've lost something. For a while I toyed with the idea of flying over there to break the news of my engagement face to face, but that seemed a bit dramatic and it could be risking death by

Manolo's old scythe. Anyway Maria wouldn't stand for it. So I took the easy option and rang her. I wouldn't say she took it well, but she took it. We were both kind of quiet and choked up, but what's left to talk about once you've said it? I was getting married. End of.

CHAPTER EIGHT

I'LL CRY IF I WANT TO

There was no way of knowing that our engagement party would turn out to be a watershed in my life. On the contrary, I felt surprisingly light and untroubled in the days leading up to it. I'd even loitered in the kitchen watching Maria wrap bacon around prunes and fiddling with little bits of smoked salmon and cream cheese as she did try-outs for the food on the night, thinking how much I was looking forward to it. A lot of my family would be there, the aunts and uncles and cousins you never see unless someone gets married or kicks it, and I was especially looking forward to dancing the night away with Bee, Coxy and the kids. They're a good party family, my sister's lot. Me and my nephew John had been having a giggle on the phone recently, rehearsing his Best Man's speech. I've told him it's ages away but he's only fifteen so he's keen as mustard. Not bad for a youngster either. He's got a dry touch to his delivery that I really rate and odds on he's going to be a monster bird puller in a few years. I couldn't wait to let him loose on some of the girls from the fashion desk at the party. Everyone at work was talking about it, shit gags about Woking and what have you, all good-natured stuff and I'm buzzed, happy, excited. I'd even gone to Oswald and got kitted out with a new suit for the occasion. Very tasty, single breasted, navy blue lightweight wool, slim across the shoulders and a lairy crimson lining. I was styling.

It took me a while to recover from my phone call to Pilar, but the usual sadnesses and regrets aside, I was quite settled on the idea of marrying Maria. Monogamy welcomed me into its straightforward simplicity. My mind was unfettered by the usual dodges and half-truths that until then had been my stock in trade. I suddenly had all this *time* on my hands to get on with things that needed doing. I was feeling purposeful, mature, quite smug actually. Of course, I could still flirt with women – like Bill at *The Times* used to say, 'Just because you've ordered, doesn't mean to say you can't look at the menu,' but I was nearly getting off on the idea of being faithful to one woman. The flower girl was popping into my head at odd moments, but totally uncalled for so I put that down to old habits dying hard. The death throes of a compulsion I'd all but beaten and left behind.

The week before the party had been mental busy on the paper. All of our elusive and often lethargic freelancers must suddenly have had a spurt at the same time because the fax was red-hot with copy. Most of it late, but some good unsolicited, original stuff. There must have been something in the air because after a fortnight of calling around and chasing stuff I'm suddenly inundated and having to spike half of it due to lack of space. This paper could pay the debt of a Third World country with all the money we piss away on kill fees. We frequently buy and commission stuff which we never print simply in order to stop other papers getting their hands on it. Still, it's all overtime and there's no harm being seen to put in the hours, especially the way Maria gets through the cash. I was working steadily and conscientiously, scheduling each piece as it came in rather than tossing it onto Philippa's desk for her to sort out. Philippa is the secretary-cum-assistant on Features and could do my job standing on her head. Mercifully there's enough discrimination left in the modern workplace to keep the Philippas of this world in their place and the lazy mediocre bastards like me sitting pretty. I felt like the King of the Universe when I finally left the office on Thursday and jumped in a cab. Just as it's pulling away from the kerb I look over to the flower stall, all locked up for the night and covered with a tarpaulin, and I wondered. I really should go and see that girl and get her manuscript. I'd been avoiding her for reasons I didn't quite understand so I resolved to go over first thing in the morning before work and have a chat. What was I being so didgy about anyway? She was just a flower girl, right? But in my tricky little brain, I'm calculating what I'm going to wear tomorrow, mentally going through my wardrobe.

Friday morning I got up late and took my time getting ready for work. I wasn't rushing after all that overtime. Maria had gone off early, so I mooched around having a shower and listening to a bit of music. I gave myself a bloody big gash with the razor which pissed me off no end. I also get a bit of shaving rash in the lower neck area and that had flared up too. It's Maria's fault. I've told her, it doesn't matter if it says Armani on the box it's still cheap shit. If you want to buy me some aftershave please go to St James' and get me some Floris. So anyway, I've looked better but I'm not avoiding a flower stall on the strength of it. After a bit of a delay with roadworks on Ken High Street the cab pulled up outside the stall and our eyes met before I'd even climbed out and paid. She had an inscrutable look on her face that I couldn't really read. It wasn't saying, 'Where the fuck have you been?' But it wasn't saying, 'Good to see you' either.

'Hello, Mark, what's up?' Hands dug deep in her apron, looking at me head on.

'Not much. Well no, tell a lie, it's my engagement party tomorrow night.'

'Bloody hell, you work quick, it was only a couple of weeks ago that you were burying the bodies.' She winked at me and I went wobbly for a moment. She's got these really beautiful soft brown eyes and those dimples when she smiles. So pretty.

'I've known Maria for years. Maria, that's my fiancée.' It sounded stupid somehow. I don't know that I'd ever referred to her as my fiancée till that point. She was just Maria.

'So, you're after some flowers for the lucky lady, eh?' She had that piss-take sparkle in her eye, very playful. I reckoned this one could be a bit naughty with some encouragement

'No, I'm not as it goes. I came by to get that manuscript we talked about, but I can buy some if you want me to.' Shut up, Mark.

'Oh that,' she said, all casual, and pulled up the canopy covering the stall and fiddled around looking in boxes until she emerged with a large transparent plastic folder and handed it to me. It weighed a ton. I'm no expert, not having got that far with my own book, but this had to be 140,000 words minimum, double spaced and immaculately typed. I stared at the title on the top: *Welcome to the Pleasure Dome.*

'You do this then?'

'Well, I'm not pimping for somebody else if that's what you mean.'

'No, I didn't mean anything by it, I just wondered.'

'Wondered what a girl selling roses was doing writing a book.' She wasn't being touchy, her voice was calm and pleasant. 'I've wondered myself to tell you the truth.' She jingled the change in her apron and looked a bit wistful for a minute, 'I probably just needed to get it out of my system. I actually like flowers you know, the meaning of them and that.'

'Yeah, I picked up on that.'

She smiled and seemed pleased that I'd remembered. She picked up a little sprig of violets and held it up to show me. 'Just a bunch a violets, yeah?'

'Come on then, what's the significance?' I'm teasing a little but she just laughs and I can see she's the sporting type, not one to take offence over nothing, not like some women I've known. Not like Pilar, Jesus, talk about touchy.

'They've got a very old-ladyish image, but it's a raunchy little bloom, I'm telling you, it's the flower of Aphrodite and you know what that means?'

'I could guess.'

'Some people claim they're for virtue, which I suppose doesn't have to be a million miles away from desire.' I have to think about this for a minute because there's a message in there somewhere, but before I get a chance to catch up she's rabbiting again. 'You see a lot of violets in old tapestries in museums and things. They represent scent and consummation.'

'You know what Coco Chanel said about scent?' She'll be impressed that I know this.

'No, what?'

'She said that you should put perfume anywhere you want to be kissed.' I didn't think it was too saucy for a Friday morning, but she was blushing and didn't know where to put her face.

'You think this is all bollocks, don't you?' she asked, sounding a bit unsure.

'I've never really thought about it, but no, I don't think it's bollocks. It's interesting. What about these then?' I say, pointing to a bucket full of tulips.

'Prosperity.'

'Oh, yeah, how come?'

'Because they're force fed shit in big sheds in Holland and we buy them by the wagon load and sell them for a fat profit.' We have a giggle and look right into each other's eyes as we do so. My stomach lurches. She really has got the loveliest warmest eyes that make you feel like she's got her arms around you, and an absolutely flawless complexion. I bet she's soft to touch. 'Look, take the violets, call it a thank you if you like for looking at the book. Put them next to your bed. They don't last that long, but it's supposed to be a good omen if they flower for longer than three nights in a lovers' lair.' I must have looked a bit worried because she touched my arm very gently and added, 'Don't worry if they die, it's usually the central heating that does them in. You shouldn't take any notice of me anyway, I'm too superstitious by half.'

'Oh, yeah, read all the horoscopes and do the cards, that sort of thing?'

'Something like that.'

'Yeah, well, you're a girl, it goes with the territory I suppose.'

We just sort of stood there looking at each other until she said, 'Mark ...'

'Yeah?'

'I've got a customer.' I turned around to see a red-faced middle-aged man looking impatient.

'Oh right, I'll love you and leave you then. And I'll get back to you on this.' I held up the manuscript.

'Thanks, but only if you've got the time and can be bothered. Oh, and have a good party.'

'Cheers. Later, yeah?' But she's already onto Rupert the red-nosed bastard and slapping bunches of flowers against a large sheet of paper and doesn't look up. I feel like a total prick walking into the office with a little bunch of violets and Philippa opens that huge gob of hers and cackles, 'Oh, look, our Mark has discovered his sensitive side.' I make no explanation and get on with my work, but not before I put my violets in a cup of water. I spend the day watching them like a guard dog and smiling enigmatically every time I get a dig from anyone in the office. I keep the manuscript on my lap, not daring to to put it down on the desk or even in the drawer in case Philippa gets one of her clearing-up heads on and bins it.

I am daydreaming about our little encounter and it occurs to me that I don't even know her name. I wonder what she's called. I wonder too about what she said about being superstitious and into the stars. My sister Bee is into it big-time and of course I take the piss, but I've come to have a grudging respect for her beliefs. She's quite the witch on the quiet, my sister, with maps of the heavens on her kitchen walls and shelves full of books. She does charts and readings for people. One day I was sitting in her kitchen having a cup of tea and I don't know what made me do it, I just came right out and asked her why she married Coxy.

'Venus in Aries,' she says.

'What's that mean then?'

She has this naughty little smile on her face and won't answer me until I reach over and tickle her knees – she's got very ticklish knees, my sister – and she blurts out, 'Good in bed.'

'Dirty cow.'

'Well, we didn't get three kids by reading about it.' We went on to have a pretty juicy conversation about baby-making sex as opposed to your straightforward rump. Bee reckons it's religious, but I won't go into that now. Mark it down for later.

I tell you what I do find quite interesting though – unlike everyone else on the planet, Bee's not cock-a-hoop about me and Maria getting married. Apparently Maria has her moon in Virgo and this is a bad match with my own though I couldn't tell you for the life of me what it is. I thought this was shit until Bee pointed out that mum's moon was in Virgo, then I began to see what she was getting at. Like I say, I don't plan my life around it like Bee does, but I can't dismiss it out of hand.

After work, I take a taxi home again. I've got to stop doing this, it's costing me a bomb, but I don't want my little bunch of flowers getting crushed on the tube. I'm just about to put the key in the lock when the door opens and Maria is standing there in her coat ready to go out. She's wearing lipstick and she's put her hair up. She's been growing it for the wedding and she looks good. Seeing the little bunch of violets her mouth opens in a big aaaahh, and she kisses me and says, 'They're so sweet, Mark, I love them, thank you. Listen, I can't stop, I'm just off out to meet that production director and have a pizza and a chat before we start on that crappy animal documentary next week. Don't stay up late, big day tomorrow.'

'Yeah, I'll see you later, babe,' and I give her a quick kiss, relieved to have the place to myself. I like living with somebody,

111

really I do, and there have been moments like the other morning when I was in the bath and Maria in the kitchen ironing a shirt for me when I've felt downright pleased with myself. But when you've lived alone for as long as I have, you get to like your privacy.

The first thing I do is put the violets in a glass of water and place them next to the bed. I turn the radiator off in our room, to see if they will survive. I know I'm being a bit of a girl for doing this but it doesn't stop me. In the fridge is a load of canapés that Maria was trying out for the party, so I pull out two plates and a can of Tennants, check the machine for messages and settle down on the sofa with *Welcome to the Pleasure Dome*.

I've read some good opening lines in my time, but this girl had me by the goolies from the kick-off. When I did manage to put it down for a second, I'd stop only long enough to have a quick slash and get another can out of the fridge. It's about a family living on an estate near the Plumstead Marshes. It backs onto a sewage works, which is pretty apposite when you read the shit that goes down in the house. This has to be her story, because there is no way you could know this stuff unless you'd lived it. The dad is your bog-standard out and out loser. When he isn't pissed he's down the bookies or passed out on the sofa. When he has a win on the horses everything is sweet and it's bikes for the kids and a new dress for the wife. But if he's on a losing streak or just maudlin drunk everybody has to duck for cover. The kids get a regular slap but he saves the best of his temper for the mother and it's pretty coruscating stuff, but described with a total lack of emotion, almost clinical, and I'm surprised she can write like this. I'm seeing basic errors, thinking, I would mark this and that, but overall is a general feeling of excitement and every now and then I have to say out loud to nobody, 'Fucking hell, this isn't bad.' It's a monster topic, violence, and I've got nothing in my life to compare it to, really. There were no rows in our house and my dad was a good bloke. Nevertheless I recognise the culture of my childhood and realise how far from it I've travelled. It gives me a very funny feeling.

Four hours went by in ten minutes and it was only when I heard Maria's key in the lock that I looked at my watch and saw that it was nearly midnight. I don't know what made me do it, but I quickly stuffed the manuscript under the big cushion on the sofa and closed my eyes, pretending to have dropped off. I've always been a bit sly but this didn't seem like any way to carry on with the woman I was about to marry. You're supposed to share things, right? I'm not sure about never having any secrets but by and large I reckon you've got to air it out. Maria was full of it when she came in. Had a total change of mind about the production director. Turns out he was a very switched on guy and far from being the short pilot series she was expecting, this Nick Rogers has managed to screw three six-parters out of Channel Four. Apparently abandoned animals are the new rock and roll and Maria is pretty high on this. It's a change of direction, away from the serious documentaries to something more commercial, and I'm pleased for her. Freelance production isn't the steadiest line of work and getting two months' work is a big deal, let alone nearly two years. The money is very good too and she's more buzzed about her job than she's been for ages. It'll make a nice change if she can find something other than the wedding to talk about. She stops blabbing and touches my arm and looks at me like she's got bad news.

'Look, Mark, I know I said I wanted to start a family as soon as we got married, but this is too good to turn down. It'll be so much better for me to establish my reputation with Channel Four now, then when we do start having babies I'll be in a secure position. I don't want to put the wedding off or do anything drastic but would you be really upset if we didn't try for a baby for a while?'

No, my sweet, I would not be upset. In fact it'll be a huge fucking relief. But instead I just pull her into my arms and tell her, 'I want you to be happy, Maria. If we have to wait, that's all right. We've got years ahead of us.' She cuddles up then slowly works

113

her head into my lap where she unzips my fly with her teeth and expresses her gratitude for my understanding.

The day of the party, Saturday morning comes up bright and sunny. Maria sits up in bed like a bolt and announces that she's going to give the flat a bloody good clean. What is it with women and cleaning? I'm about to say, 'Off you go then' and roll over and go back to sleep when I remember the manuscript I stuffed under the cushion the night before. As she leans to swing her legs out of bed I pull her back and pin myself on top of her. She's all warm and puffy from sleep and even though her breath is a bit sour I kiss her long and deep then slowly work my way down her body and return the favour from the night before. I must have hit the spot because she nearly lifts the roof off and as I climb back up the bed I see her lying there with her eyes still closed and mouth open in a kind of surprised smile. I have a dreadful feeling of emptiness, almost nauseous as if I hadn't eaten for days. Everything about this scene feels very wrong and out of nowhere comes the thought, there's no way I can marry you, Maria. As I turn over to look at the bedside clock, I notice that the violets are dead.

I'm pretty good at keeping my feelings to myself and we manage to pass the rest of the morning without Maria noticing anything is up with me but I'm definitely didgy. I keep telling myself that I'm just a bit confused and that it will be all right, whatever that is. I fuck off to the gym and have a wank in the steam room but I really can't settle. As I pack my bag to go down to Woking for the night, I slip the manuscript very carefully under my shirt and zip the bag up tight. We load up and are on our way to the Veg Palace by half three. I don't say much on the drive down but I wouldn't have been able to get a word in anyway. Maria is wittering on about how much her dad has forked out for the booze and the food and what a great bloke he is. I'm just kind of muttering in agreement because I can't be bothered to argue with her and yes, it is good of him to stump up because I certainly couldn't afford it. I'm tempted to point out that a couple of grand is loose change to her old man and I'm really starting to brood as we get closer to Woking. She's going on and on and, I'm thinking, shut up you spoilt little bitch. She's always had everything she's wanted and while she's no snob – impossible given her lineage – she really doesn't have a fucking clue how the other half live. She thinks it's cute that my dad was a park-keeper, little realising how grim it could be stretching out his wages from the council from week to week, just enough to feed and clothe us and put a roof over our heads, but not much else. I don't feel sorry for myself, but it really sticks in my craw some-times the way she goes on. As we pass through the gates of Veg Palace I give myself a mental lecture about chilling out but it's not easy. The manuscript is bugging me and it's whirling round in my head even when I'm not reading it. There's something so baldly honest and unvarnished about the way she writes that I'm moved. If she could spell, I'd probably be jealous, but fortunately there are enough basic errors with grammar to salvage my dignity. Can her book really be that good or am I experiencing the early symptoms of a breakdown? I definitely do not feel right and I want a drink. Once we get inside I'm calmer but Diane must sense that some-thing is up because she shoos me to the staircase and tells me to take a nap or have a bath and just relax while she and Maria finish up the preparations. I am relieved that the Veg King is out playing golf because I don't fancy making nicey-nicey with daddy. Diane has put us in Maria's old bedroom for the weekend – a princess suite complete with teddy bears and posters of Brian Ferry. The double bed is covered in a primrose satin eiderdown and of course there's an en-suite bathroom in matching primrose. I run a deep bath and splosh half a bottle of Radox in. I get the manuscript out of my bag and lock the bathroom door.

By 7 p.m. we're suited and booted and waiting downstairs for the first guests to arrive. The Veg Palace looks pretty bloody magnificent with big church candles throwing off a lovely soft light around the room. There are flowers everywhere and I don't know what any of them are, let alone what they mean, but the scent is

115

heady and I can't help but think of my flower girl. That smell, so sweet and heady. Maria has gone the extra mile tonight and even painted her nails to show off her ring to maximum effect. The ring looks different and Maria tells me this is thanks to Diane who got round the back of the stone with a toothbrush and a bit of Fairy Liquid to really make it sparkle. Maria is wearing a dress that is both sexy and demure. It's made from a dark blue material which sparkles as she moves. It has long sleeves which I like and nearly reaches the floor. The sexy bit is the neckline which is not so much plunging as wide, showing off Maria's neck and upper chest to good effect.

The first little group to turn up are her new colleagues on the animal documentary and they're all standing around telling her how lovely she looks. I'm nodding away trying to look like a cat that got the cream, but even though I can see that she is beautiful I can't *feel* it. As more people start to arrive I watch her from across the room and I'm back in that detached mind-set which makes me feel like I'm watching a fly-on-the-wall documentary. I see it all, but I'm not part of it.

The Veg King jolts me into life: 'Mark, I want you to meet my partner Ron.'

I turn and put my hand out and what grabs it is the largest human creature I've ever laid eyes on. Ron pumps my hand, nearly crushing it. 'Pleased to meet you, son.'

Ron has got to be six foot five in his stockings and weighing in around the eighteen stone mark so I don't want to be rude but I definitely don't want to be his new best friend either. I edge away when I see Bee, Coxy and the kids come in. They've all scrubbed up well, even Coxy looks human and I'm touched by the effort they've made. I figure if they're here mum can't be far behind and sure enough Patsy tiptoes in on a pair of very high heels and a skirt with a slit up the side that would be considered risky on a woman half her age. I kiss her hello and say, 'You look nice, mum,' and she seems really chuffed that I approve, like she didn't want to let me down on my big night. Big Ron hasn't found anybody to talk to, he's still loitering in my orbit, so I make the introductions and I see him give her the eye, a right come on. Mum's flirting outrageously from the off and she hasn't even had a drink. I'm shocked at the spectacle of my mum being pulled and obviously loving it, so I back away and have a chat with Coxy about the roofing game. I'm really hard on Coxy and I know I shouldn't be because he obviously dotes on my sister and his heart is in the right place. He says if me and Maria buy a house he'll stick a new roof on it as a wedding present. That's not just a few coppers we're talking and I'm bowled over by his generosity. 'Fuck off, Coxy, I'm filling up here, what you trying to do to me?'

'Well, we're family, ain't we,' he says simply. But the moment passes quickly and he comes back with, 'Here, I got to tell you this one about a bird with three geezers in the back room of a pub,' and he's back to his old self with a blue, blue joke. The awkward first hour passes quickly because with a do like this, especially an out-of-towner, everybody turns up on time. By 8.30 the place is full and there's a lot of booze flying about. It really takes off. I'm looking at it dispassionately, thinking that the evening is a success already, but I really don't care. Like it's not even my party.

Funny things, celebrations. There are always a few characters overcome with the emotion of it all and either crying in corners or picking fights with the biggest bastard in the room. It has always amused me the way people carry on at parties, but that night was my turn. I'm avoiding Maria, like really avoiding her, and every now and then someone grabs us for a photo opportunity and I tell you, it's painful having to put my arm around her and smile. So I keep busy, doing the rounds, working the room, pausing for some tasteless humour with the blokes from work and keeping an eye on my mum and big Ron who have been stuck on the love seat in the corner since they got here. I get the feeling that my sister is following me. I keep catching her out of the corner of my eye, and sure enough when I nip upstairs for a jimmy she's waiting on the landing when I come out. I smile the happy smile of a man having the time of his life at his engagement party. Bee's having none of it.

'What's the matter with you?'

'Nothing. It'll pass, I mean really, nothing.'

'What do you mean it'll pass? What will pass?'

'Give it a rest, Bee.'

This is all I fucking need, my sister playing *In the Psychiatrist's Chair* at my engagement party. I'm steeling myself for a bit of an inquisition but instead she just says, 'Suit yourself' and trots back down the stairs. As she's disappearing into the crowd I get the urge to call her back, but swallow it. I'm standing at the top of the landing and I physically cannot get myself back down those stairs. My fight or flight instinct is working double time and I disappear into Maria's bedroom, our bedroom, and lock the door behind me. I've got to finish that book. I read over a hundred and fifty pages in the bath that afternoon and came out looking like a walnut. There's only about four chapters to go and I can't wait till tomorrow. So I'm lying there on the bed, with the door locked and my legs spread apart with that big heavy pile of paper resting on my groin. It feels strangely intimate to be alone here like this with her book, like I'm locked in a room with the girl herself. She's describing the way the father keeps crashing the car but escaping with nothing more serious than concussion and bruising. Nothing that would keep him in hospital and out of the home for long enough for everyone to relax. Can you imagine wanting your dad to be in hospital? But there's worse to come and I can't stop reading because I'm getting closer to her with every line. It's fucking spine-chilling, I tell you, because you just know that however sweet things are, a nasty episode is never far away. Every time she hears her father's key in the lock – and it could only be her dad, there's no way you could make this stuff up – I'm holding my breath, almost unable to bear the tension. A little girl, delighted that her daddy is home, each time hoping that he'll walk through that door pleased to see her, but each time letting her down either by being sick or passing out, or pissing his trousers or giving everyone a good hiding. I can hear the party going on beneath me and I know I've got to get back down there, but I don't want to leave her. I want to crawl inside the pages and take her away from the horrible bastard, fold her in my arms and tell her that it's all going to be all right. I'm willing the mother to take a knife to the fucker and off him, but she's paralysed by fear and the hope that he'll turn back into the man he used to be. There's something about the fear of a child that I just can't stomach and the scenes where she's got her pillow over her head so she can't hear him beating the shit out of her mum make me wild. I'm turning this way and that on the bed with this fucking manuscript like I'm making love to it and at one point I'm biting the bedspread because I want to cry out when the old man stabs the dog. Suddenly there's a knock on the door then the sound of somebody trying the handle. 'Mark?' Maria. I quickly throw the manuscript back into my bag in the bottom of the wardrobe and rush over to open the door. I must look as guilty as fuck because she says very suspiciously, 'What's going on?'

'Nothing. Just wanted to have a crap in private, is that all right with you?' I'm sharp and she feels the sting.

'I'm sorry, I was just a bit worried, that's all. I haven't seen you for over an hour, everybody keeps asking where you are.' I put my arm around her shoulder, innocence itself, a brotherly hug and I know I want to feel more than this for the woman I marry.

'No, look, Maria, it's me that should be saying sorry. I didn't mean to snap, I'm just a bit overwhelmed with it all.' I make a face of sincere contrition. She grins.

'It's going really well, isn't it?'

'Yeah. Brilliant. Come on, let's go down.'

Back into the fray and I start drinking big-time. I'm physically grafted to the bar and work my way through one bottle of champagne, chatting to people as they come and go, then another.

In the distance the Banana Rajah is in full flow boring the bollocks off some poor sod when he catches my eye and bellows, 'Stay there, I want a word with you.' I'm not normally aggressive on a drink, but I'm standing there swaying and muttering to myself, 'Yeah, come on then you fat cunt, do your worst,' but of course by the time he actually gets his fat drunken arse across the room I've lost my bottle and say nothing. The Veg King goes to launch into one then stops and leans right into my face and says, 'You're totally pissed, aren't you, son?' I can feel his hot breath on my face and the booze fumes wafting up my nostrils. He's laughing now, totally paralytic himself of course, and his face takes on the dimensions of some grotesque caricature. That big fucking gob wide open and a bit of dribble escaping down the side. He's sweating and his face is red, he's leaning right into me and if he doesn't back off I'm going to smack him, I don't care how big he is. I see my moment when he raises his arm to put his hand on my shoulder and I duck under him and excuse myself with the memorable words, 'I think I'm going to puke.' It's a lie but it gets me my exit and I fly up the stairs two at a time, back into the bedroom and turn the lock. I've got to finish that book.

By this stage I'm too pissed to care what Maria or anybody else thinks and I'm ploughing through the pages, actually sitting on the loo this time, with my strides round my ankles. Sometimes it takes me ages to have a piss when I'm drunk even though my bladder can be close to bursting and I don't want to be wasting precious time standing there swaying about, turning on taps and trying to persuade my waterworks to get going. So I'm pretty comfy all plotted up like a girl and I'm reading on and on and I've even stopped looking at my watch, because I truly do not care. She's just shopped the father to the police and I'm nearly at the end of it but I still don't know what's going to happen. This girl is a natural storyteller, there's no way you can go on a creative writing course and be taught this, you've got to be born with it. There are tiny twists all over the place and and the plot is as tight as a drum, the kind of book you always want to read but can never find. I can't believe it was written by a girl, they just don't think like this. As I finish the final page and pile all the paper back together my bladder gives my dick the green light and I have the most luxurious, long piss. I mean I'm going like a racehorse, it's pouring out of me. The sweetest slash of my life, no two ways. I must have lost every ounce of alcohol in my body because by the time I do my flies up I'm as sober as a judge, wide awake. I go to the door and I unlock it and slowly stick my head out. My nephew John is standing on the landing in the queue for the toilet so I hiss at him to come over.

'Go and get your mum for me.'

'What's the matter, Uncle Mark, you got the shits or something?'

'Never mind that, just go and get your mum quickly for me.' The other people queuing for the loo are all looking and I can feel them wondering what's going on with one half of the happy couple locked in his bedroom. I shut the door on them and it opens again almost immediately and Bee and John come in. I point at my nephew and say, 'I can't talk to you with him here.'

'He's staying.'

'Bee, this is private.'

'I don't care. How's he ever going to learn to be a man if he's never around men?' This one came out of the left field somewhere and rather than try and get my head around an answer I motion for them both to sit on the bed. 'So, come on then, what's it all about?'

'I can't marry Maria.'

'Obviously.'

'What do you mean obviously?'

'Well, obvious to me, but don't worry, I shouldn't think anyone else has noticed.'

'I noticed, mum.' John speaks up.

'Did you, love?' she asks all interested. 'What tipped you off?' Brilliant. This is turning into a panel game.

'Well, it's the way Uncle Mark had his arm around Maria when everybody was taking photos.'

'How many ways are there to put your arm around somebody for fuck's sake?' I'm affronted.

'You didn't pull her close to you. You know, when you really like somebody you pull them close to you, but you looked like you wanted to get her away from you.' I feel like clipping the observant little sod's ear.

'Is there somebody else?' Bee asks.

'No. Well, yes and no. No, not really.' Bee just nods at me to continue so I think, nothing ventured and just lay it on the line. 'Do you think it's possible to fall in love with somebody just by reading a book they've written?'

'Yeah. Course.'

'What do you mean, yeah, course? It's fucking ridiculous. Totally nutso.'

'No it's not, it's beautiful. I'd get wet if Coxy wrote a note to the milkman.'

'Mum!'

'Shut up you, you're here to listen, not talk,' Bee says to John, then to me, 'So what's she written then, confessions of a stripper?'

'She's not like that!' I surprise myself with the force of my reaction.

'Calm down, I'm pulling your leg.'

Bee's tutting away, mumbling 'stupid sod' to herself and she's right. I try to marshal my thoughts and start with the toilet where I left the manuscript. I hand it to my sister and say, 'This has changed my life.'

Bee starts reading and says straight away, 'I like the title.' She reads on a bit more, nodding to herself, like she really gets this. I stammer out a few sentences by way of explanation.

'Look, I don't know if this is her story, but even if it isn't there's so much of her in it. It's so revealing, Bee, do you know what I mean? I'm reading this book and I'm thinking, I know this girl, I really know her.' Bee just keeps nodding like it's all making perfect sense to her. She amazes me sometimes, my sister.

'What's her name?' she asks.

'I don't know.'

'You're in love with a girl and you don't even know her name. Have you ever actually seen this girl, or are you pining from a distance?'

'No. I've met her and she's nice. Really nice, she reminds me a bit of you. She's really pretty, Bee, really sweet.'

'That's a dead giveaway.'

'What is?'

'You using the word pretty. Normally when you speak about your girlfriends you describe them as fit or horny or tasty or even beautiful, but never pretty.'

'What am I, some kind of case study for you?'

Bee ignored my complaint and told me what to do. 'First off, you've got to tell Maria that the engagement's off.'

'What, now? Tonight?'

But before we can name the day, there's a hammering on the door and loud voices and the three of us nearly jump out of our skin. I can hear a woman crying – Maria – then a man's voice shouting, 'What the fuck is his game, locking himself up here all night?' It's the Veg King. I have a choice, I can confront it now or I can backslide.

CHAPTER NINE

GET ME OUT OF HERE

Naturally, I backslide. And this is how much of a good liar I am, because when I answer the hammering on the door I'm contrition itself. I go right into one, nearly manage to make myself cry and I'm looking imploringly at the Cucumber Kaiser. 'I'm sorry, Graham, but I've gone and got myself totally bolloxed. I was in bits down there in front of everyone, filling up, I was.' This stops the bastard in his tracks and even Maria slows her sobbing. Bee's right on it with the alibi.

'Go easy on him eh, Maria? He had a skinful and doesn't know whether he's batting or bowling. My John came up to look for him and found him sobbing his heart out. I think it's all been a bit much for him. It's not just us girls that get emotional, you know.'

The Veg King is standing there looking nonplussed and says, 'Well, I still think you're out of order. You've made my Maria look a right mug, going on the missing list like that.'

'No, dad, leave him,' says Maria. She folds me in an embrace and soothes me, stroking my hair and whispering, 'It's all right, my baby boy, it's all right, we'll be fine, mummy's here.' I nearly puke at this and John's on the beam, standing behind Maria and putting his fingers down his throat making a retching motion just out of the Veg King's line of vision. Bee's more professional.

'Come on, Graham, let's go downstairs and have that dance you promised me. Leave these two on their own to sort it out.'

The Veg King trails silently behind my sister followed by John

125

and then we're alone. Maria clocks the manuscript on the bed and says, 'What's that?'

'Oh, that. It's just some proofs of a book about the War that I brought down for John. He's got some project at school.' I stroll over to the bed, gather up the papers and sling them in my bag in the bottom of the wardrobe very nonchalantly. I'm so fly I scare myself sometimes.

'You're such a good man, Mark, fancy thinking of him when you've got all this going on. You really look out for that boy.' She glances at me coyly. 'You're going to be such a lovely daddy.' She's got her head cocked on one side as she says this and her eyes are a bit glassy. Oh God no, please, not drunk endearments. She stands in front of me smiling and swaying slightly. 'I really want your babies, Mark, let's have a baby, let's do it tonight. It would be so romantic to conceive at our engagement party.' Fuck me, the surprises keep coming tonight.

'What about your animals?'

'Work's not important. Money means nothing. The only thing that matters is us. You're the most precious thing in the world to me.'

Maria is doing her best impersonation of a woman in love and I'm feeling doubly sick because she probably means it. She's clinging and grasping and as I look at her, I think, where has my fucking friend gone? Who is this suffocating bitch? I cup her face and look at her the way I've seen them do it in the Calvin Klein ads and say, 'We're not thinking straight tonight, Maria. Let's just go to bed. I don't want sex, I just want to hold you.' This line is the absolute tried and trusted guarantee of a ride, except tonight I don't want to get my way. 'Sod everybody downstairs, just get into bed and let me hold you.' I'm saying this thinking to myself, you, you cunt, are constitutionally incapable of having an honest relationship with a woman. I have to wonder how much Maria really knows me because if she genuinely saw me in the round, not just a convenient hanger to drape her fantasies from, she'd know I was lying. But she doesn't, she really doesn't and for a moment I despise her. Maria locks the door then walks back to the bed and slowly begins undressing for my benefit. I look at her little breasts and I think, shit, I don't even fancy you. I get an image of my flower girl and the way her bust swells under her gilet. I couldn't give you exact dimensions, but a nice handful and then some. I want Maria to put her bra back on, or a T-shirt or nightie or something and just get her tits away from me. I'm as soft as a flopsy bunny, turned right off. But she plunders on and the next thing you know she pushes me flat on my back and sits on my face. I can't even be bothered to be polite and have a good sniff. She smells bad, a sort of ammonia whiff and I realise it's the fucking drink. I can smell the booze coming out of her and I want to smack her arse really hard and just push her off me. I've never hit a woman in my life but I could punch this one sky high. I ease her off me and mumble some excuse about feeling sick and just roll over and close my eyes. They're backing up with tears, I can't stand it. I don't recognise the woman she's turned into and I want the old Maria back, my mate who would tell me to buck my fucking ideas up, not this clinging vine that suddenly wants to be inseminated. I'm thinking, turn that fucking light off and go away, get me out of here.

I must have slept in a permanent state of red-alert because at 6.15 I open my eyes and get straight in the shower. Maria is still asleep and doesn't stir when I open the curtains and find that the morning is dull, misty and quiet. Woking is still deep in dreamland, so I creep down the stairs and and see that the Veg Palace is like a fucking war zone. There's a body of indeterminate sex I don't recognise under a duvet on the sofa and I'm thinking, sod this, I'm not hanging about to clean up. I hear footsteps behind me and Maria has woken up and says, where are you going, stay and have a cooked breakfast with mum and dad. Sorry love, but I'm going now. She wants to know where I have to be this early on a Sunday morning and I say my sister's but this is a lie as I just want to get back to the flat and be on my jack. The idea of going home and seeing Maria's stuff everywhere is bad enough, let alone the woman herself. I feel so guilty I can't look at her. 'Poor Marky, needs some space,' she says in this pathetic baby voice I've never heard her use before and I don't know that my nerves can take much more. I run upstairs and get my gear, throw on a jacket and kiss her briefly by the door. 'Call me,' she coos from the front porch but I'm across that gravel double quick and into the car as she calls out, 'I love you, Mark Tucker.' I raise a hand, start the engine and I'm gone.

Once I get the other side of Woking I'm fine. Really chilled. There's no traffic and I'm flying along getting green lights all the way. I fiddle about in the tape box and at random pull out Bjork's *Debut* album and slot it in. It's not my tape, it's Maria's but I'm in the mood for a change. There's all these harps going on and I'm thinking the wrong tape must have been put in the box but then her voice breaks in and she sings this little ballad, 'Like Someone in Love', and I am totally blown away. I mean finished, like I've had the wind knocked out of me or I'm dosed up with tranks. I rewind it and play it again and again and again and I can see my flower girl and I'm rushing on it. I swear to God I can almost smell her standing there on that stall surrounded by all those blooms, looking so clean and so confident. I get this weird kind of tingling sensation that starts in my bollocks and ends in my throat. I'm burning up and kind of tripping at the same time. What the fuck is going on here? I'm having this weird sort of biochemical experience and it's coming from everywhere. I've really got the ache for this woman, but I don't just want to fuck her. Not even. I don't even know that I could look at her the way I'm feeling at the moment. Maria slides across the front of my brain and right out the other side. Ashes, gone, just like that. The feeling subsides as Bjork gets a bit funkier and I'm nearly in London. The power of rational thought is beginning to kick in and I get my Henri Temple-Golden head on and I'm giving it the old, 'Now, Mark, what we have here is a classic case of avoidance. You have woken up to your real feelings about your fiancée and you want to use this new woman to springboard you out of your current situation. You seem to be unwilling to confront your emotional pain and are clearly seeking ways to get round that. An idealised vision of love is offering you what you think is an escape route. But perhaps this woman merely represents what is missing from your life at the moment. Am I making sense, Mark?' I buy the theory but only for about two minutes because I know for fucking sure that something is up here. I rationalise: you like the look of her, you like the cut of her jib and when you think of her you feel happy. What's so fucking complicated and significant about that? She's a woman, you're a man, it happens. But not like this it doesn't, not with me anyway.

By the time I get to Maida Vale I'm feeling brisk and business-like. I settle myself by the fire in the front room with the manuscript, some plain paper and a pen. I'm going to read it again and make some notes so that I have something constructive to say when I see her tomorrow. If I can put my personal feelings to one side for the moment, this is actually the work of an extremely talented person who deserves a result. Her spelling is poor and I get the feeling that maybe English wasn't her best subject at school but she's totally authentic and fuck me she's got stamina. There's a lot of it, her book, but I never once felt bored reading it, even when I was half thinking, I wouldn't have done it like that. I was telling myself I could do better, but honestly, I couldn't. I'm too lazy for a start. So I stick to what I'm good at, make some calls, pull some strings, help the girl out.

129

CHAPTER TEN

TEA IN KILBURN

Monday morning I'm up with the lark. I had spent all day and all night reading her book and making notes and for once in my greedy life I didn't have a drink. Maria called and said that she was going to stay in Woking for a few days because her outfit are filming at some RSPCA centre in Chobham which is just down the road from the Veg Palace. Oh, and guess what? Daddy is going to buy her a car so she can get from location to location. I know exactly what she's up to. She's had a chat with the Veg King and he's told her to stay there until I apologise. Let him come grovelling if he wants you, nobody treats my princess like that. She thinks if she holds out in Woking for long enough I'll crack and do a midnight raid to get her. I'll come grovelling and tell her I can't live without her. Dream on, baby.

I'm in Ken High Street by half eight but the flower stall isn't open yet, so I mooch up to the office where I have a coffee and quick chat with the early birds. By nine o'clock I'm back over there but she still hasn't arrived. I have no idea what time she opens up because I'm never normally at work before ten. I dick around in the office, not really concentrating, then go back over at quarter to ten just as she's unloading boxes from the van with Pete.

'Good morning,' I say brightly.

'Mark, what's up? How did your party go?'

'Yeah, not bad. How you doing?'

'I'm late this morning, we overslept.' We. She's got a boyfriend, maybe even a husband though I can't see a ring.

'I read your book over the weekend.'

'Bloody hell, that was quick.' She looks a bit abashed. 'What did you think? Any chance?'

'A more than average chance if you ask me.'

'No.' She stands stock still. She really cannot believe what I've just told her.

'Yes.'

'I don't believe it, you're just being nice.'

'To be honest, I'm as surprised as you are, but straight up, it's a winner. You must have some idea of how good this is?'

'Well, I like it, but then I would, wouldn't I?' A couple of punters approach the stall, she's still unpacking and looking a bit stressed.

'Look, we'll get together for a chat when you've got more time. Do you fancy a drink after work or something?' My bum goes when I say this because if she turns me down I'll be in bits.

'I can't, Mark.' I'm in bits.

'Well, no worries, some other time.' Totally downcast.

'I'm not fobbing you off, it's just that it's not easy to get out. I've got a daughter.'

'Well, can't you leave her with her dad?' This is a bit fucking bold but I want to know her set-up if only to put me out of my misery.

'She hasn't got one. Well, when I say she hasn't got one I mean we're on our own.'

'I'll come round to you then.'

'That would be brilliant.' She looks like she means it. 'Come for your tea tonight. We eat about six o'clock by the time I've packed this lot up and collected Phoebe.' Phoebe, sweet name. She scribbles her address on a piece of paper and hands it to me. I know exactly where this is. It's the council flats opposite Kilburn Park tube. I had a mate who lived there years ago, it was a bit of a toilet but I know people refer to that area as Brondesbury now. It's what's politely termed as a 'transitional neighbourhood'. You can imagine how much work I get done that day. Absolutely dick. I spend all day mooning around looking vacant and switching my phone to voice-mail every time it rings. I still don't know her name. I should have asked. What if I can't find her place and I have to ask somebody? What am I going to say if I have to stop somebody in the street? 'Excuse me, do you know where I can find a really pretty woman with long curly brown hair, cute dimples and a daughter called Phoebe?' Cool it, Mark, you're getting all worked up. Free-floating anxiety, it's a terrible thing but it dogs me for the rest of the day. I'm worrying about the inside of a gnat's arsehole by the time it gets to half five and reckon on making my way to the tube. No way am I turning up on a council estate in a black cab. She'll think I'm a total prick.

I'm coming out of Kilburn Park tube at ten to six and as I do so a black cab pulls up on the other side of the street. She steps out with a little girl of about five in thick Coke bottle glasses. The child is pulling something on a lead and after a bit of encouragement a whippet jumps down onto the pavement. I stand there looking at the three of them thinking it's a sweet scene. The little girl is wearing suede hotpants with long laces at the sides which she's twirling round, doing a bit of burlesque on the pavement. My flower girl nudges her to behave while she pays the cab driver and Phoebe instructs the whippet to 'sit still and be a good boy.' I walk across the road and she looks up, surprised to see me. For a moment I think she's forgotten.

'Sorry, you were expecting me tonight, weren't you?'

'Yes of course, I just didn't expect to see you coming across the street, that's all. Mark, this is my daughter Pheobe.'

'And this is little Frank,' says Phoebe pointing to the whippet.

'Little Frank eh? Where did he get a name like that?' I ask.

'He's the son of big Frank, champion racer.' My flower girl is standing there looking at her daughter and smiling indulgently, all proud of her little girl. It makes me want to kiss the top of her head.

'Come on, Phoebe, let's get indoors and get Mark a cup of tea, shall we?' She looks hot and flustered, her cheeks are glowing and her face slightly damp. I think I'd like to run my tongue down her face and taste the sweat which I guess would be salty but sweet.

'By the way, what's your name?' I ask.

'God, I'm sorry, it's Sara. My name is Sara.' Sara, eh? Not what I was expecting. I was expecting a Michelle or an Alison or something. I follow Sara and Phoebe and little Frank down the steps and across a courtyard and up some more steps and down a ramp and I'm wondering if I'll be able to find my way back out of here later. All the time we're walking Phoebe is explaining little Frank's pedigree. Apparently he's the product of an accidental union between big Frank champion racer and a whippet bitch called Beverly. Beverly? Beverly has two pups, a boy and a bitch. The bitch comes out thoroughbred greyhound and the dog is a hundred per cent whippet. No genetic crossover at all.

'Don't you think that's wicked?' she asks me.

'Yeah, really wicked.' This little girl is a bit of a boffin. Very bright, very grown up for her age, speaks very well. Confident too for a kid with such thick glasses. She's swanking about her bib and hotpants, telling me how her nan bought them off a woman at bingo for a fiver and how pleased she is because they match her school shoes which are bright red patent. Doesn't look like any school uniform I've ever come across but this is inner London, so I make allowances. She's got a pretty little face but you can't really see it because the bins dwarf her features and give her an air of vulnerability at odds with the outfit and patter. I follow her along thinking if I was her dad, I'd never let go of her hand – she looks so incorrupt and tiny, despite the gob. We reach the flat, which is on the ground floor of a three-storey block, the front door is lacquer red with a shiny brass knocker and two large tubs of flowers either side. Looks immaculate compared to some of her neighbours, some of whom don't bother with curtains, save an old sheet nailed up at the window. She searches in her bag for keys and says to her daughter, 'Don't push, Phoebe, I'm going as quick as I can.'

'Little Frank's hungry, mama.'

'So am I, love, now just calm down a minute.' She's getting a bit agitated and I want to help her with her bags and stuff but I'll probably just make it worse, so I wait. She finally finds the key and looks at me apologetically. 'I'm sorry, Mark, it's always like this, we just can't seem to get ourselves organised, can we, Pheebs?'

'I'm organised, mummy, so is little Frank. It's you that isn't organised because you stay up late every night reading and writing. You should go to bed earlier, like us.' She hugs her dog's neck and he licks her face in agreement. Sara rolls her eyes but says nothing, pushes the door open and welcomes me in. It's small and there's stuff everywhere. A design nightmare. There are toys on the floor and a basket of washing in the hall and we haven't even got in the kitchen yet. The kitchen is also small, but it's tidy and the floor is sparkling clean, like in the ads.

'Come on, Phoebe, get that dog out of my kitchen, take him out to the garden while I unpack the shopping and put the kettle on.'

'Can I give him a biscuit, mama?'

'Go on then but only one.' The little girl takes two Bonios from a cupboard and gives one to little Frank once he's sat down and lifted his paw. The other one she puts in her own mouth.

'Phoebe, will you stop eating those dog biscuits, it's disgusting. I'm going to make your tea in a minute. Have some bread and butter if you're hungry, or there's fruit in the bowl.' Phoebe declines the offer of human food and wanders off with her dog. Sara asks me distractedly to please sit down, mumbling to herself, 'That kid won't eat her dinner now. She does this every time, comes home and stuffs her face with dog biscuits.' I'm strangely comfortable sitting there in her kitchen. There's a nice homey vibe about this place, it's warm and smells of clean washing. I plonk myself down at the table and pick up a children's book and start reading. Sara is busy unpacking the shopping and making a cup of tea. We don't speak. We don't need to. I'm quite happy sitting there with my book. 'Do you take sugar?' she asks.

'No thanks,' I say and don't even look up. I realise that I'm totally at ease with myself. This is double weird. Sara brings the mugs of tea over, puts them on the table then hunts around in her bag, coming out with a packet of Bensons. It figures. Every girl I have ever been out with has smoked and there's something reassuring about the fact that she does too. I've never smoked myself for the very good reason I'm not very good at it. I occasionally have a tug on a spliff if I'm out at a party but I always cough my guts up so what's the point? She lights her fag and looks at the book I'm reading. 'Getting stuck into *Owl Babies*? That's Pheebs' favourite book, that is. Every bloody night since she was about two years old I've had to read it to her. They're so funny the way they get fixed on something, kids.'

'Have you always been on your own with her?' It's a pretty direct question but it feels cool to ask.

'Yeah, from day one. My family all live around here so I've got plenty of support.' She pauses and exhales a long cloud of smoke. 'It gets a bit lonely though.'

'I can imagine. Look, tell me to fuck off if I'm being nosy but was it your choice to be on your own or her father's?'

'Mine.' She doesn't elaborate so I switch subjects and fortunately we have a very ripe topic of conversation. I pull *Welcome to the Pleasure Dome* out of my bag and thump it on the table. We're straight into a discussion about the structure of the book and bits I think she needs to lose. I keep pointing out to her that I'm no expert but she listens attentively and takes it all in. Some writers you really have to handle with kid gloves because they can get very precious about their stuff, but this girl doesn't seem to mind a bit and is taking a pen and drawing a line through pages and pages of stuff that I thought was superfluous to the story. She's nodding away and going, 'Yeah, yeah, I see what you mean, that's a good point, I hadn't thought about that.' She's humble without being annoying, practical and workmanlike. So workmanlike, in fact, that I find myself trying to move the conversation round to me so I can get her to take some notice. I find myself telling her how I broke my leg when I was four by jumping off the climbing frame at nursery under the illusion that I could fly. She laughs uproariously at one point to reveal perfectly white teeth, not a single filling that I could detect. I find myself staring at her mouth which is soft and wide. She clocks me looking and shifts uncomfortably. Smooth bastard that I am, the conversation moves back to the book seamlessly and the moment passes. It helps that she's so easy to talk to and really listens before she answers. There's something nearly unwomanly in the way she can keep her mouth shut while I'm talking. Call me sexist, but I tend to give female freelancers a wide berth when I can help it because they want to discuss the ins and outs of every little change you make and can get very touchy when you have to slice their work about. I tell them, it's nothing personal, it's a newspaper, stuff gets cut, but they won't have it. I've got one madwoman who writes intermittently for the paper and once actually rung me up in tears saying that my small alterations to her copy had changed the entire context of her piece and offended all her friends who 'trusted her to handle their comments with integrity'. I wouldn't mind, but it was some dopey piece of fluff about fashionistas with accessory dogs – what other context is there apart from 'these women are sad thin birds with no mates'? But Sara doesn't seem in the least bothered and is gaily putting large marks through pages of words which might have taken her months to write.

'How long did it take you to write this?' I ask.

'Nine months.' She doesn't elaborate so I'm not sure of the significance of this, but we're really getting down to it and I'm enjoying myself, my brain is grinding into life and I'm coming up with new suggestions that hadn't occurred to me when I read it before. She suddenly looks at the clock on the wall and says, 'Jesus, it's seven o'clock and I haven't got the dinner on yet. Pheebs will be starving.'

'Is there a chip shop round here?' I ask.

'About a hundred and fifty yards away. Would you mind?'

'Not at all, what do you fancy?' She calls for the little girl to come in the kitchen and tell me what she wants from the chip shop. She's back hunting around in that bag again and I know she's looking for her purse so I say, 'Come on, I'll get these.'

'No please, take it,' she says offering me a tenner. 'I invited you to come for your tea. He's our guest, isn't that right, Pheebs?'

'Are you my mum's boyfriend?' Phoebe stares at me through her thick lenses.

'Don't be silly, Phoebe.' Sara blushes. 'Mark has just got engaged.' She looks hot again and her hair is falling in wisps around her face. I get the ache for her badly.

'Oh, that's a shame. My mum really needs a boyfriend. All my friends' mums have got them. Have you got a nice car?'

'Phoebe! Go and get in the bath. You can have your saveloy and chips afterwards.' The little girl runs off laughing and Sara turns to me and says, 'I'm really sorry about that, she's a bit embarrassing sometimes, my daughter.' I laugh it off and leave to get the fish and chips thinking, don't apologise, love, I got a lot of good information there.

The evening flies by. We eat our fish and chips in front of the telly watching *Coronation Street*, then Sara goes off to read Phoebe a story for bedtime. Before the little girl turns in for the night she says to me, 'Are you going to come to our house again?' Picture it. A five-year-old girl is standing in front of you in her nightie and Barbie slippers. In her hand is a book about spiders and her dog-eared copy of *Owl Babies*. She's still wearing her glasses but her hair has been taken down from its pony tail and given a good brush before bed. She's asking if you'll come round her house again and you know it's more of a plea than a question. She's probably like this with every man who comes into her orbit because she wants a daddy. My fucking heart is melting but I just say, 'I'd love to, sweetheart. Night night, God bless.' While Sara's putting her to bed I'm slumped in front of the telly with my feet up, shoes off and tie undone feeling really comfy. I feel at home here. My defences come galloping in to tell me not to be mad and go getting mixed up with a single mother. A single mother on a council estate in Kilburn, no less. My entire life so far has been devoted to style and ease. This just doesn't fit the picture.

Sara comes back about half an hour later. 'I'm sorry about that, it takes ages to get her to go to sleep. I have to lie down with her until she drops off. She gets really clingy and frightened if I leave the room before she's asleep.' She sighs and pulls her hair out of its plait, running her fingers through it and scratching her head. It's not a provocative pose, she really is just scratching her head at the end of a long day. 'Do you fancy a drink?'

'Love one.'

'I'm not sure what we've got. I'll have to go and have a hunt around in the kitchen, should be a drop of scotch if you fancy it?'

'Lovely.'

She comes back with two fairly small measures and this gives her away not as tight, but just somebody who doesn't drink very much. I finish mine in one gulp and she's apologetic and gets me a refill. She drinks hers very slowly and doesn't even seem to be aware that she has a drink there most of the time. Not like Maria. Maria gets through a bottle of wine on her own making the dinner. She needs to watch it, that one, or she'll end up like her mum and dad. We kind of drift off the topic of the book and start talking around it, agents, publishers, what have you. She really doesn't have a danny about the business so I casually assume the mantle of adviser until we can steer this project into safe waters. It's an excuse to ring her up at the very least. I'm certain I wouldn't be so fucking big about it if I didn't want to bite her flesh because if I'm frank my nose is slightly put out of joint by the fact that this woman has managed in nine months what I couldn't achieve in years. I'm larging it to cover up for the fact that I'm a bit of an inadequate in the writing stakes. I'm acting like some benevolent despot, 'You stick with me, darling, I'll see you right.' With another woman I'd be tempted to lie and exaggerate my contacts, but there doesn't seem much point with Sara as she wouldn't have heard of anybody even if I did roll off a list of names. There's also a strange compulsion to be honest with her. No bragging, just telling it like it is. I tell her plainly that I have a mate whose sister is an agent and I'll have a word and see what they suggest.

'Would you? Really? You're so nice.' Then her voice changes and she asks guardedly, 'Why are you doing this?'

'Because I want to help you. It's a good book.'

'Look, don't think I'm being rude, but what's in it for you?'

'I don't know. Nothing, I suppose.' I'm confused now. What am I supposed to do, tell her the truth? I want to help you because I'm falling in love with you and I'm looking for any excuse to be in your life.

'But you can't be doing it for nothing. Nobody does anything for nothing,' she insisted.

No, you're right, darling, especially not me. I had to think for a bit because by this point I'm not fucking sure about anything apart from a strong urge to snog her. My head's all over the place. I stand up and say, 'Well, it's up to you, but all I'm proposing I do is get the number of this agent for you, make a bit of an introduction and then the ball's in your court.' She looks at me sheepishly.

'I'm sorry about that, I don't mean to sound suspicious or ungrateful. I'm just not used to people helping me out.' She doesn't sound self-pitying when she says this. It's a fact of life for her. I remember some of the scenes from the book and I get it. No, I don't suppose you are used to people helping you out, love. All you ever got was a slap for your troubles. She walks me to the front door and scribbles her number on a piece of paper. I take it but it's surplus to requirements because it's memorised instantly. I want to tell her that the violets died but enough's enough for one night. We say goodnight and I ask her just friendly-like to give me a hug. She puts her arms around my neck and pats my shoulder. It's not sexy, just affectionate, but I feel the swell of her bust against my chest and catch my breath. She's just as soft as I thought she'd be. I walk away and hear her door close behind me. There's a fucking colony of butterflies in my stomach. I'm alive.

CHAPTER ELEVEN

YOU MAY BE FEELING
HOPELESS AND AFRAID

It was a very mild evening so I walked all the way from Sara's in Kilburn to Maida Vale. No big deal you might think, just ten minutes down the road, but for me who takes a cab for even the shortest distance it was daring, romantic even. I'm still tingling from our little embrace and I don't want the feeling to end. I'm all stirred up and feeling high and optimistic. London looks beautiful and the opening bars of 'You Make Me Feel Brand New' are playing on my lips. I see a gang of teenage boys outside a kebab shop staring at me. I laugh and they have a little laugh back with me. Tonight London is a friendly place and instead of seeing a gang of boys about to nick the wheels off a car or sell a couple of rocks, I see a gang of boys just hanging around outside the kebab shop because there's fuck all else to do. If I smoked I'd offer them a couple of fags. I'm losing my edge of suspicion and sort of chuckling to myself. Sure it's a complicated situation, she's got a kid but love will find a way. Love will find a way? Come on, Tucker, get a grip. But what convinces me that something is stirring inside my crafty heart is the fact that I don't want to fuck her. I do eventually but not yet, not now. Usually at this early stage with a bird I'd be scheming the fastest route to the bedroom, but for the first time in my unblinking penis-led life I want to take my time and play a longer game. I want the suspense to nearly kill me. I want to fall in love properly.

Good job I walked because my little reverie was short-lived. I open the front door of the flat, switch on the light in the hall and from the front room I hear, 'Where have you been all evening?' Fuck, Maria. What's she doing back here? I go in the front room and switch on the light.

'What are you doing sitting here in the dark? You scared the shit out of me.'

'We need to talk.' Must we? Fuck, shit, piss.

I look at her face and it's all puffy where she's been crying. She looks like a bush baby or something, squinting at me through glassy eyes like she can't see properly. Must be how Phoebe looks when she takes her glasses off. Concentrate on the matter at hand, Mark, don't start drooling over some myopic kid. I need a drink. 'Do you want a drink?' but as I say it, I see that she's already got one. There's an empty bottle of wine on the floor and a second one open. Bollocks, I really do not need this. I go into the kitchen and get a glass then join her on the settee.

'Aren't you going to take your coat off?' she asks. There's the old subconscious at work for you, because no actually, I don't feel like stopping. I feel like getting up and going right back out that door and just keep on walking. I want to get back the beautiful feeling I had before I saw you, you miserable drunk pain in the arse. I leave my coat on and don't say anything.

'What's happening to us, Mark?' Her voice wobbles when she says this and I know that whatever I say a fresh round of tears is on the way.

'I don't know, Maria. Really, I don't.' Liar.

'Everything was all right until the party, what's changed, Mark? Why are you pulling away from me?' She's weeping steadily now, her voice all over the place. Shit.

'I don't know, Maria. Maybe I'm getting cold feet.' This is

brave, but it's not even close to the truth. It's enough for her though. She clutches the straw and brightens immediately.

'Well, that's natural. I was talking to Nick and he said he felt exactly the same way before he married Lisa.' Great, now the whole fucking world knows our business. Her enthusiasm for this marriage is extremely off-putting. 'I think it's quite normal for blokes to feel like that, especially guys like you who are used to a lot of freedom.' Not like this, it isn't, love. I say nothing because I've got about as much appetite for a pack of lies as I have for the truth right now. She's going on and on and on, working herself right up, you can hear the relief in her voice. Fucking hell, Maria, do you really think so little of yourself that these crumbs are enough? Where's your fucking dignity? What happened to the girl that used to tell me to fuck off at the drop of a hat? Bring her back, she's easier to deal with than this tear-sodden one. She's drying her eyes and blowing her nose and she's got the face of a kid at Christmas. Look, I'm all better now, we're going to live happily ever after. I don't know that I can stand to hurt her any more tonight, so when she suggests we go to bed, I follow heavily behind. Once we get under the feather she's like a performing seal or something, like she needs to give me a really good ride to convince me that we're happy and I'm going along with it and trying to pretend that it's Sara who's tonguing my arse and massaging my balls, but that just makes me feel dirty, because I don't want sex with Sara to be like this. This is fucking playacting and it's churning me up and making me feel sick and empty. I just want it to be over with so I'm banging her really quickly trying to get there and as I do the tears start to roll. It's my turn now, there's no holding them back and Maria is cradling me like a baby, mistaking my tears for a surfeit of emotion and whispering, 'I love you too, baby, I love you too.' Jesus.

Tuesday morning I'm up with the birds, shaved and ready for work by 7.15. Maria is just getting up as I search for my keys and coat and she catches me before I have the chance to slip out. She's yawning and stretching, standing there in front of me totally naked and all I can think is, put some fucking clothes on, will you. 'Where are you going this early? I was going to do you a fry-up.' This scene is traditionally the stuff of wet dreams, a naked woman rubbing her tits against me while simultaneously offering egg and bacon, but I just want to get her away from me. Last night's booze and fags are heavy on her breath and I need to get out of there. Pronto.

'I can't, babe. Gotta fly. There's an editorial meeting at nine and I was so caught up with the party last week that I haven't sorted anything out.' Back to my old slippery self, the lies are just rolling off the tongue. But she's grinding her fanny against me now, her arms are tight around my neck and I can't get out of it without seeming at best ill-mannered.

'Don't go before I've had my brekkie, Marky Mark.' I'm perplexed for a few seconds, thinking, what's she talking about, but as she slides to her knees and takes my knob out of my trousers I get the picture. I'm not even remotely turned on and I'm standing there with my keys still in one hand and my coat in the other. I don't even put them down, I'm just passively letting it happen, then I feel the tears welling up in the back of my throat again. I'm trying to bite them back, but it's no use. This is so totally over and the maddest part of it all is I feel I'm being unfaithful to Sara. What the fuck is up with me? I pull away slowly so her teeth don't catch and zip myself up. I don't say a word, I just leave her there on her knees with her mouth open. I resist the urge to slap her face and tell her to get up. I close the door behind me and run down the stairs three at a time.

I'm all over the place so I just keep walking, need to work this off before I get to the office. A dozen cabs pass me, but I don't hail a single one. Typical, try finding one when you're late for work. I'm walking, walking, walking, nearly breaking into a trot at times and before I know it I'm at Notting Hill. I'm starving by this stage, didn't even have a cup of tea before I left the house, so I go in the first café I come to and order a bacon sandwich. There's a copy of the *Mirror* on the table so I'm leafing through it, slurping my mug of tea and chewing that beautiful bacon sandwich on white bread, soaked through with grease, and I'm feeling quite reborn by the time I pick up the crumbs from my plate and lick them off my greasy finger. I wash it down with a long slug of tea and I'm back to normal. I'm just about to fold the paper up and put it back when I see the horoscopes and read mine. It says, *Crunch time for you Sagittarius, the moment of truth has arrived. Promises like pie crusts were made to be broken. Abandon the guilt and set yourself free.* You can fuck off, Justin Toper. Jesus Christ, I'm turning into my sister. I'm much more relaxed when I leave the café, so I order a cab and inch along in the rush hour traffic. It would have been quicker to walk but enough already. My phone goes and I see from the display it's Maria calling from the flat so I switch it off. It's quarter to nine by the time I get to the office and just as I'm paying the cab I clock Sara's white van pull up on the other side of the street. I watch for a few seconds then disappear inside my office block before she catches me spying.

I've never figured this one out, but the more I like somebody, the less I make a play for them. I can't stop thinking about Sara so I'm going to avoid her for a while. I desperately want to hear her voice so no fucking way am I going to ring her up. Go figure. I do ring my mate Des Calder though. He's the one whose sister is an agent at one of those big firms with offices all over the world. Des works at *The Times* editing foreign news, I haven't seen him for some months now but I've never leaned on him for a favour before, so I shouldn't think he'll mind too much. He can only say no. But he doesn't of course. He's pleased to hear from me, says he's heard on the grapevine that I'm getting married and congratulations, mate, we must get together for a pint sort of thing. When I ask him if he'll speak to his sister for me he gives me her direct line at work and says, ask her yourself, just say I gave you the number and take it from there. So I call her. Fiona her name is, Fiona Calder and I know she's pretty powerful so I'm not hoping

147

for too much of a result, but maybe just a recommendation of somebody who could help Sara. Sara what, she asks and it's embarrassing because I don't know her bloody surname, but Fiona's casual and just says, bike the manuscript over and I'll check it out and get back to you.

I can't very well play it cool when I need to find out not just her name but get back the manuscript which I left on her kitchen table, so I trot over to the stall. There's a light drizzle and she's looking a bit cold and pissed off but pleased to see me nonetheless. She's not wearing any make-up and she looks tired but her skin is perfect, a natural beauty. I tell her that I've spoken to Fiona Calder at the agency and she's wildly impressed, thinking I'm some sort of media god, but I tell her the truth. It's just a mate's sister doing me a favour, getting in through the back door if you like. I'm thinking of offering to drive over to Kilburn tonight and pick up the manuscript but before I can do so she says she'll bring it to the stall tomorrow morning, that way she can tidy it up a bit tonight. I'm disappointed, but I don't push it. I ask her what her surname is.

'Oh God, it's a bit embarrassing.'

'What? Come on, tell me. I'm dying to know.'

'O'Mara.'

'Sara O'Mara,' I say. 'It's good, got a real ring about it.'

'Oh, I hate it. Having a name that rhymes, it sounds so stagey, I don't know what my mum and dad were thinking.' She trails off mumbling then quickly brightens. 'You scored a big hit with Phoebe last night.'

'Oh yeah, how come?' I'm doing a bit of a peacock now, chest out, all proud.

'Because you let her dog sit on your lap. People can be very funny about dogs and my Pheebs takes it personally. Little Frank is the moon and the stars to her.' She smiles distractedly, 'Oh, and you had a spud in your sock.'

'A what?'

'A hole in the bottom of your sock. We call them spuds.' Great, so I'm sitting there last night with my shoes off and half my feet hanging out of my socks. I make a mental note to go into Barkers and stock up at lunchtime. She's kind of taken the wind out of my sails, but I try not to let it show, or she'll see what a vain bastard I am, that something as insignificant as a hole in my sock could torment me.

'Well, I'll let you get on then, Sara O'Mara.'

'That's not fair. I don't know your name. What's your surname?'

'Tucker.'

'Tucker!' she screeches. 'I bet you got a few rhymes to go with your name at school eh?' For some pathetic reason, I'm hurt by her laughter. I'm trying to go along with the joke, but I'm proper stung, so I just say my goodbyes and slope back to the office with the vague promise to go back in the morning. I'm sitting there at my desk thinking, cheeky cow, laughing at my name like that. She can go fuck herself if she's going to take the piss out of me. Hello. Earth to Mark. Are you reading me? Get a fucking grip, Tucker. But it's no good, I'm on a downer.

The morning drags on and I can't snap out of it. I'm beginning to think I could do with a bit of psychological help, maybe take the talking cure but no way am I in the mood for Henri Temple-Golden, so I call my sister. It's the usual pandemonium when she answers the phone, the sound of the telly blaring and Robbie pulling on her, asking for biscuits. 'Can you just piss off a minute, Robbie, I'm trying to talk to Uncle Mark.'

'You shouldn't swear in front of the kids like that, Bee, they'll pick it up.'

'You can fuck off. Now get to the point, I'm busy.' Charming.

'I'm all over the joint, Bee.' I'm whispering so the people in the office can't hear me, but neither can Bee because there's so much noise at her end.

'What? I can't hear a word you're saying, speak up.' She's really fucking grumpy and I feel like giving her a mouthful.

'I need to come and see you.'

'Well, come over then. Don't keep ringing up, just get your arse over here. I gotta go, Robbie's trying to stick his sword down the dog's throat, I'll see ya.' And that's it, she's gone. She really pisses me off sometimes, my sister, she can be so blunt. Christ, I'm touchy, so I think, sod it and walk out of the office and jump on the tube to Victoria where I catch a fast train to East Croydon then a three-minute cab ride to Bee's. I'm on her doorstep within half an hour. It's quicker to get to the suburbs than get across town some days. I wonder if Sara's ever thought about moving a bit further out of London for the kid. Could I stand it, I wonder, living round the corner from my mum and sister if we got married? Where the fuck did that come from? Get married? Move to Croydon?

Mystic Meg opens the door before I have a chance to ring on the bell and shoos me indoors quickly. 'Come on, come on, get in or the dog'll get out.' I follow her into the kitchen where she pulls a couple of cans from the fridge, hands one to me and takes a big slug from her own before speaking. 'Sorry, Mark, but I'm having a right day of it. Robbie's bunking off, telling me he's got belly ache and can't go to school, but he hasn't stopped eating all morning and now he's trying to kick the shit out of the dog. I'm supposed to be on duty at three o'clock, I'm going to have to call in sick myself.' My sister works at the Mayday Hospital in Croydon and it's really badly paid, horrible work. Slopping out bedpans and washing old geezers down in bed, I don't know how she does it. She's probably glad of the excuse to get out of the house. I certainly couldn't cope with three boys and Coxy. The house is in a right state, there's washing hanging up everywhere and shoes and boots and toys all in a jumble on the floor. Bee looks washed out, really drained and quite ropey, standing there drawing deep on her fag and looking thoughtful. I've come to moan about my problems but something's up with her, I can tell.

'What's the matter, Bee?'

'I'm pregnant.'

'Is that good or bad?'

'I don't know, Mark. I've had enough dirty nappies to last me a lifetime. I'm not sure I can go through it all again. We're just getting on our feet moneywise as well.' A solitary tear rolls down her cheek. I give her a cuddle and she gently cries on my shoulder.

'I thought you were on the pill,' I say, brushing the tears off her cheek.

'I was. But I'm thirty-five and I smoke so I had to come off it.' She's sniffing loudly and I'm thinking, please don't snot on my jacket, I've just had it cleaned. 'They offered me that long-term injection but I didn't fancy it. We were using johnnies for a while but you can imagine how well that went down with Coxy, so I've just been trying to be careful. I'm normally good at knowing when I'm ovulating but I must have got it wrong.' She wipes her forearm across her face taking a trail of tears and snot on her sleeve.

'How can you tell?' I'm fascinated, I really want to know. I think it might be nice to know a bit more about a woman's body than the quickest way to get it humming. Bee's always been very matter of fact about this kind of thing, very down to earth, I suppose it comes from being a nurse.

'Well, usually, you get this kind of clear sticky discharge. It's the mucus surrounding the egg as it travels down the fallopian tube. You can tell from your mood as well. Normally when I'm ovulating I swing between being really snappy and really randy. Like a bad mood that only sex can get you out of. Nature's way of making sure you have babies, I suppose.'

'I thought women only got ratty when their periods were due.' I'm all ears now.

'It's just like being due on, you feel the same, all bloated and you can't stop eating sweeties but it passes after a couple of days. Oh Mark, what am I going to do?' She's crying again now. There's a lot of it about.

'Have you told Coxy?'

'Not yet.'

'Have you thought about an abortion?' I hesitate when I say this because I know my sister's feelings on this issue. She's mental pro-life, not out of any religious convictions, she just thinks it's bad juju to kill a soul.

'No way.'

'Yeah, but Bee, you've already got three.' I'm going softly, softly, but I really think she should consider it.

'There's a life inside me, Mark, I can't go tearing a baby out of my body. It's all wrong.' She's wiping her eyes with a piece of kitchen towel now and lighting a fresh fag with the butt of her old one. 'Besides,' she says, drawing deeply, 'Coxy wouldn't hear of it, he'd do his nut if I offed one of his unborn children.' Her words play around in my head for a while because I've never thought about it in those terms. I've got a couple of girls pregnant in my time and in both cases there was absolutely no hesitation on either part to get rid of it and no regrets. One of the girls had it done in her lunch hour. You have casual sex, it happens, no big deal. It's the first time I've thought about it in ages and now it makes me feel a bit funny. Unborn children. Put like that, abortion sounds sinister. What the fuck is happening to me? All this talk of sticky mucus and the rights of the unborn child, it takes my mind back to Sara. I don't think I'd ever be the sort of prat who marked his girlfriend's periods down in his diary but it might be interesting to get a bit closer to a woman on this one. Standing there in Bee's kitchen with our cans of beer makes me think back to that conversation we had about baby-making sex a couple of years ago. Bee reckons there's absolutely nothing on this earth to compare to it. She says it's deeper and harder than any other kind of sex and your head goes all trippy. Afterwards she does a shoulder stand for as long as she can hold it, to make sure all the spunk gets right in there. I'm not sure I want to be having a mental image of my sister in the nude doing a shoulder stand, but it's there all the same. Suddenly I remember my mum.

'What happened to mum on Saturday?'

'Oh fuck, it was hilarious, I haven't told you yet, have I?' Bee cheers up straight away and goes right into storytime, telling me how she and Coxy are trying to persuade mum to get in the car, but mum won't be peeled off big Ron and insists that she's going home with him. Ron lives in Byfleet or somewhere and mum goes back to his place with him. Doesn't get her arse back to Croydon until teatime on Sunday.

'Dirty cow, going with a bloke she's just met at a party.' I'm pretty disgusted at the thought of my mum with that huge animal.

'Oh, like you've never done it on a first date.'

'I can't believe you're defending her, Bee.' I'm totally appalled at the idea.

'Oh wind your neck in, you. It's done her the world of good. She was as happy as a sandboy when I spoke to her Sunday night.'

'I still think it's disgusting.'

'Yeah well, never mind Patsy, eh. What's occurring with you?' We get another couple of cans out of the fridge and settle in around the kitchen table. Robbie and the dog come in from the garden and Robbie curls up on Bee's lap and just sits there quietly while we're talking. He's a big kid, Robbie. He's six or seven, I can never remember their ages exactly, but after playing up all morning he's now as docile as a baby, leaning his head against her boobs and looking really comfy. She's a sweet mum, my sister. Her boys all get a regular bollocking but she's pretty free with the cuddles. Sitting there pouring my heart out at her kitchen table I start to ache for a baby, a girl specifically. I can see Sara and me and Phoebe and a little baby girl all happy together. I thought it was only women that had biological urges, but there's real yearning there in my guts to take a little girl by the hand – it's physical. Bee listens carefully to everything I have to say and she's nodding away like she does, going, 'Yeah, yeah, right.'

153

'You gotta let her go, Mark.'

'Which one?'

'Maria, of course. To be honest, I've never thought she was the one for you.'

'Thanks for telling me.'

'Like you'd have listened. Besides, I may not be Maria's biggest fan but as a woman seeing another woman dangling, I think it's cruel to drag it out if you know for sure that it's curtains. Go home tonight and tell her.'

'Oh fuck, Bee.'

'Don't try and worm out of it, Mark, you'll only make it worse.'

'Yeah, I know you're right.' I let this horrible fact sink in for a minute, slowly resigning myself to the task ahead. 'What about Sara, how should I play it with her?'

'Very slowly.'

'Yeah, I think so too, but why?'

'Because she's got a kid.'

'What difference does that make?'

'All the difference in the world.'

I nod, but I'm not sure I know what she's getting at. I hang around at Bee's until the other two come home from school, do a bit of wrestling on the carpet, my devoted uncle number, then call a minicab back to the station. As I'm standing on her doorstep saying goodbye my heart sinks. I know what's ahead of me and I'm not looking forward to it.

'Good luck,' says Bee.

'Yeah, you too, love.'

We have a little cuddle and Bee makes that sign with her fingers next to her ear that means gimme a ring and then I'm gone. There's a train from East Croydon that goes to Olympia so I jump on that and steel myself for the evening ahead. I'm really shitting it as I get off the train and walk to the taxi rank. In about ten minutes' time I'm going to be having a really horrible experience. I'm standing there waiting for a cab but there's a big fucking queue, loads of people pouring out of some exhibition, so I think sod it and go and sit in the pub across the street. I pick up a copy of the paper and flick through it while I'm having my pint and I remember that I should have sent a piece down for the late edition and I haven't done it because I was so distracted and pissed off this morning. A surefire bollocking is on the cards from Cullen tomorrow but at least I've got tonight to come up with an excuse. I linger and have another pint until I finally get up the nerve to go home and get on with it. Just as I'm going out the door, Henri Temple-Golden is walking in with a middle-aged guy in wire-framed spectacles and a bald head. She does a quick double take then says something to baldie who goes inside, looking backwards to check me out as he does so. I'm just smiling politely, how you doing, nice evening etc and looking at her ratty hair thinking, you're a bit of a stranger to the brush, ain't you, love? 'It's been a while, Mark, why don't you call me?' she says in a very confident way and I say sure, I've got your number. She reaches into her pocket and pulls out a little card. 'Not this one you don't. It's my home number, call any time.' The card says simply henri in a lower case modern font and a St John's Wood phone number. Not her business card, I'd wager. I pocket it and say, see you around, have a good evening. 'Yes, you too, Mark,' she says very sincerely. If only she knew.

I'm at the flat in under ten minutes and trudge up the stairs, dragging my feet and pausing for one last deep breath outside the door before I put the key in the lock. I go in and it's totally dark and silent. She's sitting in the front room getting drunk and being weird again, I just know it. I turn on the lights, but it's totally silent, except for the humming of the fridge. Nobody home. The front room looks different, like she's had a tidy-up or something. Then I go for a slash and I notice that all her make-up and bits are gone from the bathroom. I flick the light on in the bedroom and the wardrobe door is open with my stuff shoved up in one corner and a big empty space on the rail where her clothes used to hang. On the bed is an envelope. I open it up and the ring falls out. I'm feeling a bit sick and panicky as I read the note with it: *You might as well tell me who she is, because I'll find out if it's the last thing I do. There is no other possible explanation for the way you've been behaving and I am not going to be made a fool of. You know where you can put your ring. When you're ready to come and explain yourself properly you can find me in Belsize Park. I'm going back to my old room at Terry and Joseph's. I must be an idiot because I still love you, but I'm so humiliated I can't stand it. Maria. PS. You owe my dad £1700 for food and drink.*

Talk about out of the blue. Totally wrong-footed me. I ring her at Terry and Joseph's and Joseph answers the phone and tells me very tartly that Maria is busy and I should call back another time. Fucking poof. The coward in me rejoices because I don't have to go through the excruciating business of breaking off my engagement but I feel curiously cheated, deprived if you like. There is no doubt in my mind that I am a total cunt. Poor Maria, I've fucked her over again. I hang my coat up, taking the keys from the pocket and pulling out henri's card. I put it on the table under the mirror in the hall with my keys. I wander round the flat noting the empty spaces where her gear used to be and I'm proper choked because I know that this is it. Our seventeen-year friendship is finished for good and it's all because of a woman I haven't slept with, haven't even taken out for a meal or to the pictures. I'm going fucking mad, this can't be right. My brain feels like it's got electrodes tied up to it or something and I'm being bombarded by all these contradictory messages. What are we going to do with all the engagement presents? How am I going to tell everybody the wedding's off when they were only dancing at our party a couple of nights ago? Have I just made the biggest mistake of my life? No, it's for the best. She was never right for you, Bee thinks so too. There's only one thing for it. I get the brandy off the counter in the kitchen and I keep drinking until the voices in my head get a bit quieter. I want oblivion, I want to pass out. My wish is granted.

CHAPTER TWELVE

WE CONTINUE TO TAKE
PERSONAL INVENTORY

I woke up in the same spot I passed out on the settee. I never expect hangovers to be pleasant but this one was in a different league. The remorse was something else. I hadn't just got drunk and said something to embarrass myself, that stuff is the everyday meat and potatoes of living and making a tit of yourself. No, what I'd done was lose my best friend, totally sober, then I got drunk. Oh God, Maria, I'm so sorry. Outside, the rain was coming down in sheets and a quick glance at my watch told me that I was already half an hour late for work. Fuck. I stood in the bathroom looking at my raddled face and whiskers and wondered if the whole Sara thing wasn't just a few condensed moments of madness. She was expecting me to pick up the manuscript, but I reckoned on giving the whole thing a wide berth. I was in enough trouble. It was Wednesday, I was going nowhere. Work could whistle for it.

I spent three days sitting in the flat, watching telly, eating toast, drinking tea, not shaving and not answering the phone. By Sunday I had grown restless from being cooped up watching daytime shite on the telly and pacing the flat. I spent a lot of time in front of the mirror in the hall checking myself and wondering who I was. I remembered the card Henri Temple-Golden had given me in the pub doorway on Tuesday evening and sifted through the heap of mail on the hall table until I unearthed it. It's one of the most tasteless, almost offensively pretentious little cards I've ever seen but I wondered if I hadn't been too quick to dismiss her and her ideas. She was a funny-looking bird and possibly I was holding her looks against her. It's often the way with me and women I don't like. I simply find them ugly and therefore cannot take them seriously. I wondered if it was impolite to call her on a Sunday, but figured with a name like Temple-Golden it probably didn't matter. She picked up the phone after two rings and said, 'This is Henri.' Very odd. For a moment I paused, not knowing how or even if to continue. I identified myself and she couldn't have been more pleased if I'd been the man from Littlewoods telling her she'd won the pools. 'I knew I would hear from you again, I knew.' Her enthusiasm was discomfiting but I told myself it must be something they teach them at shrink school. I briefly sketched my situation, the engagement and break-up with Maria, the presence of a third person in my affections and suggested that maybe I swing by her office in Primrose Hill for another try. 'Perhaps a less formal approach would be helpful. Possibly we could meet for lunch sometime?' My head's spinning a bit at this and I'm wondering if I'm going to have to spring for lunch as well as her fifty-minute fee. She intuits my reticence: 'There will be no charge of course. I think you would benefit from a more informal, friendly exchange.'

'I didn't feel that comfortable on those cushions to tell you the truth.'

'You don't have to tell jokes to mask your discomfort, Mark. Without pain, there can be no growth.'

'Well, you're the expert. Are you sure about this?'

'It would be a pleasure. Do you have plans? We could meet today.' Fuck me, she must think I'm a right lost soul, put me straight to the top of the list. Either that or I was right and she really did try to make a pass at me that time we met before. No harm if we meet in a public place though, so I arrange to hook up at a brasserie in Primrose Hill. I arrive ten minutes late to find her perched on a stool at the bar, heavily perfumed with her hair piled bird's nest style on top of her beaky face. I reckon it's an attempt at the 'I've just spent the entire morning shagging' look, but I check out the dumpy body in the voluminous clothing and think, you'll be lucky, love. I ask the bartender for a beer while we wait for a table, but she closes a damp hand over mine and whispers in a very breathy voice, 'I'd prefer it if we didn't drink. It's important to be totally honest about what you feel. Substances are blocks to feeling, Mark.' I feel like telling her to please herself, because I always have a drink on a Sunday lunchtime, but I think, no, come on, Mark, go along with it, you might learn something. We're seated quickly at a table in the window, something I'm given to understand is only for favoured customers, and Henri smiles beatifically at the staff, Lady Bountiful herself. I'm nursing my Virgin Mary wishing it had a vodka in it while Henri explains her theories on men who cannot commit. 'I want us to think in terms of the struggle to become whole and the centrality of intimacy to that wholeness. The repeated seduction of women is a classic device to avoid real intimacy and so keeps you further and further from your ultimate goal, resulting in shallowness of feeling and confusion.' My roast beef arrives and I chew on a fatty bit of meat wishing I had a nice bottle of claret to go with it. Henri's blabbing on about the importance of not rushing into committed relationships and I'm thinking, fuck me, you can't win. I look around at the other diners, all drinking wine, then turn back to Henri who is fingering a large stone on a long chain around her neck in something approaching a foxy, teasing air. I'm bored with discussing my failure to commit to Maria and get to the bit I really want to know about, which is Sara. Is it possible to fall for somebody, so quickly and over so little? 'Well, of course, all things are possible,' says Henri knowingly, a snide little smile on her ugly boat, and when I tell her that Sara sells flowers she laughs indulgently. 'Just a little Pygmalion fantasy, I'm sure. A woman who will not challenge you, leaving you to continue to behave in the way you choose uninterrupted.' I reckon she's taking a lot for granted saying that about a woman she's never met, so I tell her about the book. She doesn't look so sure now, but dismisses Sara again by telling me that I really need to concentrate on my own needs for growth and stop distracting myself with 'sensual frippery'. Frippery? Excuse me, lady, but I've cancelled my wedding on the strength of a desire to kiss a face so beautiful it gives me stomach ache. I think of Sara's perfect skin and study the pockmarks under Henri's make-up. I reckon there's a bit of snobbery in there somewhere, and I'm thinking, yeah, you stuck-up jewshrew, you couldn't hold a candle to her.

'Henri, do you believe in love at first sight?' I'm bold and on the attack.

She carefully rests her knife and fork on her plate of roasted vegetables and does that irritating ladylike dab with the napkin in the corners of her mean little mouth before looking me right in the eyes and replying, 'But of course not. Such feelings are merely an infantile justification of sexual attraction. Possibly you feel guilty about the breakdown of your relationship with Maria and need to justify your lust for this other woman by dressing it up as something more significant.'

'Look, this isn't some dolly bird I picked up in a bar, she's a grown woman with a daughter and a lot of natural talent.' I'm really on my high fucking horse here and it strikes me that I was never so quick to rush to Maria's defence.

Henri smiles and says 'Aha' as if suddenly all the pieces have fallen into place. 'Does the daughter play some part in your attraction for this woman?'

'I'm not with you.'

'It's perfectly natural to feel desire for children. It's a completely misunderstood phenomenon.' Henri says this with a flourish, moving her mineral water around her teeth like it's mouthwash.

'Are you trying to say that I'm some kind of fucking nonce?' I'm gonna slap this bird in a minute.

'Not at all, but your defensiveness flags up an area that we might want to look at more closely.' Henri is pulling her diary out of her bag and I think, no fucking way am I wasting another minute listening to your obscene insinuations. What is it with this bird, why can't she just be happy for me? I reckon I'd have been better off going out to lunch with mum or Bee, at least they've got some common sense. I don't hang around for pudding or coffee and say I'll be in touch. I feel angry and confused and tell myself it's my own stupid fault for ringing her in the first place. I buy two good bottles of red wine on the way home and spend the rest of the day drinking, wondering what the fuck I'm going to do.

Go to work for a start. Monday morning I get up, neck four Nurofen to get me through the day and jump in the shower. It hasn't stopped raining since last week and there's not a single fucking cab to be had so I'm reduced to getting on the tube with all the other drenched commuters, stuck in that damp, stinking carriage with all those dripping brollies and not a single bloody happy face. The day is about to get much, much worse. I barely have time to hang up my sopping raincoat when Cullen comes roaring across our big open-plan office and barks, 'I want to see you now.'

'I'll just get a coffee.'

'I said now!' It's embarrassing because everybody has heard him and there are a lot of faces watching for my reaction. Suddenly it goes very quiet, even the phones stop ringing as if to maximise my shame. I try to maintain my composure, what is left of it, and trail behind him along the corridor until I get to his office. 'Come in, close the door and sit down.' I meekly obey. 'What fucking time do you call this?'

'Quarter to ten.'

'Don't be fucking facetious, Tucker, I've a good mind to fire you this minute.' I go to stutter out some excuse, but he puts his hand up to stop me. 'I don't want to hear it, I've had enough of your bullshit to last me a lifetime. From this moment your cushy little contract is finished. You either go back to working full-time for the same salary or you can clear your desk.' I swallow hard. This is a lot heavier than I was expecting. 'Did you really think you could go on taking the piss out of this paper and we wouldn't notice? I've got guys out there with more talent in their toenails than you and they work more hours for less money.' He reaches into his desk and pulls out a piece of paper and hands it to me. 'You can take this as a written warning for your consistently unprofessional conduct. I wouldn't mind your little dodges if you at least did the work, but last week was the final straw. Not even a phone call. Philippa tried to cover for you, though God knows why she bothers, but I knew you were skiving and you needn't think you're getting paid for it. I've had enough of you, Tucker, and if you so much as steal a paper clip from these offices I'll have you out of that door so quick your feet won't touch the floor. Do you understand me?' I swallow and nod. I'm burning up like a boy getting told off by the headmaster. I feel small and humiliated and my head is getting hot. He clocks me squirming and I couldn't claim that he looked like he was enjoying himself, but he obviously thought I had it coming. He softened his voice slightly for the final thrust of the sword. 'From now on you work eight till five with an hour off for lunch. If those hours don't suit, you'll have to find another paper to work on but don't bank on getting a reference from me.'

I nod in agreement. 'Fair enough, Matthew.'

'I'll say it's fucking fair enough; now get out of my office and do some work before I change my mind.'

Jesus Christ, that was nuclear. Normally a bollocking is water off a duck's back to me but this time I've had a proper slap. I spend the morning at my desk working diligently and avoiding the sympathetic glances I keep getting from Philippa. The blokes all seem to be avoiding me, like I'm tainted with something contagious they might catch. Fair dos. Nobody wants to be associated with a loser and let's face it, even allowing for self-pity I'm a fuck-up, a nobody, a waster and a joke. I watch the clock until it says 1 p.m. exactly, get up, put my coat on and pop out to get a sarnie. It's still pissing down. I'm undecided as to whether I'm gonna go over to the stall until I turn the corner and see Sara loading the white van. I run across the street dodging the traffic and arrive dripping and breathless.

'Mark, where have you been? You look terrible, I mean you don't look very well.' She's soaked to the skin herself and there's a raindrop hanging from the edge of her nose which I badly want to remove with my tongue.

'It hasn't been the best week of my life, no. Look, I'm really sorry I haven't been to get your manuscript but things went arse-up last week and I'm only just getting back to normal.' She's struggling with buckets of flowers and the boxes, they're all wet and starting to bend, so I help her load up.

'Thanks, you're a gent.' She's the only one who thinks so. 'So, what's occurring, how come your life is in tatters?'

'The engagement's off.' You can tell from the look on her face this was the last thing she was expecting, but I wouldn't say she looks too crushed on my behalf.

'But why? You only had your party the other week?'

'Long story.'

'Sorry, I didn't mean to be nosy. Oh, don't put those boxes there, slip them on the top of this one here.' There's obviously some order to this that I don't understand.

'How come you're packing up so early?'

'Because I'm absolutely fed up with this weather. I've had a whole week of it, business is really slow and I can't afford to stand around here getting wet and paying a childminder while I'm not earning. '

'Isn't she at school then?'

'No, she's got a tummy bug, that's what's made my mind up really. I'd rather be at home on the settee watching the telly with Phoebe.'

'And little Frank.'

163

'Oh, yes, we musn't forget little Frank.' She loads the final box and turns to look at me, then executes this little display of tenderness that nearly does me in. She touches my cheek and says softly, 'I'm really sorry about what's happened to you, Mark.' Her fingers linger for a couple of seconds, then it's as if she realises what she's doing and quickly draws her hand away. 'Look, if you're feeling fed up and fancy coming round just to chill and watch the telly, please do. You don't have to talk if you don't feel like it. Phoebe will be pleased to see you.'

'I'd love to, but I'm in trouble at work, gotta keep my nose clean.' Fuck Matthew Cullen. A couple of hours with a beautiful woman, a four-eyed little girl and a whippet might be just the ticket for my battered ego.

'You are having a bad time of it, aren't you?' I want to tell her everything, but I just offer to take the manuscript away and say I'll be in touch. She hands it over, it's a bit damp around the edges, but it'll do for Fiona.

'Look after yourself, Mark. And call me. I mean it.'

'Yeah, I will.' I mean it too.

I grab a sandwich from the Pret à Manger next to the tube and go back to my desk. I reckon I may as well work through lunch, but I haven't turned into a complete saint, so I book a bike on the company account to get the manuscript over to Fiona's offices in Soho. Just as the messenger is collecting the package from my desk, Cullen walks past, but even he wouldn't think I had the brass neck to go taking a liberty so quickly after my dressing down and the incident passes without comment. It gives me enough of a fright to make me say a silent prayer of thanks and make a genuine resolution to stop taking the piss. I treat this job with total disdain but the fact is if I lost it I'd be gutted. And I wouldn't find it easy to get another job. You have to do something pretty radical to get sacked from this place. It's the beginning and end of the line for London papers in here and if I drop another bollock it's back to regionals. I shiver at the thought. I'm thirty-four years of age and

I've got fuck all to show for it except for a trail of broken hearts. My so-called book hasn't even got a title, let alone text. I have no mates to speak of. I never bothered keeping up with the blokes I went to school with and even though I go out for the odd pint with colleagues past and present, there isn't anybody I could talk to properly. I've always been too busy with the ladies to worry about building friendships and if I needed to talk, I always had Maria. Maria, Maria, I wonder how she's doing. I'd ring up and ask but she'd only tell me to fuck off, or worse still expect an explanation. I think of giving Bee a bell, but she's got enough on her plate. So that's it, I'm on my jack with nobody to blame and nobody to talk to but myself. I've got a job, but only just and I've got the flat, but it doesn't seem like much of a consolation from where I'm standing at the moment.

About half-past two I get a call from the main reception down-stairs and Doug, one of our so-called security operatives, who does jack shit apart from polish his lapels and read the paper, calls me and says there is a package for me. 'Can't you send someone up with it?' I ask, all shirty.

'No, come down. I think you'll enjoy the surprise.'

So I trot out to the lifts and wait ages and while I'm standing there I'm thinking what a lazy bastard Doug is. He just can't be bothered to move his fat lily-white arse up the stairs. He really is an idle sod that Doug. A bunch of paramilitaries could walk through the door with a case full of Semtex and Doug wouldn't even look up from his *Mirror*. After a very long ride down in the lift, which stops on every bloody floor before reception, I march up to Doug's little desk and say, 'Come on then, what you got for me?' Doug gives me this funny look, then purses his lips like Larry Grayson. I could smack him, but then he pulls up this big, and I mean massive, bunch of flowers from inside his cubby hole and gives them to me.

'Where did these come from?' Then my heart sinks and I realise it must be Maria. Oh for fuck's sake, no. Please, I can't stand it.

'That bird who runs the stall across the street brought them over about an hour ago.'

'Did she say anything, why didn't you call me?' I go hot and cold all over.

'She said not to, but asked me to give you this note.' I grab it off Doug and tear the envelope open. It's one of those cheap manila ones that your mum used to put your dinner money in, and inside is a piece of lined note paper torn from a spiral bound pad. It said simply: *Yellow roses for friendship, white roses for purity. Chin up. You'll fall in love again. Sara.* What a turn-up. I leave the flowers with Doug on the desk and say I'll collect them on my way home. It's a big old arrangement and I don't want to draw any unnecessary attention to myself what with trying to keep a low profile and all, but I'm totally made up. Chuffed as monkeys I am, and I spend the last couple of hours of the day opening, closing and reopening my little note from Sara and reading it. *You'll fall in love again.* Damn right I will, sweetheart.

The day drags. I haven't worked a full day for a while and certainly not five days in a row for a very long time. I can't believe it's still only Monday. I take the tube home, which for me is like wearing a hair shirt, and I'm sitting there with my fuck-off floral tribute and enjoying all the attention from my fellow travellers who are clocking me wondering what my story is. I get this sudden compulsion to go to a church. Not just any church, but the big one on the corner of Warwick Avenue and Clifton Gardens. I nearly jump off the tube one stop early at Warwick Avenue, but sanity prevails and I stay put. The moment passes, but I'm left with a lingering image of this church and the sure conviction that one day I'm going to get married there. I can see it, all dark and foreboding in the rain, but inside lit softly with stained glass and candlelight. Weird one. Me and my sister were both baptised into the Church of England but that means absolutely dick. The Anglican Church don't seem to ask anything whatsoever of their flock, not even a belief in God. Getting married in a church was never an option for me, which is why Maria and I had settled on a trendy secular do at the Chelsea Town Hall. But there's this very strong image of me kneeling at the altar in a navy blue suit. My bride is wearing pink, but I can't see her face. Very odd indeed.

That evening I make myself a meal, something I haven't done for a long time. Nothing fancy, just some fresh pasta and parmesan cheese but at least it made me go to the shop and buy some food for my bereft fridge. I ate my tea with my feet up in front of the telly and watched *Coronation Street*. I'm not a regular viewer of anything, but when I watched it over at Sara's the other night there was a really fit Indian bird whom the local crusty was trying to pull and I was wondering what had happened. Maria knows the bloke who plays the crusty. He used to work at Scribes West as a cellarman when Maria was on reception and she had a necking session with him once at the staff party. Said it was the best snog of her life. I can't quite believe it to look at him, but he has got these very thick lips and it's often the way that these skinny little dudes are full of surprises. I toy with the idea of calling Maria, but not yet. No, not yet. I call Sara instead. I have the perfect excuse. She picks up the phone and I can hear music in the background that I recognise. I say hello, I just rang up to say thanks for the flowers and that I biked your manuscript over to Fiona. And by the way, what's that record I can hear playing in the background.

' "Three Plus Three", the Isley Brothers.'

'No shit. One of my favourite albums. *Summer Breeze*.'

'Yeah, I suppose *Summer Breeze* is the obvious choice, but I prefer *Moving Down the Highways of My Life*.'

'Oh, listen to the muso.' And that's it, we're off. We don't stop. The conversation's dipping in and out of different topics and just skimming the tops of a few others, like a butterfly. The old brain is ticking over nicely, we keep interrupting and finishing each other's sentences. We're laughing a lot and after three quarters of an hour we still haven't run out of things to say. I'm having a good time.

'How's the girl then?' I enquire after Phoebe.

'Asleep. She was really knackered when I picked her up from the childminder's. She must have woken up from a bad dream or something because she was inconsolable for a couple of hours. Wouldn't stop crying. I was getting worried, she got really hot at one point.'

'So what did you do?'

'Roasted a chicken.'

'That's the secret, is it?'

'Works for my lot.' My lot. A family. A small one, but a family nonetheless. I haven't even got a fucking hamster.

'So how did your chicken turn out?'

'Beautiful. Little Frank nearly made himself sick he ate so quickly.'

'A chicken man, is he, little Frank?'

'That dog goes on total surveillance the minute a bird goes in the oven. He just sits in the kitchen staring at the oven door until I bring it out.'

'Do you give him some for his trouble?'

'Yeah, course. What about you, what did you have for dinner?'

'Just a bit of pasta, but it was nice. I watched *Coronation Street*.'

'Oh brilliant, I missed it putting Phoebe to bed, what happened?' So I'm actually giving this girl a blow by blow of a soap opera. I am not being a man I recognise. This is up there with some of the most banal conversations I've ever had, the type I have with my mum or sister and I've never felt happier. What the fuck is going on here? Usually after five minutes of this shit, I'm off the line sharpish, but I want it to go on, I want to know every bloody boring detail of her life, because to me nothing has ever seemed more interesting. I ask her what she does at weekends with Phoebe and she says not much, just mooch about, take the dog for a walk, go over to my mum's or my sister's, go to church.

'Go to church?'

'Is that a bad thing then?' she asked a bit nervously.

'No, not at all, it's just that I had this funny vibe about that church on the corner of Warwick Avenue and Clifton Gardens on my way home from work tonight, I nearly went in there.'

'You're kidding.'

'No, straight up.'

'That's our church.' It goes very quiet on the line for a second or two. It's spooky and we both feel it. I try and get it back on track.

'You a regular churchgoer then?'

'Not really, it's just that there's this great priest over there that I've known since I was a kid. My dad used to take me and my sister on Sundays.'

'Religious was he, your dad?'

'No, just Catholic. He used to sit in the back row playing cards with his mate Eamon.'

'Did your mum go?'

'No, mum's a bit of gypsy. Me and Pheeb are kind of neutral but it's somewhere to go on a Sunday morning. You should come with us one day, it's a bit of a laugh. Father Tom lets Phoebe take her dog in with her. Told her that he got a special dispensation from the Pope for little Frank. You want to see her face, she takes it so seriously.' She pauses. 'It's my birthday as well.'

'What, this Sunday?'

'Yeah, this Sunday, 1st May.'

'How old will you be, if you don't mind me asking?'

'Thirty-nine.' This one knocks me sideways because I had her down for about thirty-two, thirty-three. This bird is in very good nick. I go quiet. 'Hello?' she says.

'Yeah, I'm still here, just a bit surprised, that's all.'

'How old are you then?'

'Thirty-four. Thirty-five in December.'

'Nice age.'

'Is it?'

'It was for me, that's when Phoebe was little.' I'm taking all this in, trying to figure out the chronology of her life. She must have had the kid at thirty-three if Phoebe is five now. I really didn't have her down for thirty-nine. It must be those dimples.

'Why did you call her Phoebe?'

'Have you ever read *Catcher in the Rye*?'

'Read it? I fucking lived it for a year or two.' Then I get it. At exactly the same moment we both quote Holden Caulfield's incantation, 'My sister Phoebe kills me!' We just fell about after that. Much hooting and oh my God, I loved that book so much. This is way cool. We move on to families and I tell her some about mine. She reminds me of Bee and for a minute I get a mental image of that fucking rook Temple-Golden telling me I've got a problem because I'm in love with a girl who reminds me of my sister. Maybe I have, but I really couldn't give a flying one. 'You've got something about you that reminds me of my sister.'

'Is that a good thing?' she asks.

'Yeah definitely. I mean, she's my sister so she gets on my nerves, but she's a sweetheart.' We move on to fathers. Both of ours are dead and I told her that mine had a stroke on my sister's wedding day.

'Bit heavy,' she said.

'Yeah, it was a bit. How did yours die?'

'He tried to cross a dual carriageway when he was pissed and a lorry knocked him up in the air. My mum says it's because he wasn't wearing his glasses and couldn't see. He was as blind as a bat, my dad, they used to call him Batty O'Mara. It's probably where Phoebe gets her shortsightedness from. My mum won't have it that he got knocked over because he was drunk.'

'Still loves your dad then?'

'Totally.'

'Must have had something about him.' I'm thinking about the father in her book and wondering.

'He had something all right, I think they call it alcoholism. He was a bright man my dad, he used to work in the print and read a lot, but I reckon he flipped out with the drink and saw himself as this Othello figure to mum's tormented Desdemona. You know that kind of "love you so much I have to kill you" scene?'

'I think so.'

'Do you know what my first thought was when I heard he was dead?'

'Tell me.'

'I thought good, I hope it bloody hurt.' She's kind of edgy and see if I give a fuck when she says this. This is getting a bit intimate for me, I'm not sure we should be talking about how we feel about our parents. I want to get off the line, so I tell her I'll call her about Sunday. She's casual. Sure, whatever. We say goodbye, leave it on a nice note. I put the phone down and take a minute or two to let it all soak in.

Slow it down, Mark, you nearly got closer than you wanted to back there. I have a riffle through the CDs and find my Best of Sinatra. I move it forward to track eight and turn it up really loud. Those horns and strings come booming across the room then Sinatra starts in on *Nice and Easy*. I'm actually crooning into my mirror above the fireplace, giving it the old Sinatra pointy finger and singing at the top of my voice, having the time of my fucking life. Then I'm riffling through again looking for *Three Plus Three* by the Isley Brothers but I know I never bothered to get it on CD. I've got it on vinyl in a box knocking around in mum's loft. Marcus. That's who'll have a copy of it. I ring him and he picks up the phone straight away. No problem, I'll tape it tonight and bring it into work tomorrow. I'm buzzing, it's happening.

CHAPTER THIRTEEN

HIGHLIGHTS AND HANG-UPS

I'm flying for a couple of days, really content in my own little world, scheming and dreaming of all the things to come. I'm still undecided about the church gig because even though the hand of fate is clearly at work in my well-disordered little universe, I still balk at the prospect of a fifty-minute Mass on a Sunday morning. We'll be there together one day, so where's the rush? I avoid the flower stall, but I can still check her out and see what she's up to because there's a very good little vantage point on the corner of Derry Street and the High Street where I can spy on her unnoticed. It's at such an angle to the stall it's unlikely she'd ever be looking in this direction. Most of her trade is either walking along the High Street or coming down Ken Church Street. She looks well from what I can tell in the distance. She's wearing her hair up, but there are big clumps hanging down from the sheer weight of it. That girl has got a lot of hair, I'm telling you. She kind of slipped it in on the phone the other day that her hair was naturally curly and not permed. She was swanking, check out the mane baby, kind of number. I'd love to, sweetheart, but I'm really mulling this one over. I'm letting things unfold at their own pace. I'm thinking change, when it comes, has to be natural. I'm thinking organic.

I managed to hold out until Thursday when the rain stopped and the sun finally came out and London was too beautiful not to want to share it with her. I can't believe I just said that. Me, share? Daft, but true. Work had evened out from its grisly nadir on

Monday and I was as back to normal as I was ever likely to be, chatting easily with the other blokes, starting to fuck around a bit more. Marcus came up trumps. He made me this crystal clear recording of *Three Plus Three*, which sounded mental when I got it home and I kept playing it over and over. Mrs Murray must be having kittens down there but sod her, I didn't buy a flat so I could have some old lady run my life. There's real definition in the sound, the kind you only get from a Bang & Olufsen system. I reckon Marcus' place in Notting Hill is rocking at the weekends and no shortage of ladies to share it with either from what I can glean. He's very low key, doesn't brag, properly discreet, but you just know from that lopsided grin on his boat that this guy keeps himself very fit in the boudoir. We had a pint after work on the Wednesday and I told him about Maria. If he was shocked he kept a pretty straight face and just shrugged it off, 'If it ain't right, it ain't right.' I didn't tell him about Sara, not just because he might think me unstable. For now it's my little secret and I don't want to break the charm. He said come over to Notting Hill one night and have a drink with my lot. I can't imagine what sort of a posse he's got going on over there, but I'm intrigued when he lets slip that he's forty-three. No kidding, you'd think this guy was thirty. That's two people who've shocked me with their ages in the last few days. People just don't seem to be ageing like they used to. Or I'm just getting older myself. Whatever. I still can't disabuse myself of the notion that it's all over if you haven't married and mated by thirty-five, but there's clearly a different point of view out there.

Thursday lunchtime presents me with the perfect opportunity to see Sara. Just as I'm trying to get a freelancer off the line and go for lunch, Philippa tells me there's another call waiting. I'm giving her the 'take a message' look, but then she shoves a piece of paper under my nose which says FIONA CALDER. My freelancer is quickly dispatched and I pick up line four.

'Fiona, what's up?'

'You didn't tell me how good this book was.'

'Yes I did.'

'Yes, you probably did. My point is this. Your Miss Sara O'Mara could be the next big thing.' My Miss Sara O'Mara – I wish she was. Fiona continues, 'She's got a definite voice and doesn't pull her punches. There's a terrible shortfall of strong young women writing at the moment. The Bridget Joneses are very amusing of course, but they're girls, not what you'd think of as women, they don't have the gravitas. Is she pretty?'

'Yeah, very. Well, I think so.' Gravitas, my arse.

'Would you say she's photogenic?'

'Possibly, she's got a lot of hair and very pronounced dimples.'

'Mmm. Could be promising.' Bingo, bingo, fucking bingo. My stomach is dancing, she's going to love me when I tell her this.

'Shall I get her to call you?'

'I'd rather you got her over here by the end of the day so that I can sign her up before anybody else does.'

'You're the only person who's seen the manuscript.'

'Good. Let's keep it that way.'

'Do you really think she's that good?'

'Yes, I really do. Where did you find her, by the way?'

'She runs the flower stall across the street from my offices.'

'How extraordinary.' This Fiona's no snob, but I know that she and her brother Des were educated at England's finest and she probably cannot conceive that anybody who hasn't had the same could achieve anything. It's a little victory for the common man, or woman in this case, and I'm really excited for Sara, underscored though my enthusiasm is with a bit of dented pride. I can get very touchy over other people's successes. Every book review in the paper is a rebuke for my own failure of effort. I'm often resentful, I have to admit.

'I'm just going out for a sandwich, Fiona, I could drop by the stall and pass on the message.'

'That would be very kind, thank you. Please ask her to call me at the office and if possible come in by the end of the day. I'm going to Val d'Isère tomorrow and I'd like to have this tied up before I go.'

'No problem.' I'm physically licking my lips at this point. 'So, do you think you could place this book then?'

'Place it? I intend to have a minor bidding war.'

'How encouraging.'

'Yes, I rather enjoy this aspect of artist representation. I like the deal.' I bet you do, you little tigress.

'Well look, Fiona, thank you. I'm sure Sara will be very pleased to get your message.' Play it down a bit, Tucker, keep your cool, no point going into raptures yet.

'No, thank *you*, Mark. I shall be expecting her call. Goodbye.'

I don't know anybody who still says goodbye like that. It's all see ya; later; bye. She's a nice-sounding bit of posh, this Fiona, proper received pronounciation, the real deal, just the kind of woman you want in your corner if you're up against a publisher. Lovely voice, clear, modulated, persuasive. This is a right result, no two ways.

I'm over at that stall in less than a minute. I tell her. She can't believe it. Believe it, I tell her. She's jumping up and down on the spot she's so excited and she's totally blanking the queue of lunchtime punters. Then she throws her arms around my neck and is still kind of jumping up and down on the spot and I can feel her body moving against mine and it's too much for me, if you know what I mean. If she keeps this up I'm gonna want to get stuck in and I'm no street corner merchant, I like a nice bed with a big cover, so I gently back off. I leave her with Fiona's number. Let me know how you get on, I say.

I'm pretty high all afternoon, there's kismet in the air. I work very fast and thorough throughout and I can nearly see my desk again, I've cleared up so many loose ends. About four o'clock the evil spectre of Cullen arrives by the side of my desk and says he wants to see me in his office. He's not shouting, he sounds quite calm, but I know it's curtains. I go hot, cold and clammy. Obviously he's been thinking about it since Monday and has decided that my face just doesn't fit any more. I can't take all the extremes of the last few weeks. I'm either flat on my arse or up in the air, I want things to even out a bit. I trail heavily down the corridor to his office, resigning myself to the fact that this is total meltdown. Everything, it seems, must go. Maybe I'm having a premature mid-life crisis.

'Sit down, Mark.' He's calling me Mark, he's definitely gonna sack me. 'You've done well this week.' Yeah, but not well enough. 'When you actually pull your finger out and get down to it, you're good.'

'Thanks.'

'You're not in the clear yet, Tucker, don't get your hopes up.' As if I would. 'But you can clock off early for the weekend if you like.'

'It's fine, I've only got an hour to go.'

'Suit yourself, but I thought you'd probably be ready for a drink, unaccustomed as you are to working full-time.' I have to smile at this.

'Well, cheers then. I will. Thanks very much.' I stand up.

'I meant what I said. I'm not giving you a licence to sit back and put your feet up. Don't go thinking you can slip back into your old ways unnoticed. I know you use our account to bike your personal business all over London, but I want you to understand that I reward effort. You don't have to take the piss all the time to get what you think you deserve. Do you understand me?' I nod. He dismisses me from his office with a wave of his hand and I'm running down that corridor like it's the end of term. Another result. As I leave the building and turn out of Derry Street I see that Pete is on the stall. No sign of Sara, she must have gone over to Soho to see Fiona. I'm really jonesing to find out how she got on. I don't go for a pint, but I do treat myself to a cab back to the flat. I'm indoors by half four and at ten to five the phone rings. She's

CHAPTER THIRTEEN

breathless, I can't understand much of what she's saying but I think it's positive.

'Slow down, start again,' I have to interrupt.

'Sorry, sorry, sorry. OK. Well, I went to her office which was out of this world, have you ever been in there?'

'No, I know where it is though.'

'I've never seen so many books in all my life, and they're all her writers, there must be hundreds and the office itself is a beautiful set-up in one of those big houses on Soho Square. I thought she was a really nice woman. There's something very decent about her.' Sounds like it went well.

'Decent?'

'Well, sort of respectable, but warm. She looks like she's a good mum.'

'I didn't know she had any kids.'

'Five.'

'Fuck off, nobody has five kids any more.'

'She does. She's the sort of woman who could run the country in her spare time, do you know what I mean?'

'Backbone of the nation.'

'Yeah, you could see her in India a hundred years ago colonising the place.'

'Brilliant. So did she talk to you about any publishers?'

'She said there are three she thinks will have a nibble. They're not giants, but they've got enough money in the bank to pay a decent advance.' When she says decent advance, I'm thinking four, five grand. I'm pleased for her, four or five grand is a lot of money for a single mother on a council estate in Kilburn. So I ask her if she's going to go on holiday with the proceeds.

'And the rest. I'm going to buy a house. I'm shopping at the weekend.'

'Well, hold on, love, you don't get that kind of money for first novels.' I'm trying to let her down gently here, she's got a bit carried away, love her.

178

'She reckoned she could get me twenty-five minimum.' Two and a half grand? She's being exploited.

'Twenty-five hundred?'

'No, divvy, twenty-five thousand.' Her words hang in the air. I'm speechless.

'Say something, Mark. Don't you think that's very good? It sounded like a lot to me.'

'Is it a lot, sweetheart, it's the bloody jackpot. I'm sorry to space out on you, but I'm still taking it in. Do you realise how unusual this is?'

'I think so, but I'm not a publishing expert, the closest I come to doing deals is haggling at Covent Garden over the price of freesias.'

'Trust me. It doesn't get any better than this.' My voice trails off and my heart sinks. I really do want to be pleased for her, because she's a good writer and deserves a result, but I have to admit to a healthy portion of masculine pride here. It should be me doing the hunting and gathering and getting the big piles of cash. I'm the one who should be sleeping by the cave door, protecting the women and children. I don't mind her earning, but this whopping advance effectively puts her out of my league. She's just gonna streak by me now, thanks for the favour, see you later number. Shit, this wasn't what I had in mind at all.

'Look, I've got to go now, Mark, and ring my mum and my sister, but I'll be in touch, yeah?'

'Sure.'

'Oh, by the way, we're not going to church on Sunday. Pete said he'll lend me the van so I can go down to Herne Bay on Sunday with Phoebe.'

'Fancied a day at the seaside for your birthday?' I wonder if she'll ask me to come.

'I'm going to look for a house to buy.'

'In Herne Bay?' I've only been to Herne Bay once years ago and

I didn't like it much, it's just a low-key working-class seaside town on the Kent coast. No great shakes.

'I love Herne Bay. I've always wanted to live there. We used to go there for holidays when my sister and I were small. It was the only time we were ever really happy together as a family on those little trips. My only good memories of that time.'

'Yeah, but living there all year is a different thing. You might not like it so much on a wet afternoon in November.' And more importantly, I don't think I could like it even in a heatwave

'I know it's not ideal, but I want to get out of London as soon as I can. It's not bad on our estate, most of the people are nice, but it's little things. Like not being able to hang the washing up in the garden because next door will probably chuck their cat shit over the fence, or one of the kids upstairs will throw something out the window. It's very noisy too, people playing records all night. It drives you mad.'

'I suppose Phoebe will get a bit more freedom as well, if you move out of London.' I'm trying to be positive, but I'm on a downer, no two ways.

'Yeah, that too. I can't let her walk to the sweet shop on her own round here. I'm not picturing some dream cottage set-up for us, just somewhere with some open space, you know, the beach, some fields, somewhere she can go with her dog. Somewhere we can take our bikes.'

'You a serious cyclist then?' She laughs at this question.

'You must be joking. I'm out of breath after two hundred yards, but it's something to do with Phoebe at the weekends, take the bikes down to Regent's Park, have a ride around, check out the people.'

'Sounds very nice.' I wonder if I could ever be happy just doing normal stuff. I envy her.

'It can be. I've really got to go, but listen, I owe you one, right.'

'You don't owe me anything.'

'But I appreciate everything you're doing, I wouldn't want you to think that I didn't.'

'I know you do, Sara, I know. I'll see you around, yeah?'

'Definitely.' The line goes dead. She didn't ask me if I wanted to go to Herne Bay for the day with her. But I suppose that's it now, she'll be off. Big book deal, money in the bank, nice little place on the coast. Next thing you know she'll be falling in love with Martin Amis. Great.

*

I spend Saturday cleaning my flat. It has to be done occasionally and I accept that, but I'm going through the cupboards thinking, where did Maria put the Flash, so I ring her up in Belsize Park and ask her. Terry answers the phone, he's Miss Manners herself. 'Mark! How good to hear from you, how are you coping with bachelor life?'

'That's why I'm ringing up, Terry, would you ask her where she put the Flash to clean the bathroom with, I've looked everywhere.'

'Still a wag with the humour, I see.'

'No. I really want to know where the Flash is. I'm standing here in my underpants and a pair of flip flops about to wash the kitchen and bathroom floors. I don't want to have to go out dressed like this. I would expect a man of your grooming to understand that, Terry.'

'Flattery will get you everywhere, you little studmuffin, now hold on and I'll give her a shout.'

There's this really theatrical bellowing up the stairs. He's singing her name, Ma-Ree-Ya. Never miss an opportunity for a showtune, these boys. You can hear him telling her what I've said as she's coming down the stairs. I hear her feet approaching on the boards, click clack, click clack across that great room of theirs and she snatches the phone up and says, 'Are you seriously calling me up to ask me where the Flash is?'

'And to ask how you are, my sweet.' This little bit of cheek does the trick and she laughs. What a relief to hear my mate chuckle again. I've missed her.

'I suppose you want me to come over and clean the flat for you too?'

'If you wouldn't mind, oh and would you pick up some shopping on the way?' After the initial good humour, it all goes very quiet on the line and I ask, 'How are you?' Never had such a banal question seemed so loaded.

'I'm all right as it goes.' She sounds it.

'Maria, come over later. Or I'll pick you up, yeah? I know I've got some explaining to do.'

'Don't strain yourself.'

'Sorry, I didn't mean it to sound like that.'

'I think I prefer you when you're taking the piss, Mark. But I will come round. I'm having dinner in town at 9.30, so I could swing by the flat on my way, say around seven, half seven.'

'Perfect.'

'Later.' And she's gone. Phew, that was easy. I don't know what made me ring her like that but I must have had some instinct telling me this was the right time to do it. That was a piece of piss. A very pleasant surprise. And she's obviously not sitting around moping if she's having dinner in town. I'm pleased for her. There was a time when that little manoeuvre would have pissed me off no end, I'd think she was trying to make me jealous (and succeeding) but now I saw it for the survival mechanism that it was. She's nothing if not a survivor, that Maria Weller. I really admire the way she picks herself up and gets on with it, she's always been a right trooper when the heartaches come along. Course, she won't be able to resist getting a few digs in later and I'd better have a cheque ready for her dad, but this might be a good opportunity to get some closure. We need it. I still don't know where the Flash is so I call again.

'You've run out. You'll have to go down the shop and get some.'

'Thanks for nothing.'

'You're welcome, I'll see you at seven.'

If I say so myself, I do a pretty immaculate job on the flat. Took a load of sheets and towels down the laundry, changed the bed, scrubbed the kitchen from top to bottom, swept and mopped the floors. I even ironed a shirt for Monday. About six o'clock I'm relaxing in the bath, something I never seem to make time to do. I'm a full-time shower man me. I'm lying there reading some nutty book about aromatherapy that Maria left in the cupboard along with about half a dozen bottles of oil. I've only heard the rumours about aromatherapy but according to this book you can treat ailments, alter your mood, reduce anxiety etc, etc. Apparently they can do everything except Hoover the front room these oils, so I think I'll slosh a few in the bath. I grab Frankincense, Juniper and Grapefruit. It says use ten drops, but they mean ten drops in total, not ten drops of each. Within minutes my skin is burning and I'm having a full-on home-made chemical peel. It's really bloody painful like I've just sat in a load of nettles and I have to turn the shower on cold and hose down the backs of my legs and bum which are the worst affected. I can't believe women just leave this stuff lying around. Maria is unmoved by my suffering when she turns up at the flat, she just thinks it's hilarious. I give her back her bottles and say, please get these things out of my house. She looks right at me when I say this.

'You hit the nail on the head there, Mark. This would never have been my place.'

'Don't be stupid, it would have been half yours, you would have been my wife.'

'Yeah, but your heart has never been in it. When I get married I want it to be because the guy really loves me and wants to, not just because it seems like the thing to do and I'm pushing him into it.' This is a simple statement of some basic facts and she sounds sad when she says it. She's not at all aggressive or proud. She's admitting defeat and she's giving in pretty graciously. I'm humbled because if the boot was on the other foot I don't know that I'd be that big about it. 'I know there's someone else and to be honest with you, now I've calmed down, I'd rather not know who it is.'

'It's not what you're thinking, Maria.'

'It never is, Mark.'

'But nothing has happened. I've met somebody I like, but I swear I haven't laid a finger on her.'

'Spare me the bollocks, please. Don't insult my intelligence. Haven't you taken enough?'

'I think you gave it away, Maria. I might have taken it, but I never asked for it.'

It goes very quiet for a few seconds. She takes a big breath as if she's going to launch into one, then stops herself. 'Well, if that's how you really feel there's nothing else to say, is there?'

'No. I don't suppose there is. But I'm not having an affair, you must believe me.' She shrugs as if to say, whatever, and walks towards the door. I follow. 'So who are you having dinner with, anyone I know?' I ask, just to be polite, but quickly wish I hadn't.

'Yes, you do actually, it's Marcus.' A sharp shot of anger tears through me, but who am I to complain? Didn't waste much time, did he? I'm thinking mildly racist thoughts as I take the cheque out of my pocket for her dad and hand it to her. She just looks at it then looks at me, shakes her head and walks down the stairs calling behind her, 'I feel sorry for you, Mark, you really don't get it, do you?'

'No, but you're going to be fucking getting it tonight, aren't you, you tart?'

I immediately regret my childishness, which gives her the upper hand. She pauses on the landing and looking at me very coolly says, 'I've been getting it for the last couple of days if you must know. And very nice it's been too.' Stitched me up like an old kipper, she did, and left me standing there in the doorway listening to her footsteps receding down the stairs and the main door downstairs slam shut. She's gone. In under ten minutes I'm showered and out of the door. I don't know where I'm going but I'm not coming home alone. There's nobody I can call up for spontaneous sex as they were all voided in the wake of the engagement. I'm seething, really fucking boiling with rage and temper, I could almost cry. I want that easy feeling, that peaceful calm that comes from either a skinful or unloading inside a woman.

CHAPTER FOURTEEN

SLIPPING AND SLIDING

I spent Sunday morning moping and wearing remorse like a yoke. My mission on Saturday evening proved successful, if bedding a twenty-one-year-old modelling hopeful from Manchester on the sofa while her mate passed out in the next room counts as such. I met them of all places down the gym. I'd gone for a sauna to try and sweat out some of my fury and we struck up a conversation in the lounge area around the jacuzzi. They were staying with a friend in Paddington for a fortnight so they could hawk their portfolios around the agencies. They were, as they explained in broad accents, 'having it large' which I came to understand meant a lot of late nights, pink drinks and powder. After the gym we jumped into a cab and headed for the central zone. Sober, I fancied Clare who was the more demure-looking of the two in a simple sweater and jeans. After a couple of drinks Becky, who was a bit maggoty but wearing a backless top, seemed like a better prospect. We tagged around town, I paying for the drinks, like you do, while they whispered, giggled and went to the toilet together a lot. Somewhere around drink five I toyed with the idea of taking them both on, but realised I was too pissed for a marathon. In the end the choice was simple and I fucked Clare on the sofa because Becky had passed out on the bed. It was moderately fruity, but not really that satisfying because I kept thinking of Sara and felt like a dog. Afterwards, Clare went and got in bed with her mate and left me to cosy up with a sleeping bag surrounded by overflowing ashtrays.

They were both awake by nine and looking as fresh as daisies. They watched morning kids' TV and ate bowls of cereal while I decided I was getting too old for all this. I had them in a minicab to Paddington by eleven and slumped on the bed grateful to have the place to myself again, even if I did rattle around aimlessly not sure what to do with myself. Maria's departure had left a hole, no matter how annoyed I might be at her powers of recuperation or even relieved to be done with the whole business. I screened my calls for most of the day which was handy as Henri Temple-Golden tried twice to get in touch. The first time she left a rather breathy message along the lines of picking up where we left off, then tried an hour later and hung up. I know it was she because I 1471'd.

The business with Sara had left a bitter aftertaste. In my dejected and cast-down state I felt sure that she wouldn't be in touch, that I'd simply been a useful stepping stone to a better life. I kept playing the Isley Brothers' *Three Plus Three* but couldn't get high on it. I was listening to the swansong of a love affair that never got off the ground. I wish I was the kind of man who could simply be happy for her, but I was too invested to be that big. Considering I haven't even kissed this girl you'd have a case for thinking me unhinged, but there's something about her. Something very good and very strong and very simple. Given her history she should be damaged goods, but she seems remarkably unaffected. I get the feeling she doesn't complicate her life unnecessarily and I could do with having somebody like that around. Someone I could just sit still with. She's had her share of shit but she's marched on. She's not a drama queen, she gets on with her life. If only I could be so resourceful.

By Sunday afternoon I'm medicating my hangover with a couple of cans, watching sport on the telly and feeling quite depressed with the way my life is unravelling. It seems cruel and unjust. Surely even an arsehole like me gets to meet a nice girl and settle down. I think of calling Maria just to give her a bollocking, but

188

decide to be a man and call Marcus instead and tell him where to fucking get off. But when he picks up he's so bloody matey, all, 'Hey bro, how you doin?' that he gets me on the back foot and I waver. He must know that I know, but you wouldn't think so to listen to him. Says he's pleased to hear from me, that he was going to call me today and I must be telepathic because he's got a little trip in mind for tonight and thought I might want to come along for the ride. Oh yeah, I say, all intrigued, but he doesn't give anything else away, just instructions to call by around six. This sounds a bit early but he assures me this is a good time if we're to miss the rush. I don't have a clue but I'm guessing along the lines of some terminally hip musical outfit playing a secret gig some-where. Not usually my scene but what the hell.

He's waiting on the pavement for me when I pull up. I'm thinking he must have Maria stowed away in the flat and he doesn't want to let me in, but he's all excited, rubbing his hands and laughing. If this is a man with a guilty conscience, I'm a choirboy. He jumps in the car, ejects my Best of Blondie, which I thought was a bit of a fucking cheek as he's shagging my ex-fiancée, and slots in a Teddy Pendergrass tape and tells me to get on the Westway and head out to Park Royal. Park Royal? I always thought it was a load of industrial estates over that way but curiosity is piqued. I ask him why the Pendergrass tape and he says enigmatically, 'Just the thing to get us in the mood.' It's gotta be women he's got lined up and I'm thinking he must have set me up on some sort of blind date which is not what I'm in the mood for and I'm wondering what kind of weird psychological strategy he's got on the go to confound me. Don't get me wrong, I'm not one to hold a grudge for long but I was hoping to give the opposite sex a wide berth given my current run of luck. 'How much cash are you carrying?' he asks. I have a quick scan through the wallet at the lights and I see I've got sixty-five. No problem, says Marcus, you can stick your credit card behind the counter but tip in cash. I start thinking along the lines of a casino and now I'm really going off the idea, because I've never been in one in my life and don't want to start now. I totally resent spunking money on gambling. I don't even do the Cup Final or the Grand National because I'm such a miser. It's turning into a magical mystery tour and once we're round the back of North Acton cemetery I'm starting to get didgy. 'Patience, brother, patience, this is it,' and he points to a shopfront in a quiet street. There are lights on inside but the blinds are drawn. We park up, get out the car and Marcus presses the doorbell. A female voice answers and Marcus just says his name and the door is buzzed open. Before we cross the threshold he winks at me.

Inside it looks like a dimly lit dentist's waiting room. A very clean-looking place with comfortable chairs and nondescript prints on the wall. A radio is playing softly and behind the desk is a woman of about forty, quite attractive, who looks up brightly when we come in. She stands up and kisses Marcus, greets him very warmly and tells us to take a seat. He's obviously no stranger to the place. We're a bit early, she explains, the girls aren't quite ready yet but they should be out in a minute. 'What girls?' I whisper. Marcus looks at me and smiles and says, 'Working girls, man, haven't you sussed it yet?' I'm thinking what's he talking about, working girls, then I realise. We're in a knocking shop, a massage parlour, a whore house, call it what you like but these girls are for hire.

'I'm not sure about this, Marcus.'

'Relax, boy, you'll be fine.' Marcus certainly looks chilled. He's leaning back in his chair with his eyes closed and smiling to himself.

'How much is this going to cost?' I'm on the point of outrage now, being dragged over to this fucking shit part of London so I can drop a load of cash on some brass. This is so not my scene. I've never paid for it in my life. Never given it much thought at all in fact. Don't get me wrong, I've got a lot of respect for prostitutes, they provide a vital public service but they're for old men who want to get their arses slapped, blokes who don't want to upset the wives with unorthodox demands in the bedroom.

'Chill, boy. It's eighty quid plus tip. Trust me, it's worth every penny.' But before I have a chance to protest, a group of girls come into the reception area in single file. There are six of them and I'd say not a single one was over thirty. There are two black girls who giggle when they see Marcus, obviously a regular. He stands up and kisses them hello, then reaches into his wallet and peels off eight twenties which he drops on the desk. The three of them disappear through the door marked Private, Marcus with a hand on each arse, and I'm left sitting there on my jack with four girls in front of me. Part of me is very indignant on Maria's behalf and I'm wondering if she knows this is the kind of thing lover boy gets up to. All my instincts are telling me to get up and run but the woman behind the desk must see how uncomfortable I am because she comes and sits beside me and smiles and says, 'First time, babe?' like I'm some fucking schoolboy. She pats my arm and says, take your time. Quite apart from anything else I'm embarrassed. There are four prostitutes standing in front of me waiting for a decision but it still feels rude to look. They've got these white uniforms on, like beauticians or health club attendants and they look very clean and tidy. There's a tiny blonde with good curves but she's got too much make-up on for my liking. Another tiny, this time an Oriental, but they're not to my taste either. I had a thing about Asian babes for a while, but when I actually pulled one it was like fucking a little girl and it made me feel perverted. They've got this very thick hair, Asian women, like a horse's tail or something, and the combination of the tiny bodies and coarse hair sort of puts me off. The third girl looks like Miss Average, mousy hair hanging straight, nice enough face but nothing to do cartwheels for. That left me with one option. A tall Slavic-looking woman with very high cheekbones and lovely cat eyes. She's got long legs and a full bust and as I check out the tits I think of Sara. Fuck it, I'm here now, so I get up and hand my card to the

191

receptionist who winks and says, 'Enjoy yourself, it's eighty pounds for the first hour and fifty for every half-hour after that.' The Slavic girl smiles at me like a sympathetic dental nurse, takes my hand and leads me through the door marked Private down a long corridor. We pass another door from behind which the sound of laughter can be heard. Marcus. He's a dirty dog, that one, all cosied up with the two black girls doing God knows what to them. Now there's a bloke you wouldn't have thought had to pay for it. He's worse than me and I find his depravity reassuring.

My Slavic girl takes me into a room with a long massage table in it and tells me to take my clothes off and lie down. I'm pleased she knows what she's doing because I wouldn't have a clue where to start. She starts rubbing my back and as she leans over me I can feel her breasts pressing against me and I'm warming to the task. You've spent your money now, Tucker, you might as well enjoy it. She's very professional, very sweet and I won't give you a blow by blow, but it wasn't as sleazy as I expected. I was very impressed with the house condoms which are my all time favourite, Trojan Reds. I discovered the Trojan Red in San Francisco one summer. Unlike those nasty Durexes that are all pink and slimy and roll off your cock, the Trojan is a good, snug, unlubricated prophylactic in an opaque cream colour. You get a lot of sensitivity, but you're not frightened it's going to come off. They're the Rolls-Royce of johnnies, I'm telling you. My Slavic girl is skilled in the ways of love and knows how to get a man where he wants to be. I come quite quickly, nerves I suppose, but she says for another tenner I can take a Viagra and we can have another go. I decline her kind offer and we spent the rest of the time mostly chatting. I fiddle around with her for a while but she politely stops me, saying it's nothing personal. We had quite a nice little chat while we were tidying up with the Kleenex. She came over from the former Yugoslavia about three years ago with her daughter. Her husband was killed in the war. Rather than begging or taking work for less than the minimum wage, she thought she'd work in a massage parlour. I ask her what she'd rather be doing if she had the choice and she tells me that she has a master's degree in biochemistry and eventually when her residency papers come through she'd like to do research for one of the big drug firms. Bloody hell, I've fucked a scientist. I don't know what kind of ignorance makes me think all prostitutes are drug addicts, or stupid or just slags but this little experience has definitely given me a fresh perspective. A lot of these girls must be single parents trying to make ends meet. I think of Sara again and feel a proper bastard for resenting her success. I look at this Slavic girl, Dana her name is, as she puts fresh towels on the bed, ready for the next punter, and she's smiling away, asking me about my work and family and I'm wondering, how can you be so nice when you have to fuck strange geezers just to put food on the table? It's a right lesson in humility, no two ways. Before I leave I dig out my fifty and give it to her. She's chuffed to bits. You're welcome, sweetheart. Good luck. I have almost another forty minutes to wait for Marcus to finish but the receptionist is sweet, gets me a beer and tells me all about her two boys and how they're in this motorbike club that tours around the country in the summer doing displays, jumping off ramps and through rings of fire. Her eldest is eleven and the youngest only six and when I say they sound a bit young to be riding motorbikes she says, rubbish, they've got four-year-olds doing wheelies. I get a picture of all these little kids whizzing about on motorbikes and it makes me feel very, very happy, the idea of all these tinies in helmets giving it a bit of throttle. It's that broody streak in me coming out again.

When Marcus finally tears himself away from his double portion we get back in the car and he's full of it and says I was mad not to take the Viagra. 'You're crazy, boy, it's the best. Next time.' I explain why there won't be a next time. It was an experience I'm glad to have had from an anthropological point of view and I'd be interested to know what Henri Temple-Golden would make of it. I daresay she'd put it down to my famous fear of intimacy but I don't see how you can accuse a bloke who can't keep his trousers up of that one. I felt strangely confidential and relaxed as we drove along and told Marcus that I was ready for something more soulful in the love department. It all comes out about Sara and Marcus doesn't laugh or think I'm stupid, he says it sounds like the real thing.

'And what about you and Maria, is that the real thing?' It stings, but I have to ask. Marcus laughs gently.

'I don't think so, bro, we're just two people who've had their eyes on each other for a while. It was bound to happen sooner or later.' I'm struck by the thought that we're being very grown up about this and I'm not sure I like it.

'Not if I'd married her it wouldn't have.'

'Yeah but you're not, are you?'

'The pair of you didn't waste much time, did you?'

'We don't have to. We're adults.'

I couldn't fault his logic, but I wondered if Maria was feeling so cool about it all. She's the type who has to convince herself she's in love to justify having sex with men. She's fallen in love a lot, often for very short periods of time. We drove along in silence for a while, then I did the unthinkable and asked for his advice. 'Say you can't stop thinking about somebody and you're really burning for them but you're frightened you're going to fuck it up, what do you do then?'

'Come on, bro, if you feel like this about the girl and you haven't even slipped it to her yet something big is happening. You gotta go for it, man.'

So I do. Because I'm being too chicken shit and indecisive waiting for her to make the overtures. If she's who I think she is she'd rather cut her leg off than make the first move. I just need to be a fucking man and put it on the line.

CHAPTER FIFTEEN

THEN, I GO AND SPOIL IT

Monday lunchtime I'm over at that stall full of purpose. She's really pleased to see me and very excited about her trip to the coast. Said she had a lovely birthday, the weather was brilliant, she and Phoebe had a great laugh, bla, bla. She wants to go back next weekend, without Phoebe this time, so she can have a really good look around, suss out where the schools are and so forth.

'You're serious about this move then?' Please don't move to Herne Bay, please stay here in London.

'Yeah, deadly. Can't wait. Now I've made the decision it feels right. I'm ready for a fresh start.' She looks straight at me when she says this so I think, come on, Tucker, make your move.

'I'll come and have a look round with you if you like?'

'Really?'

'Yeah, really. When are you going?'

'I'm packing up early on Friday and driving down so I can book into a bed and breakfast, get settled for the weekend.' I get an immediate image of us tucked up in a little boarding house but it soon evaporates. 'Why don't you drive down and meet me there on Saturday?'

'I will. What time?' I'm deflated, but I'm not giving up.

'I'll meet you on the pier at noon.'

'Whereabouts on the pier?' She laughs at this.

'It's only tiny, we won't be able to miss each other.'

'Okay, see you there.' Despite my efforts at playing it cool, I'm

195

smiling broadly. I'm worried I might be looking a bit too happy about this.

She smiles back and says, 'Yeah, see you there, I'll look forward to it.'

'Me too.'

Goes without saying, it's the longest week of my life and I'm counting the hours until Saturday at noon. Normally when I've got a hot date lined up, I spend the days beforehand going down the gym, doing a lot of sit-ups, maybe have a couple of sunbeds and a quick trim with the nail scissors. It makes your dick look bigger, no doubt about it. But I desist. I don't want to tempt providence and I'm getting very superstitious, reading my stars in the paper, avoiding the cracks in the pavement and acting very out of character. I work hard to keep Sara off my mind and Cullen off my back. Cullen's obviously pleased with the work I'm doing and when he walks past my desk says things like, 'Keep it up, Tucker, this is more like it.' I smile at him ingratiatingly and even manage a spot of conversation about cricket. As I'm leaving work on Friday, coming down the escalator into the main reception hall, Doug shouts my name and points to a bouquet of flowers on the front desk. 'Same girl?' I ask.

'Same one.' He hands them over and with them is another brown envelope. I tear it open and the note says, *Fiona rang last night. She got me a £30,000 advance. How cool is that!? I owe you a massive favour. Looking forward to Saturday. Love, Sara. (Yellow lilies for gratitude, anemones for sincerity, crocuses for gladness and freesias for trust.)* Thirty grand, eh? Gratitude, sincerity, gladness and trust, eh? Wouldn't mind a bit of passion, sweetheart.

Friday night I can't sleep and Saturday morning I can't wake up, but I drag myself out of bed and jump in the shower. I don't know what to wear, but I don't want to go overboard so I settle for jeans and a white shirt with my pigskin jacket. Trainers or loafers? Suede loafers, definitely. Go better with the pigskin. Or do they? For fuck's sake, Mark, just get dressed and get out the house. I can't eat because I'm so nervous, then I'm starving by the time I'm half-way down the M2 and stop off at the services and shovel in a greasy sausage roll which sits like a rock in my stomach. I can't work out whether it's the butterflies or the sausage roll that is making me feel so sick, but I'm definitely didgy. I'm half an hour early so I park up along the front and go in a pub and have a pint. Much better. As I'm draining my glass, I look at my watch and it says five to twelve, so I make my way to the pier. She's right, it is tiny, a little Victorian structure with a clock tower, and as I'm getting closer I can see her standing there waiting. She's leaning on the pier rail reading a paper with her back to me and her hair is being blown all over the place by the wind. The weather is changeable, mostly cloudy but the sun is very warm when it does break through. She must have sensed me approaching because just before I get there she turns around and smiles. I kiss her hello on the cheek just as the pier clock strikes twelve. High noon, my stomach flips over and I have to use every ounce of determination I've got not to wrap her tight in my arms. She says she's starving, she's been up since six walking around the town looking at the different areas and trying to decide which neigh-bourhood she likes best. It's quite busy with Saturday shoppers and she suggests we find something to eat before the restaurants get packed. She's gassing away, really full of it, and I'm grateful that she's rabbiting on so much because I'm feeling uncharacter-istically shy and lost for words. It's a relief just to nod and say 'Great, yeah, oh really?' She's looking very well, very fresh and healthy and she's wearing jeans, loafers and quite a tight white shirt. Funny how we're dressed the same. Her blouse isn't tarty or deliberately provocative, but she's got a fair old bust going on under there and her buttons are straining just a little. I imagine what it would be like to undo those buttons and catch my breath.

'There's a really nice seafood place just up this lane,' and she leads me along a tiny, dark alley – fuck knows how she found this place – and through a plain blue door. They say hello, how are you, where's the little girl? They're very friendly and she explains that she and Phoebe came in here for lunch on her birthday last Sunday. When the waiter comes over she looks at me a bit nervously and asks, 'I hope you don't think I'm showing off, but would you mind if we ordered champagne? Don't worry, this is my treat, it's just that I feel like celebrating.' I don't mind at all and we get through most of the first bottle before the meal arrives, so we order another. She's telling me all about her phone call with Fiona and get this, she can't even remember the name of the publisher. 'She did tell me, but I wasn't really listening, all I could think about was what I was going to do with the money. She says they won Publisher of the Year last year.' I know exactly the firm she's talking about and mention their name. 'That's it!' I ask her what her next book is going to be about.

'What next book?'

'You are going to write one, aren't you?'

'No, I don't think so. I haven't got anything left to write about. It's all in *Pleasure Dome*.'

'But Sara, you could have a good career doing this.'

She thinks about this for a moment then just shrugs and says, 'Well, maybe, but I'm not giving up the flowers. I've already applied to the local council for a trading permit.' I absolutely piss myself when she says this. Can you imagine Helen Fielding or Jeanette Winterson saying, 'I'm not giving up the cleaning job'?

'What's so funny?' She looks perplexed.

'You are.' She laughs with me out of politeness but I don't think she gets the joke. I go to pour more champagne in her glass, but she shakes her head and says she really can't because she's feeling quite drunk already. She is a bit red, so I order her some water and ask what Phoebe's up to in her absence. We're having another one of those totally banal conversations that make me so happy. Her mum and her sister are taking turns to look after her, and I ask what her sister's story is, married, kids?

'No, my sister reckons she's gay.'

'What, don't you believe her?'

'No I don't. She hates men, but that's not the same thing as being gay. It doesn't automatically mean that you love women. She's really fucked up, my sister.' She tells me a bit more about Bridget, who drives a bus in Brent and has a part-time girlfriend called Heather. She says she feels sorry for Heather. I ask why.

'Because Bridget won't go down.'

'What, like oral sex, won't go down?'

'Exactly. I mean come on, what good is a dyke that doesn't go down?' I'm tempted to chuckle in a slightly seedy fashion the way I always do at gay gags, but she's not being deliberately funny, she's really full of sympathy for the poor unloved Heather. I don't know how she stocks her reservoir of compassion but it puts me to shame. I tell her about my sister who's got the opposite problem, too many kids and another one on the way.

'Yeah, that's really tough, I sympathise totally. If I got pregnant I wouldn't hesitate this time, I'd definitely have an abortion, but it would be a real tragedy for me.'

'So why do it?'

'I couldn't do this again, Mark. I love Phoebe and I haven't got any regrets, but if I do it again it's got to be for keeps. I've got to know that I'm going to settle down with the father, have a proper family.' She goes red and I can't make out whether it's the drink or she's embarrassed at giving so much away. I swallow hard and ask about Phoebe's dad.

'He wasn't a bit of me, but I didn't work it out until I was pregnant. He was a drinker too and that's what really made my mind up. I know what they're like to live with and I wasn't having that with a child around.'

'And he doesn't see her at all?'

'No. He saw her once when she was less than a day old and I haven't heard a dicky bird since.'

'So was it just a mad fling then?'

'Do you know, I've never really been able to figure it out. There was a woman on the radio the other day who was saying that the human being has got this evolutionary programme in its brain which makes them fall in love for six weeks exactly, just enough to cover two ovulation cycles so that the woman gets pregnant. It certainly wasn't much longer for us.'

'Maybe it was a gene thing, you know, maybe you got some kind of primeval sense that you wanted his genes. An old mating signal or something.' I'm getting into this now, it's pretty fascinating and I'm looking for any explanation other than the obvious one that she might have loved him.

'Yeah, maybe,' and she's staring out of the window again. I wait a minute, let her have another think before I dive in with the next question because this I really want to know.

'So was he your last boyfriend then?' My arse is up in my throat now.

'No. There was Brian.' Brian? I try not to cackle, but she clocks me smirking and has to smile. 'I know, terrible name.' We look at each other, I mean really look at each other, and those brown eyes of hers are too, too much. I want to lean over and kiss her.

'So what happened with Brian then?'

'He hung around for a couple of years, but I think it got too much, dealing with another man's child.'

'So what happened then, he just fucked off?'

'I think it was when Phoebe started calling him daddy that he really got the wind up. He was a bit younger than me too and needed his freedom. I think for a while he fancied playing daddy, before it got too real.' She paused to light a fag. 'He was an engineer and his firm offered him a three-year contract in Dubai. He pretended that he was really torn about what to do for the best but I knew he was relieved to find such a neat exit.'

'You must have been really cut up.' Say you weren't, please say you weren't.

'I was upset for Phoebe. She kept asking me if he would come back if she was a good girl. She blamed herself, thought he'd gone away because she'd been naughty and that's what really did me in. There's no way I'm getting involved again unless the guy is prepared to marry me and adopt Phoebe.'

Fuck me, that one took the wind out of my sails a bit. 'That's a tall order, Sara.'

'Yeah, I know. But it's the bottom line. I want a love story.' She's got a take it or leave it expression on her face, but she can't look me in the eye. A love story, eh? She's obviously uncomfortable so I switch subjects.

'Here, talking about science programmes, did you know it's a proven fact that men think about sex every three seconds?'

'What, even when they're eating?' She makes a point of eyeing the huge forkful of swordfish poised in mid-air.

'I'd say especially.'

This is bold for a lunch date and I decide I need to cool it, especially when she stands up and says, 'Come on, let's go, I need some fresh air.' I follow her back down the alley thinking, you're getting closer, you're getting closer, don't push it, don't push it, just let it happen. I put my arm around her shoulder and kiss her on the cheek and thank her for lunch; she smells like a rose garden, very floral, very feminine. She doesn't seem displeased that my arm is still around her but as we turn the corner she peels away, so I just fall into line beside her which takes a bit of effort, because the girl has got a stride on her.

'Come on, let's walk along the promenade, I want to show you some of these beach huts, they're mental.' She leads me down the steps from the main road onto the promenade, which is a very wide concrete sweep that curves around the bay. Jammed right up against the sea wall are rows and rows of beach huts all painted crazy colours, some done up like Union Jacks, others with beach scenes and one was festooned with an oversized Elvis head. They're mostly uniform in size, but every now and then there are slightly bigger places, more like surf shacks, decorated with painted sunrises and hanging baskets. It's pretty cool down here, not the retirement community I expected at all. Yeah, I could hack a bit of this in the summer, it might not be so bad at all. We're nearly at the edge of the bay and she asks could we sit for a while on the beach. We find a little windbreak and the sun comes out and it's very warm. She makes a pillow with her denim jacket and lies down. I'm just sitting there for a few minutes, looking at the sea, and when I turn round to say something to her, she's asleep. Totally out for the count. I wouldn't have thought shingle was that comfortable to sleep on, but she's not bothered. I take the opportunity to give her a thorough checking out. I prop myself up on one elbow and watch her sleeping, loving the way her stomach and bust rise and fall with her breathing, and through the gap in her shirt I spy a white lacy bra. She's pretty solid, this girl, not what you'd describe as slender, but she carries it well. Her hair is being blown across her eyes and nose so I can only really see her mouth which is hanging open slightly. There's the slightest hint of a snore which makes me feel very tender and protective towards her so I take off my jacket and place it over the top of her. I'm tucking her in like she's a baby but the action of doing it wakes her up. She suddenly shoots up and says, 'I'm so sorry, I didn't mean to fall asleep.' I tell her not to worry, go back to sleep, but she's apologising and looking at her watch and scrambling around in her pockets looking for her cigarettes. We're going to have to do something about the smoking. 'Oh, God, I'm so dry after all that champagne, I wonder if there's a little van where we can get a cup of tea?' She stands up, but I grab her hand and pull her back down. She looks a bit surprised but she doesn't stop me. I'm encouraged that she hasn't told me to fuck off, so when she's sitting back down again I take the fag from her fingers and throw it away. She looks at me as if to say, 'What you doing?' so I pull her face to me and just rest my lips on hers. No tongues, just an innocent kiss and let me tell you it was fucking beautiful, total fusion. I gently push her backwards until she's lying on the shingle and lean over her and kiss her properly. She's a bit hesitant at first then her arms go up around my neck and she pulls me closer to her. Oh, Sara. She's not Deborah Kerr and I'm certainly no Burt Lancaster – there was a bloke who could fill out a pair of swimming trunks – and this is definitely not fine powdery white tropical sand we're lying on, but this is my *From Here to Eternity* beach scene. Sara O'Mara and Mark Tucker snogging on the shingle at Herne Bay. Magic. We must have been lying there necking for about a quarter of an hour and when she pushes me off I think she's going to say that's enough. But she doesn't, she says come back to the bed and breakfast with me, come to bed with me, Mark. It's pretty direct and I swallow hard and tell her she'll have to hang on a minute because I've got a hard-on sticking out of my jeans and I'd rather it settled a bit before we started walking. She giggles at this then puts her hand on it and squeezes very gently. Jesus. 'Have you got any johnnies?' she asks and I lie and say no, because I don't want her to think that I've been planning this all along. I've always got Trojans in the glove compartment but I don't want her to know that, so we go through this fucking charade of me going in and out of every bloody shop in Herne Bay looking for a packet of three. The local shops don't sell them and we've just missed the chemist which, inexplicably, closed at three. I try a couple of pubs but even the men's toilets don't have any. 'I'm sure Herne Bay is going to be a lovely place to live, but bring your own condoms,' I say to her, thinking fuck, fuck, fuck, there's no way she'll do it without one and I can't own up to the ones in the glove compartment without looking like a total prick. Just as I think it's about to slip away, she says, 'Don't worry, we'll just have to be careful, come on.' It takes another ten minutes to get to the bed and breakfast and all the time we're walking we're holding fast to one another like we've been stuck with glue and my hands are running up and down her waist and hips and I'm thinking, come on, come on, where is this fucking place? We get there and she lets herself in with a key. There's nobody around, the place feels deserted and we walk up the stairs clutching one another. Outside the door she pauses and looks at me and says, 'Are you sure you want to do this?' Are you fucking kidding?

The room is quite small, but it's got its own bathroom and a double bed. The window overlooks the garden and she walks across and draws the curtains, leaving a lovely soft muted light in the room. I sit on the bed with my legs stretched out and wait for her to join me. We don't rip each other's clothes off, we're just kissing for a long time, then slowly, slowly, start to undo zips and peel away clothing. I can't get enough of her hair and I've got my fingers dug right in, holding her head and kissing her. Usually when I'm with a woman I'm kind of hovering above the scene, judging my moves, but I'm totally absorbed in what I'm doing, lost in it. I get this very strange sensation of my past and my future slowly merging into this exact point and I'm in the now, right here, with this woman and it's perfect. I have to tell you, this was no command performance. We were both nervous, and at one point I was trembling so much I couldn't unhook her bra. Just as I'm sliding her knickers down she stops me and tells me to please be careful, go slowly, she's got a lot of scar tissue from where she had Phoebe and can get a bit dry, a bit sore. I leave it for a while and we're just rolling around, really smelling and licking each other like a couple of rutting animals and I realise what it is with this girl – she smells right. Not her perfume or her shampoo or body lotion or whatever, just her, her sweat, her skin. I could have done without the aroma of Bensons in her hair and her mouth, but like I said, we can sort that one out later. When the knickers are finally down and I slide my hand underneath her, she whimpers and I nearly come there and then. I don't know about babies and scar tissue, but there doesn't seem to be much wrong with this one. She's very wet, very swollen, very warm and I want her bad. I go easy, very gently, but she's responsive and I'm starting to lose my mind with happiness. I'm getting lost in this girl and where with another woman I might be thinking, you could do with a bit of toning up, sweetheart, I'm loving it all, the way her belly creases and her breasts hang heavy and I'm thinking this is what a woman's body should look like. She's soft, proper woman soft and I can't get enough of her. Like I said, there was a bit of fumbling and nervousness and at one point she stops me and says, 'I'm really sorry, it takes me ages to come.' Another time, I'd take this as a major insult to my prowess, but with her, it was immaterial, hitting the jackpot didn't seem to be the point of it at all. A lot of the time I'm not even moving inside her, I'm just in there and we're breathing very deeply together. I want to tell her that I love her, because I do, I've got no doubt about that and as I'm getting close to coming I'm looking at her thinking, you my little beauty are the future, you're going to be the mother of my children. I know I said we'd be careful, but I can't pull out and she knows exactly what's going on but she doesn't push me away either and when I come she pulls me closer to her and wraps her legs tight round my back getting me as deep as she can. My panic is short-lived and I think, so what if she does get pregnant? Good. When it's all over and I finally roll off, which takes a while because she's clinging on and saying, 'Don't pull out yet, don't pull out,' we look at each other and burst out laughing. 'That was fucking tremendous,' I say and start kissing her again. She pulls away and gives me a funny little look, and I get it. 'You want a fag now, I suppose?' She just smiles and gets up and lights one. I'm lying there looking at her walking around naked thinking how totally beautiful this girl is, with her long hair hanging down her back which is broad and incredibly straight. No sloping shoulders on this girl. She's got these two dimples just above her buttocks, exactly matching the ones on her face, and I think to myself, give it ten minutes and I'm having another go. She sits down on the bed and looks very thoughtful as she's smoking her fag.

'You all right?' I ask, putting my arm around her.

'I can't believe we just did that.'

205

'Didn't you like it?' I'm all worried now.

'No, not that, Mark, it was lovely but I can't believe I let you come inside me like that. It's so stupid, what was I thinking?'

'It's all right, it's all right, we're in this together.'

'Yeah, right.'

'Sara, don't be like that.' Come on, Tucker, now's the time to say it. 'I love you.' She freezes beneath my arm and turns to look at me. 'How can you say that, you don't even know me?'

'Because it's true.'

'And I'm supposed to believe it?'

'Yes, you bloody well are.' I'm affronted now.

'Look, I'm sorry, Mark, but you don't have to flannel me. I'm a big girl, I can take it. It was a moment of madness, we've had too much drink, it was a mistake.'

'Thanks a lot.' I'm sulking now, she's put a right fucking damper on the occasion. She touches my arm and softens a bit.

'It really was lovely, but it shouldn't have happened. You've been good to me but you're not really the sort of bloke I should be getting tangled up with.'

'What's that supposed to mean?'

'Well, you get through the women a bit lively.' She stubs out her cigarette and draws the sheet up to cover her modesty.

'I know what it must look like, but I'm not like that, really I'm not.'

She doesn't look at me, but says quietly, 'I think you'd better go.'

She's got tears in her eyes and she looks like she means business. Normally, I'd hang around long enough just to have a row, but I get up and get dressed. I can't believe that ten minutes ago she sucked out my soul. I stand by the door on my way out. 'I meant what I said, Sara. Think about it.'

'I'm sorry, Mark. This is all my fault, I should never have slept with you, but please go now.' I do as I am told, I'm full-on stunned. What is it with her? I've just had a life-changing encounter, proper falling in love making love, not that clinical come-trick I paid for last week. Now she's gone and booted me out. What the fuck do I do now?

CHAPTER SIXTEEN

QUE SERA, SERA

I tried to find my way back to the seafront from the bed and breakfast. You'd think it would be easy, just keep walking towards the sea, but there were all these dead ends and cul-de-sacs and I had to keep double-backing and taking side streets getting very wound up before I eventually came out in a small lane between the amusement arcade and the Wimpy on the front. Now what? I could see the car parked up about a hundred yards away but I didn't feel like driving home just yet. You never know, she might come looking for me. I sat in the Wimpy drinking nasty coffee and doodling on a serviette, going over and over what had just happened and trying for the life of me to see where I fucked it up. I meant it when I said that I loved her but Jesus, bad timing or what? She was frightened, I could tell that much. Maybe she's one of those people who can't accept good stuff when it happens to them, maybe getting fucked-over is all that she knows. But how is a man like me supposed to make a woman like her feel safe? Why the fuck should she trust me? I mean, check out the track record, and that's just the bits she knows about. I was thinking about what she said, that any guy coming along would have to marry her and adopt her daughter. It was a lot to ask of a bloke, especially one like me, but so far it hadn't made me want to run screaming in the other direction. I liked her style and in her own funny way I reckon she's a bit of a lady. She wants something solid, no second-raters, no jokers, no flakes and I definitely rate her for that. I'm angry and a bit baffled because I know something special happened back there. I wouldn't say it was total abandonment, but it's the closest I've ever been to surrender certainly. If I had to be crude and rate her performance, I'd say she's earthy, very real and doesn't go in for any of that circus ring stuff that women are so fond of these days. With a lot of birds I get the feeling that the more tricks they know, the less they really understand what fucking a man is all about. I've known a few women who are really far out in the bedroom and it's been exciting in that borderline-peverted way but it makes me wonder if they've lost the ability to enjoy the basics, just lying there and digging it instead of jumping around all the time. Sounds like an obvious thing to say about a heterosexual woman, but it was clear to me that Sara really likes men and it's not always the case. I should know. I've known a lot of girls who give it the big come on and are physically very confident. They've got all the moves and sexy clothes, big-time flirting, that almost aggressive 'are we gonna have sex then or what?' attitude. You'd think it was a promise of heaven, but when you actually get down to it, and I'm talking literally as well as metaphorically, they're too girly, a bit unsure, just too fucking amateur for my tastes. Not Sara. She really gives herself up to it and I find that proper royal-flush sexy. The kind of woman you want to stay in bed with once the fireworks are over, fall asleep together, nudge each other awake in the night to kiss and start all over again. I should be with her now under that heavy eiderdown not sitting here in the fucking Wimpy with a couple of old geezers and a gang of kids. The post-coital sprint might be all right in Park Royal at £80 a pop, but it's not all right now. Definitely wrong in fact. I could still smell her on my fingers and kept running them back and forth under my nose like some cigar aficionado and whispering her name to myself, Sara, Sara, Sara.

It must have been about eight by the time I left the Wimpy; she was obviously not out hunting for me, and as I walked towards the car the sun was just setting and it was that lovely twilight time, very

210

dusky, what the French call *entre chien et loup*, between the dog and the wolf. Oh Sara.

I do my best thinking in the car and it was just where the A2 comes into Dartford that my plan crystallised. I was remembering something that the Rook said when we met in Primrose Hill for lunch that Sunday. She suggested the way to get my feelings straight would be to write them down. Right then, lady, I will, but not for your benefit. Sara said she wanted a love story , so why not write one for her? If she really wants to know who I am she can have the whole unvarnished sorry tale. It's a challenge, literary or otherwise. For starters, who the fuck am I ? I know I'm Mark Tucker, journalist and would-be Lothario. I know that I have a sister and a mother, a dead father, an ex-fiancée, a nice car and a flat in Maida Vale. I've slept with a lot of women, one of whom I paid for. But what drives me? I have only the vaguest notion of what goes on inside my nut and nothing I like to shine the spotlight on. It's no coincidence that I came to detest Henri Temple-Golden. I can't have some ugly bird fishing around in my psyche – no way.

By the time I get back to the flat it's nearly eleven o'clock but I'm buzzed, so I make coffee, find the chocolate biscuits and dig out the laptop that has been sitting in my wardrobe gathering dust for the last year. I'm not even sure if I know how to work this thing. I borrowed it from work when I went to Rome last year to do that election feature and haven't got round to returning it yet. Amalgamated are very slack about their property. Nobody has asked and I'm not going to hand it in until they do. When I do finally manage to boot up and open a file I don't know where to start. I fiddle about writing different scenes, bits about how I first met her, what I thought the first time we spoke, how my stomach turned over when she winked at me in her kitchen, but I'm kind of hovering on the periphery looking for an in and I'm not finding it, so I turn it in for the night. Lying there, I relive the afternoon and how it felt to hold her naked body and it's tormenting me that I can't see or touch her. I still haven't washed my hands though the smell of her has all but faded. That was a pretty unequivocal 'get lost' she gave me earlier, but I reckon it could be salvaged. I know what went on in that room this afternoon, I was there. But there won't be any quick results, it's gonna take time, patience and a lot of careful footwork. This is a learning curve for you, Tucker, no two ways. I've been rejected before, sure I have, but I've never been invested enough for it to bother me. We all get the odd knock-back, but with me it's usually before bedtime and more often I have the opposite problem. I sleep with a woman and then she won't get off my back. That clinging vine stuff has always done my nut in so I'm not going to keep ringing Sara and make it worse. There won't be any quick fixes with her, I know that. Push it now, Tucker, and she could slip from your grasp. So I maintain, sit still, do nothing. Think, Tucker, think. I'm tempted to ring Bee or Marcus, but even if they did advise me, I'm basically alone, so it's best I leave it that way.

After a couple of days I begin to adjust to my own company. Sara doesn't call, but I don't really expect her to, so I just keep on keeping on, writing, eating, working, shaving, just moving through the days. I'm wondering why I've never spent any time on my jack before, why I have to fill even the smallest void with women. It's all a big jumble inside me and like a car that needs stripping down and rebuilding. I try to dissect the various parts of my life like it's an engine and mark down all the bits that are in need of repair. There are a lot of loose ends to tie up, no two ways. I need to get some closure before I can move on. In a moment of madness, half cut sitting up late writing, I rang Henri Temple-Golden at home to tell her the good news, that I'd fallen in love and been cured. It was half tongue in cheek, a bit of mischief more than anything, but she got pretty edgy and said she thought I ought to concentrate on my own 'needs for growth' rather than pouring all my energy into a new affair. 'But I've found somebody I want to be faithful to, Henri, I thought you'd be pleased.' I was teasing, being quite cruel but enjoying myself nonetheless. It went very quiet on the line, so

I plundered on, 'Be happy for me, Henri, I've fallen in love.' Click. The line went dead. Oh well, fuck her.

I want Sara more than I've ever wanted anyone but if I'm honest with myself, Temple-Golden probably had a point when she said I wasn't ready. There have been quite a few shipwrecks in my short life and I need to clear the decks. No dark corners, no unfinished business, no shadow boxing. This time I'm playing for the big money. I do the smart thing and call my mum. She still doesn't know about me and Maria unless Bee's filled her in, which I doubt as my sister obstinately refuses to do my dirty work for me. Mum's bound to have her nose put out of joint because she bought us some crystal from Allders for an engagement present that must have set her back a few bob. She's hard to catch since big Ron came on the scene and doesn't have an answering machine so I keep calling until Friday night when she finally picks up the phone. It's all, hello, love, how are you, how's Maria, have you used the glasses I bought you? I explain that the engagement is off and that I'd really like to come and see her for a chat. 'I really want to talk to you, mum, I'm a bit confused.' Either it's this little admission of need or the fact that she's all loved up with Ron, but she couldn't be nicer, come down right now, love, I'm always here for you, you know that. I tell her I won't be there until the morning because I'm busy writing at the moment. She's surprised to hear that I'm writing but doesn't take the piss as I'd expect her to as she obviously thinks I'm a bit fragile at the moment. Poor Mark might get upset. That night I'm writing, writing, writing, I can't stop. It's pouring out of me. I want to tell Sara everything even though most of it isn't flattering. Read it and weep, baby.

Saturday morning and I'm just off to mum's thinking, this time last week I was on my way to Herne Bay for the best Saturday of my life, and as I'm leaving the flats Karl comes sauntering along. 'Didn't know we had second post on Saturday, Karl?'

'We don't. This is first post. Got totally spaced last night, I'm a bit late. I've got one here for you.'

He hands me a little brown manila envelope and before I even check out the handwriting, I know straight away it's from her. Sure enough, inside are three sheets of that lined note paper. I must get this girl some decent stationery. I make a mental note to lift a load from work next week. I'm standing there on the street corner reading it and Karl says, 'Looks like good news.' I haven't read it all yet, but it's a sign and I'm so fucking happy that I kiss Karl on the cheek and say, 'You little beauty, you've made my week.'

Karl looks a bit surprised but not too bothered that I've snogged him in the street and just says, 'Oh, nice one' before he rolls off.

I get in the car and settle down and read it properly. First off, she apologises for her behaviour last week, don't know what got into me, suddenly very scared etc., and I'm thinking, yeah, yeah, come on then, do you love me or what? The good news is that her period came yesterday, slightly early so panic over. She says she didn't go to the doctor's for a morning after pill which was stupid but it all turned out fine in the end. This is very encouraging. She can't hate me that much if she didn't go for the emergency contraception option. The bad news is that the publishers have done a thorough edit of the book and are asking for major changes. She doesn't come right out and ask for my help, but somewhere in there is a veiled request. Like it, like it. This could be very good indeed, two writers with projects on the go at the same time. Gives us something more in common besides the fact that we're fucking made for each other and a very good fit in the bedroom. As if you need anything else. She's a bit fed up she says, she's come down off her cloud. Herne Bay council turned down her request for a trading permit because she's not actually in residence yet and her Uncle Pete is being difficult about her giving up the stall. He makes a lot of money from his wholesaling to the various stallholders and he's loth to give up the Kensington pitch, a little goldmine, to somebody else. She doesn't know how she's going to find the time to do it all and look after Phoebe. She's going to have to hold fire with the plans to move to Herne Bay. She's on a bit of a downer.

She closes by saying that she shouldn't think I'd want anything to do with her after last week, but if I'm passing the stall, please drop by and say hello. If I'm passing the stall? Come on, sweetheart, I go past it twice, three, sometimes four times a day and you know bloody well I do.

I've half a mind to drive straight over to Kilburn but I stick to my plan. I am not going to see her until I've finished this book and she's read it. I've done about twenty thousand words in the last week, some of it at work when I should have been doing other things admittedly, but I'm gathering pace. I reckon I'm about a third of the way through.

I arrive at mum's all pumped up and cheerful and she remarks that I don't seem very upset for a man who has just broken off his engagement. I don't give her the whole story at once, but it comes out in dribs and drabs throughout the day. Usually when I get to my mum's I'm looking at the clock and wondering how soon I can decently leave, but I just relax and help her in the garden, weeding the borders and even mow the lawn for her. 'Blimey,' she says, 'I had no idea having a son could be so useful.' It's a dig but it's fair enough. I do absolutely fuck all to help my mum and it must be hard for her not having a man around. She doesn't pump me about the break-up but you can tell she's really jonesing, dying for me to spill. She makes me a cheese and piccalilli doorstep – my all-time favourite – and we sit on the patio in those fucking horrible cheap plastic chairs that feel as though they're about to collapse on you any minute and I tell her straight up that I met somebody else. She groans. No, mum, it's not what you're thinking. I keep it pretty low-key, but give her the truth. Meeting this woman has made me look at myself and the way I behave in a different way. I might have been a bit of a dirty sod in the past, but maybe I've just spent a lot of time looking in all the wrong places for the right girl. Funny to think she'd been under my nose for two years before I woke up to her. Even if it doesn't work out – though I'm quietly confident that it will – my life will never be the same again. Mum chews on her sandwich thoughtfully then says, 'You always were a very touchy feely kid, always wanting cuddles, would have lived in my pocket if you could. You used to drive me mad and I was forever having to push you off me, prise your little arms from around my neck. Funny kid you were.' Fucking hell, mum, don't tell Temple-Golden, she'll have a field day telling me I sleep around because I felt rejected as a child. 'Who's Temple-Golden?' mum asks.

'Just some nutty shrink I saw a couple of times.'

Mum rolls her eyes as if to say, well, you've only got yourself to blame if you go getting mixed up in all that. 'No, you're just very loving, Mark, always have been.' It was a revealing moment, but we don't dwell too long on what I was like as a kid, because Patsy wants her silver lavatera planted out this afternoon. She's off to a barbecue with big Ron down in Byfleet tonight and wants it all done before she goes.

'How's it going with Ron then, mum?'

'He's a very nice man, Mark. He was widowed when his children were tiny, brought them up all by himself, he did. We've got a lot in common.' I'm tempted to point out that Bee and I had nearly left home when she booted dad out, but she's obviously convinced herself that she and Ron have this special bond, so I leave it. I ask her if she's serious about this bloke and her response surprises me. 'I think I'm getting too old to be serious about anybody. Ron's just good fun. He likes to get out and about, do things. He's lovely company, very generous., He's always saying to me, "Put your money away, Patsy, I don't take a lady out to have her show me up," oh he is funny.' She's gazing off into the distance and smiling when she says this. I think to myself, good for you, mum. We must have thought about dad at the same time, because then she says, 'To be honest with you, Mark, I've never wanted to be married to anyone but your dad, he was a good husband and father but he could be a bit boring, he was very frightened of change. Never wanted to do anything different.' She had a point. I've canonised my old man a bit what with Patsy's mid-life crisis and then him dying like that, but he was very much the feet-up at-home type. He was never one for going out boozing or living it up, just a decent steady bloke. Ideal in a dad but it must have been hard work to be married to. I don't think mum and dad were ever really friends and that must make it a strain when you're in for a long haul. Oh, I think they were in love when they got married, but they did it because that's what you did then. They didn't have our choices. I've had too bloody much choice, me, but there's got to be a balance. Me and Patsy chat about this and that while we're planting the borders and I'm quite enjoying myself. Shirt off, sun on my back, getting my hands in the dirt. Wouldn't mind a little garden myself. Nothing major, just a place for a few shrubs, maybe an apple tree or two, a swing and a slide for the kids. Don't get ahead of yourself, Tucker, one thing at a time. I ask how Bee is getting on but mum just says, yeah, fine I think, haven't spoken to her for a while, so I reckon that she doesn't know about the pregnancy. About four o'clock mum gets up from her knees and brushes the dirt off her hands and says she'd better start getting ready, Ron is coming over at half five to pick her up. I'm welcome to stay the night if I want, there's plenty of food in the fridge etc, but don't wait up kind of thing. I have a quick cup of tea and say, don't worry about it, mum, I gotta be getting back, want to get on with my writing.

'So what's this you're writing then?' she asks.

'It's a love story.'

Her eyebrows move due north a bit sharpish.

'Oh yeah. About who?'

'About me actually, mum.'

'You?'

'Yeah. Me.'

'I think you need to stick around your girlfriends a bit longer if you want to find out about love, Mark. Love's about getting through the boring bits.'

She's a bit blunt sometimes, my mum, really hurtful. I know

where Bee gets it from. It's a bit rich too, coming from a woman who booted out her husband because she got bored, but I don't pull her on it. 'It's more about what goes on on the inside, mum.'

'Oh, I see.' But she obviously doesn't so I give her a kiss and tell her to enjoy herself at the barbecue. 'Aren't you going to hang around and say hello to Ron?' Another time, I tell her, but give him my regards. I'm driving through the middle of Croydon, it's not even five o'clock so I think I'll stop in the Cartoon for a pint. The Cartoon is a kind of blues pub with live bands where I worked weekends while I was doing my A levels. Next door to it is the ABC and I check out the times of the films and see if there's anything I fancy. *Tea With Mussolini* has just started, so I think, fuck it, why not. I tell you, I cried like a baby, kept having to wipe my snot on my sleeve, the works. It's a great story about all these old birds in Florence during Mussolini's reign and it's absolutely brilliant. It's got all the ingredients of a good weepie – small boys, old ladies and a couple of dogs. The dialogue is cracking and when I'm not filling up I'm having a right old giggle. When I come out of the pictures it's starting to get dark and I'm totally uplifted, inspired, like I've had a complete emotional experience and the beauty of it is I did it alone. So what? you might think, people go and see films on their own all the time, but you've got to bear in mind that *I've* never done it in my entire life. It wouldn't have occurred to me. I've had a breakthrough.

Back in Maida Vale I have a quick pint in the pub across the street, get a few cans to take out and settle down in front of the laptop. That film really got the old nut going and I'm flying, flying, flying, it's pouring out of me. Shit, I'm enjoying this. I stay up until seven o'clock on Sunday morning, my eyes are out on stalks I'm so tired, but before I get into bed I print out everything I have so far which adds up to about thirty thousand words and stick it in an envelope with a note to Sara which says simply: *I'm pretty busy working on something of my own at the moment, but I'll definitely give you a hand with yours when I'm finished. I'd be interested to know what you think of this. Call me or write back. Love, Mark. PS. I miss you.* This is a bit bold, but I'm as high as a kite and before I change my mind stick the back of the envelope down with Sellotape, put too many stamps on it, like it's gonna get there any quicker, and drop it in the postbox so it goes off first thing Monday. I go back to the flat and sleep. When I wake up at four o'clock in the afternoon I have a bit of a panic attack. I shouldn't have done that, she'll freak. Why couldn't I just have waited until I'd finished the whole thing? Why did I have to say that about missing her? I might be going through some changes, but I'm still an impulsive bastard.

Monday, Tuesday, Wednesday go by without a word. She must have received it by now and I'm thinking, fuck, I've really messed things up, why couldn't I just hold back? But I press on with the writing regardless and have a really good week, get another ten thousand words done in the evenings and the few bits of spare time I can snatch at work when Cullen's not around. I'm getting so into this now that I can't wait to find out what is going to happen next and to be honest with you I don't have any idea until I actually write it. It's got a real momentum about it, this little book, no doubt. It's not on the epic scale of *Welcome to the Pleasure Dome*, but it will probably end up at around seventy thousand words which is a decent little novel. I might even have a word with Fiona, see if she can place it. Wouldn't mind getting a holiday in the Caribbean for my trouble, but that's not why I'm writing it. Thursday comes and goes, still no word and I've got half a mind just to give up. She's not interested, I've blown it, finito benito baby. But it isn't, because Friday morning on the way to work the post has already been, which means Karl is on holiday, and there waiting for me on the table in the hallway is a little brown manila envelope which I jump on like a lion going in for the kill. Not the lined note paper this time, but a piece of coloured paper and when I unfold it there's a drawing, a kid's drawing of some flowers and beneath it the words: *Sunflowers for pride, heather for admiration.*

I'm proud of you. Your book is great!!! Send me more. Phoebe did this drawing for you. Love Sara XX. Proud of me eh? Two kisses eh? That's the first time she's put kisses on a note. I go back up to the flat and dig around inside the junk drawer in the kitchen until I find the Blu-Tack and stick my little picture up on the wall next to my bed. This was just the boost I needed and by the time I get to work I'm buzzing. I whip through my pile of pieces, editing at a swashbuckling pace, slash, slice, there goes another one. Cullen sidles up to me just as I'm about to go and get a sandwich and asks me if I'm free for lunch. I must look a bit worried because he laughs and says, 'Don't worry, it's nothing bad, I just want to pick your brains.' So we go over to the little basement restaurant in Kensington Church Street and as we're crossing over I see Sara but she doesn't see me. It's a warm day and she's wearing a white T-shirt and jeans and even from across the road I can see her nipples poking through her T-shirt and I get a right tingle. She's so fucking lovely, that woman, and I've got a bit of a job concentrating on what Cullen is saying. He's very friendly, orders a good bottle of wine and tells me that he's thinking of reorganising the features pages. Wants me to come up with some ideas. If they're good and they work I might be in line for a payrise, but it will mean extra hours. Extra hours? I work full-time as it is. Cullen explains that if I'm to carry more responsibility I've got to be on call from sun up to late in the evening. He doesn't come right out with it and say I'm in line for a promotion but it's what it sounds like and I think, yeah, why not? I'm single, no responsibilities and plenty of time on my hands once this book is out of the way. He asks about the book in that piss-take way of his and when I tell him that I'm more than half-way through and really gunning he can see that I'm telling the truth and it wipes the smirk right off his face. I tell him I'll give the features pages some thought and we shake on it. On the way out of the restaurant he says he's going over to the flower stall to get something for the wife, it's their anniversary. I ask how many years and he tells me twenty-two. Bloody hell, twenty-two years, that's nearly a life sentence. 'Suits you, does it, married life?' I ask and he shrugs and says, 'I don't imagine life any other way.' I can't really see Cullen as a family man, but I only know him as the bloke marching about giving orders. It's hard to picture him shopping at Brent Cross with the wife. I feel envious, I want that family life and now I know who I want it with. I'd love to go shopping with Sara for a three piece suite, really I would. Just as he's about to leave me and cross the road to the stall I tell him to tell the girl on the stall that Mark says hello and thanks for the picture, it came this morning. Know her, do you? he asks. A little, I tell him.

That evening I'm in the flat sitting at the laptop and I know I have to do more than skim across the subject of the other women in my life, and let's face it, there have been more than a couple and for a while I'm stuck. What would be the best way to go about this? I want to be honest, but there has to be a limit. My windows are open and the curtains are blowing about in the breeze and I'm just kind of staring out onto the street going blank. I've got no choice but to tell her straight up. I've got to admit that I've loved other women, a lot of other women, because at the end of the day nothing works like the truth. Once I reconcile myself to this the switch is flicked and I write and I write and I write and my fucking wrists are nearly paralysed with the effort of it all, so at about 1 a.m. I say enough and go to bed. I'm wracked with strange dreams, all the women in my life coming to me in various images, none of them in their right context. I've got Maria with me in Spain and Pilar down in Cornwall and Stella living with me in the flat. There are others too. Girls I haven't seen for yonks and yonks, girls I went out with years ago. I wake up at half five in the morning drenched in sweat. I get a cup of tea and sit on the bed and try to hold on to the fading fragments of my dreams, relive them before they slip away for good. I'm very peaceful, very still. Nothing stirs outside except the milk float stopping every few yards and the sound of the milkman whistling. I feel different. I shower and shave and I'm just heading off early for the office when the phone rings. It's Coxy. Bee lost the baby last night. She's in the Mayday for another day or two while they do a D&C. 'Is she very upset?' I ask.

'She feels guilty.'

'Why?'

'Because she thinks the baby knew that she didn't want it and bailed out.'

'But that's stupid.'

'You know what your sister's like.'

'Yeah. How you doin', Coxy?'

'Pretty gutted. I love kids, I'd have a few more if it was up to me.' I ask more questions, did the boys know she was pregnant, are you having time off, what have you, but he's obviously not in the mood to chat, so I say, see you later, tell Bee I'll try and get up the hospital tonight. Christ, what a morning and it's not even seven o'clock. Immediately I call up Maria. Something tells me it's all right to do it and I've got to talk to somebody about Bee. I wake her up but she doesn't mind and says she'll come with me to the hospital tonight, meet me at Victoria Station at half five. Perfect, see you then.

Cullen's not in, must have had a night of it with the missus and decided to bunk off. Good for him. Good for me. I'm so up to date with my work that I figure I can spend the day on the book without falling behind. I type fast and furious, all about my old girlfriends, every detail, I leave nothing out. God knows what she'll think when she reads this stuff, but fuck it, I'm on a roll, there's no going back now. Philippa can see that whatever I'm doing I'm bang into it and I don't even have to ask, she just screens my calls all day and keeps getting me fresh coffee. Now there's a girl I owe a bunch of flowers, no doubt about it, she's a total sweetheart. If I get promoted I'm going to do my utmost to see that she gets my old job. She's a fucking diamond, my Philippa. I do eight thousand words that day – eight fucking thousand – I'm getting there, another ten and I reckon I'm done. I'm all excited when I get to Victoria and meet Maria and she asks what I'm looking so happy about and I tell her that work is going well and I'm getting stuck into the book. I also tell her how much I appreciate her coming with me, she's a real friend.

'That's what we are, Mark, friends. I should never have tried to make it into something else.' We're having to move a bit sharpish down this platform because the guard is just raising his hand, getting ready to blow the whistle, so I'm breathless but I want to have this conversation with her.

'It wasn't just you, Maria, I came along for the ride.'

'Yeah, but the only thing that kept us together for so long was the fear of letting go. But we've really got to do it this time, we're holding each other back. This is where the road has got to divide for me and you.'

'I fucking love you, Maria.'

'Whatever.' We can't really talk because it's a packed commuter train but I'm feeling very soothed just having her there with her understanding and strength, her big bag and all her notebooks and her electronic organiser, scribbling away, getting on with the job. I want to ask about Marcus, but I swallow the urge.

'How's the animal documentary going then?'

'Oh, you know, tears and suffering, they'll be lapping it up.' I'm pleased for her, really pleased. If she can get a result on this Channel Four gig, she'll be sitting pretty for cash and that makes me feel a lot better. If Maria had been a woman with less earning power, I could have been looking at some sort of kill-fee – a deposit on a flat, a couple of grand to get her started. That's what happened with Pilar, I just kind of continued supporting her for a year or two, sending her money so she wouldn't have to go to work. I felt so fucking awful and I wanted to show her dad that I wasn't a total cunt. You know you've got a guilty conscience when you're writing four figure cheques.

The cab pulls up outside the Mayday which is just as cheerful as

I remember. They ought to burn this place down. As we get up on the ward Maria says she'll wait outside by the lifts and that I should go and see Bee alone. I'm about to insist that she come with me, but she's right. What a brick that girl is. Dragging her arse all the way to Croydon just to keep me company. It's a bit of a miserable visit. Coxy is there with John and none of us is really saying anything. Bee is very quiet, just staring off into space and I figure they must have monged her out with something. I leave her with some magazines I picked up at Victoria, *Horoscope Monthly*, *Vogue*, etc. all her favourites, and she smiles wanly, but she's not really there. It's a total choker about this baby and even though I'm the one who told her she should get an abortion I'm pretty shaken now she's lost it. I'm definitely getting touchy and senti-mental with age. I hang around for half an hour, but I'm pretty surplus to requirements, so I kiss my sister and leave. I find Maria where I left her by the lifts, sharing a fag with some old boy in a wheelchair who'd just had the lower part of his leg removed, thanks to his love of smoking, and they're sitting there the pair of them and she's saying, 'I agree with you, I like my fags, you gotta take some risks. Yeah, they're boring, that anti-smoking lot.' Come on, I say, let's go and get some dinner. We're back on the train after a twenty-minute wait in the rain at West Croydon Station. There's another place they should burn down. We get a taxi at Victoria and end up in that trendy toilet on Albemarle Street. This time last year you couldn't get a table for love nor money, but now the place is empty. *Ça va sans dire*, we both have too much to drink and inevitably the conversation turns to Sara though I don't mention her by name. I'm trying to be pretty low-key about it all, play it down, but then Maria gives me the benefit of her theory which is that I am a sex addict. I've got an illness. I need help. I hurl a few insults about the speed with which she took up with Marcus, but I'm not defending myself too well because I'm tired and frankly, the truth is a lot more hurtful. What am I going to say, 'I'm sorry, Maria, but meeting this woman made me realise that I do not love

224

you.'? If her little theory makes her feel better, so be it. She's adamant that I'm in denial. If I can't get myself to meetings I should go back and see Henri Temple-Golden, stop being such an idiot and wrecking lives. I'm tempted to point out that Temple-Golden is a desperate middle-aged woman with a blurring of professional boundaries, but she wasn't having it. She's a woman's woman, Maria, and doesn't like to run down one of the sisterhood unless they're sleeping with me. After an exhausting few rounds of attrition I finally put her in a cab at about midnight and it's a relief to get home and be on my own. The leaflets about sex addiction arrive the following week.

I finished the book on 26 May, which strangely enough was my dad's birthday, and now it's 4 June. I went through it checking for basic errors then mailed the whole thing off to Sara about a week ago, Special Delivery, to make sure it arrived. Not bad, eh, a novel in a month? I'm feeling pretty pleased with myself. I've spent the last couple of days just chilling in the flat. It's been really nice actually, I didn't feel lonely at all. Went to the gym, nothing strenuous, just a sauna and a wank. Even went to the local swimming pool this morning and it was a right Saturday morning crowd, all the dads had been slung out and told to get the kids out of the house for a couple of hours so the wife can clean up. So I've tipped up at the pool right in the middle of family time and they've got these bizarre floating assault courses that all the kids clamber over and dive off. It was a mental scene, really noisy, these kids were just shrieking and screaming and for a while I was fed up because I couldn't do any lengths. But then they turned the wave machine on and I nicked one of those big floats from a couple of little girls when they weren't looking and just surfed the chlorine. It was brilliant. When I came out of the pool and stepped into the sunshine with my wet hair and red eyes, my mind was very clear and I knew that I would hear from Sara today. I told my sister when her birthday was and Bee looked it up in one of her spooky almanacs and reckoned that her moon and her Venus were all in the right places. You can say that again. She rang me up last night and wouldn't you know it, her mate has just come over with a book on numerology and she's worked it out, Sara and I have exactly the same numbers, we're both 34/7s. I told Bee I didn't want to know what it meant to be a 34/7 because I only had the three hours to chat. I did my usual piss-take and Bee was laughing along with me and then said, 'No, but seriously, even if it is a load of bollocks, it's still a good omen, a drop of luck.' She hesitated slightly. 'Anyway, cheer up, you miserable sod, falling in love is supposed to be about enjoying yourself. For a little while, anyway.' And of course, she's right. She's always right, my sister, it pisses me off. I need to detach a little bit now. I've done my book and I've sent it out there and who the fuck knows what strange forces are at work in my world, but this last couple of months have been a real eye-opener, a right refresher course, no two ways about it.

There are still moments when I doubt myself. When I don't know whether or not to trust my feelings and I wonder if I haven't just made this whole thing up. Sara might just think I'm some lonely wanker and is only humouring me, you know, being nice so that I'll help her with her book. But somewhere deep down is this little light that never quite goes out, I know I'm going to go on burning for this woman and while I don't like feeling out of control I'm more alive than I've been for a long time. I wouldn't say that I wrote the book *for* Sara because I needed to do this, to prove something to myself. But I definitely wrote it *to* her. I wanted her to know who I am so I told her. I've given more of myself away than I've ever dared to before, put it right on the line and left myself open for a kicking but maybe this is what falling in love is about.

This is my story and I hope she likes it. Everything you've read is line for line what I wrote and I think it's as close to the truth as I'm ever likely to get. I hope there were enough jokes in it. Whether it does the trick or not we'll have to wait and see. Right up until the last minute, I was stuck for a title, but then in bed the other night, I'm reading this book of aphorisms which Maria bought me for Christmas years ago and I come across. *Love is a kind of warfare* .... It's a quote from the Roman poet Ovid and I reckon it's perfect. *A Kind of Warfare*, yeah I like it. It reminds me of a very ritzy lunch party over at Terry and Joseph's a couple of summers ago and there were all these A-gays dressed to kill and giving good guest. A great party it has to be said, poof-city or not. So Terry's sitting in his big bamboo throne on the patio delighted to be holding court and telling some story about a couple who had just got divorced. They're all tutting and sighing and oh what a shame, then Terry says, '*C'est la guerre*, Duckie.' I tell you what, that became the catchphrase of my summer, I couldn't stop saying it. I'm over it now fortunately but I'm telling you, that little joke had legs. And he was right. It is a war. I suppose all you can really do is keep your kit bag tidy and hope for the best. I'm buzzed, happy, sometimes fraught with doubt, but not enough that it gets boring. It looks like I'm getting that promotion and a nice old wage rise to go with it. Sara's never off my mind and I'd like to think it was going to end like a movie with the happy couple walking off into the sunset, but you never can tell. I can't claim to have sworn off other women completely and had a rather nice little encounter about a week ago with a girl from work. I figured I should make hay while I'm still single, but it was a pretty empty experience. Oh well, at least it's better than coming on your own.

The phone went ten minutes ago. It was Sara. I read your book, she said. Oh yeah, I said, what do you reckon? Very interesting, she replied. It went quiet for a minute and then she said, 'Mum said she'll have Phoebe tonight if I want to go out.'

'Do you want to go out?' I ask.

'Yes, I think I do.'

'What do you fancy, dinner, pictures, a bit of music?'

'Anything, it doesn't matter. It'll just be good to see you.'

There's a bit of a gap before I reply, 'Good. I'll pick you up about half seven then.'

'No, I'll come to you if it's all the same.'

'Makes no odds to me.'

'I'll see you later then. Can I bring anything?'

'Wouldn't mind some flowers to cheer the flat up.'

'Flowers I can do.'

'Great.'

'Okay, half seven.'

Is she going to fall into my arms or let me down gently? There's no way of knowing which way the cards are going to fall, but I can feel a bit of a winning streak coming on. I'd better get this place cleaned up if she's coming over tonight. The old me would have changed the sheets pronto, but I'm not taking anything for granted. I'm just going to have a shower, get dressed and dab a bit of Floris behind the ears and hope the smell of me doesn't make her sick. I'm growing up. I'm in love. I like it.

Acknowledgements

The subject matter of this book prompted many interesting discussions with friends and colleagues, most of which were conducted in tired and emotional circumstances and cannot be recalled, but thank you anyway. The usual plaudits to my lovely editresses, Anna Haycraft and Sarah Such, for their skill and savvy. Special thanks to Professor John Connolly of The Tonbridge Institute of Human Sexual Behaviour for access to the database which got me going. Cheers, Tiger.